Praise for the Bottom Dollar Series

BET YOUR BOTTOM DOLLAR (#1)

"In a first novel that is guaranteed to please Fannie Flagg and Bailey White fans, Gillespie introduces the Bottom Dollar Girls with a flair for timing and a cheeky southern turn of phrase... Brace for a wild ride chock-full of Southern wit and down-home advice from a clutch of quirky characters you will hope to see again soon."

– Booklist

"Use your very last bottom dollar, if you have to. Just BUY THIS BOOK. You will laugh yourself sick and love every minute of it."
– Jill Conner Browne, The Sweet Potato Queen

"A winner of a first novel, filled with Southern-style zingers and funny folks."

– Kirkus Reviews (starred review)

"The characters are the kind of steel magnolias who would make Scarlett O'Hara envious."

– The Atlanta Journal-Constitution

"Laugh out loud... this perfect summer read [will] find permanent beach-house residence."

– Richmond Times-Dispatch

A DOLLAR SHORT (#2)

"Those plain-speaking, cheeky Bottom Dollar gals (*Bet Your Bottom Dollar*) return with more rollicking adventures in Cayboo Creek, South Carolina...Never a dull moment...this fast-paced screamer of a romance begs a giggle, if not a guffaw."

– Booklist

"Laugh-out-loud antics as...Gillespie continues her entertaining Bottom Dollar Girls series...Certain to please women's fiction fans of all ages."

— *Romantic Times* (Top Pick)

"As tart and delectable as lemon meringue pie...a pure delight."

— Jennifer Weiner, Author of *Good in Bed* and *In Her Shoes*

"A fine romp of a book, well-written and thoroughly entertaining."

— *The Winston-Salem Journal*

"*A Dollar Short* is meant to entertain, and it does. It takes talent to sustain this level of comic writing for over 300 pages. Gillespie keeps the ball in the air, spinning madly, until the end."

— *The Boston Globe*

DOLLAR DAZE (#3)

"Each character is lovingly crafted in Gillespie's hilarious, heartwarming, and often irreverent look at senior living in small-town America. The third book in the Bottom Dollar Girls series (*Bet Your Bottom Dollar*; *A Dollar Short*) can also be enjoyed as a stand-alone."

— *Booklist* (starred review)

"Hilarious and endearing...Gillespie's humorous style will have readers hooting out loud, and her cheeky characters will have them coming back for more!"

— Janean Nusz, *The Road to Romance*

"Readers will be chuckling over crazy man-getting antics, sighing at the complexity of life, love and matrimony and maybe even shedding a tear over the heartbreak and tragedy. This novel is charismatic and replete with poignancy."

— *Romantic Times*

Books by Karin Gillespie

GIRL MEETS CLASS
LOVE LITERARY STYLE

The Bottom Dollar Series

BET YOUR BOTTOM DOLLAR (#1)
A DOLLAR SHORT (#2)
DOLLAR DAZE (#3)

Bet Your Bottom Dollar

The Bottom Dollar Series

Karin Gillespie

HENERY PRESS

BET YOUR BOTTOM DOLLAR
The Bottom Dollar Series
Part of the Henery Press Chick Lit Collection

Second Edition | October 2014

Henery Press
www.henerypress.com

This is a work of fiction. Any references to historical events, real people, or real locales are used fictitiously. Other names, characters, places, and incidents are the product of the author's imagination, and any resemblance to actual events or locales or persons, living or dead, is entirely coincidental.

Trade Paperback ISBN-13: 978-1-940976-73-0
Digital epub ISBN-13: 978-1-940976-74-7
Kindle ISBN-13: 978-1-940976-75-4
Hardcover Paperback ISBN-13: 978-1-940976-76-1

Printed in the United States of America

To all the small Southern towns in America.
Long may you prosper.

ACKNOWLEDGMENTS

Thanks to Susan M. Boyer for steering me in the direction of Henery Press. Thanks to Kendel Lynn, Art C. Molinares and the team at Henery Press. And as always the greatest thanks goes to my readers.

One

If you don't like my driving, stay off the sidewalk.
~ Bumper sticker on Attalee Gaines's 1963 Buick Skylark

Yellow and red leaves spun around my face as I tramped up the cracked sidewalk to the Bottom Dollar Emporium. It was October in Cayboo Creek, South Carolina, and the fall air felt crisp as a pickle fresh out of the brine. The store's candy-striped awning flapped in the breeze as I rummaged in my smock pocket for my key. On my day off, I noticed, Mavis had decorated the display window with cutouts of jack-o'-lanterns and black cats. A grinning cardboard skeleton with accordion-pleated legs swung from the front entrance. As I pushed open the door, a horrible moan sounded from somewhere above my head. I screamed, but not loudly enough to drown out a terrified shriek from the shadowy depths of the store.

I was about to turn tail and run when the store flooded with light and I saw Mavis, her face pale as paste, standing by the entrance of the stockroom holding a box of Frootee Ice Freezer Pops.

"Lord, Elizabeth, I almost jumped out of my skin," Mavis said. "I told Attalee not to hook up that silly, moaning contraption, but she must have went ahead and done it. I came in through the service entrance this morning so it didn't get me."

I glanced up and saw a suspect speaker rigged to the door. I gave it a good yank.

"If I hear that sound every time someone walks in this door, I won't have a nerve left in my body," I said.

I crossed the creaking floor to the break area, where Mavis had settled herself in one of the plastic, stackable chairs. Mavis Loomis had worked as a clerk at the Bottom Dollar Emporium for going on fifteen years. Three years ago she'd purchased the business when its owner, Dora Phelps, had died from a stroke.

The Bottom Dollar Emporium used to be a Kress Dime Store back in the '40s, when retail stores still had a certain amount of glamour. The ceiling was pressed tin and supported by a series of carved wooden columns. The original sconce light fixtures still hung on the walls, and there was even a brass spittoon by the door. But the merchandise at the Bottom Dollar was anything but glamorous. We stocked everyday items—from coconut mallow cookies to Clabber Girl Baking Powder to canisters of Comet. Most of our items cost no more than a dollar.

I poured myself a cup of coffee and sat next to Mavis, who was patting her short salt-and-pepper hair with the palms of her hands.

"I like what you did with the Halloween decorations out front," I said, stirring some Sweet'N Low into my coffee.

"I'll probably catch it from the ladies' league at the Baptist church," Mavis said. "Last year they gave me grief for that witch I had hanging in the window."

A sputtering engine interrupted our chat. I glanced out the front window and watched Attalee squeal her 1963 Buick Skylark into a parking spot. Her front fender was attached to the body of the car with duct tape.

"Looks like Attalee had herself another mishap," I said.

Mavis blew on her coffee. "You know how crazy she drives. She sideswiped a telephone pole yesterday. I keep telling her she's too old to pretend she's a NASCAR driver."

Attalee swung open the front door, winded as usual from rushing to get to work on time. She grabbed one of the columns to steady herself as she wheezed like a dog with a stick stuck in its throat.

"Something's afoot," Attalee said, recovering her breath. She narrowed her eyes mysteriously.

"And what might that be, Attalee?" Mavis said with a yawn. "Bunions?"

Attalee ignored Mavis and strode toward us, stopping short in front of the candy display. She drew back and pointed a finger at a bag of Halloween candy. "Land Almighty! What on earth are these bloodshot thingamagigs?"

Mavis craned her neck to see what Attalee was staring at. "Eyes of Terror gumballs," she said.

Attalee shuddered. "Well, they give me the heebie-jeebies, gaping up at me that way. Reminds me of Burl when he was on a bender."

Burl was Attalee's late husband—a man who was fond of Old Grandad. He was reportedly tipsy when he walked into the path of a Colonial Bread truck five years before.

Attalee parked herself in the chair next to mine. Although she was knee-deep into her eighties, Attalee looked like a wizened six-year-old, favoring floral dresses with wide lacy collars and twirling her gray hair into sausage curls that dangled girlishly down her back.

"As I was saying, something's brewing. I saw a couple of men on Mule Pen Road surveying the vacant lot across from the old Piggly Wiggly," Attalee continued.

"I wouldn't be surprised." Mavis dunked a powdered doughnut into her coffee. "That road is really building up. A Winn-Dixie's supposed to open up in the old Piggly Wiggly building soon. We got a Goody's last year. Who knows what's coming up next?"

"Myself, I hope it's a miniature golf course," Attalee said. "We're short on recreation in this town. If you don't like bingo, bass fishing, or bowling, you're out of luck."

"I wouldn't pin my hopes on a golf course," I said. "It's probably going to be something dull like a carpet shop or a TireTown."

Attalee snapped open her compact and touched up her

eyebrows with a stubby black pencil. "Too bad they don't have dance halls anymore. That would liven up this place. The three of us could go there on Saturday nights. Two widows and a spinster, painting the town."

"Elizabeth's much too young to be called a spinster," Mavis said. "She's not but twenty-five years old. That's a baby still."

"Twenty-six," Attalee said. "Her birthday's three days from now. Ain't that right, Elizabeth? Shoot, in my day, you were a spinster if you were over eighteen and still didn't have a ring on your finger."

"Attalee," Mavis warned. She made a cutting motion across her throat.

"It's alright, Mavis," I said. "The word 'ring' isn't going to send me crying to the ladies' room."

I rubbed the finger where my engagement ring used to be. Sometimes I swore I could still feel it there, although I hadn't put it on in sixty-two days.

I'd only been engaged to Clip Jenkins for three weeks when he broke off it. He didn't even have the guts to tell me. Instead he'd scrawled a "Dear Jane" letter on the back of a Hardee's bag and stuck it under the windshield wiper of my Geo Metro. After that, I'd wrapped the ring in a handkerchief and tucked it away in my underwear drawer.

I lifted my chin bravely. "A comment like that might have upset me a few weeks back, but I believe I'm finally getting over Clip."

Attalee nodded. "Men are like buses. You miss one, you hop on the next one that comes along. 'Course at my age, the bus service has slowed down to a crawl."

"Amen," Mavis said. She propped her tennis shoes up on an empty storage carton.

"The hurt hasn't gone away completely," I said. "It's still there some, like a pebble in my shoe."

Just this morning, I'd been looking for a ponytail holder in my junk drawer and I'd come across an old greeting card from Clip.

When I saw his handwriting, I crumpled inside.

"Well, y'all had been sweethearts since high school," Mavis said. "It's going to take some time to heal up completely."

I nodded and went to freshen my coffee. That's when I spotted Birdie Murdock crossing Main Street on a beeline toward the Bottom Dollar Emporium. Birdie was the publisher of the *Cayboo Creek Crier*. A visit from Birdie meant one of two things: She'd either run out of Silver Luster No. 5 or she had some news to report.

I scurried to flip the welcome sign from "closed" to "open," saying over my shoulder, "Birdie's coming this way."

Attalee groaned as she got up from her chair. Her back was curled like a cashew and she jerked to straighten it. "Am I on cashier duty today?"

"That all depends," said Mavis. She stood, adjusting her name tag and smoothing the dark green smock she wore over her clothes. "Did you bring your teeth?"

Attalee's bad eye flickered behind the lens of her glasses, and she dipped a hand into her brassiere to adjust the long slope of her bosom.

"Today's Friday," she said. "Ain't you ever heard of casual Friday?"

Before Mavis had a chance to respond, the bell over the front door jingled and Birdie strode in.

Birdie was dressed in a pressed navy-blue suit that matched her saucer-shaped hat. She had a polka-dot hankie tucked into her breast pocket and carried a reporter's notebook under her arm.

"Hey, Birdie," Mavis called out. "Hope you're not here to sweet-talk me into taking out another ad. I'm tapped out since I bought that brand-new cash register."

Mavis was so proud of her cash register. It was a Samso Model CT-A32O with a digital readout and a built-in calculator that replaced the one that had been used since the 70s.

To celebrate its arrival Mavis had staged a ribbon-cutting ceremony and served sparkling grape juice and party cookies that came in individual, fluted paper wrappings.

Birdie's pumps and purse matched the navy of her suit and her silver hair floated around her face in well-trained swoops. Her appearance was marred only by the scrawl of eyeliner just a shade too high up on her lids.

"Mavis, I came as soon as the news arrived over my fax machine," Birdie said. She pulled the polka-dotted hankie out of her pocket and dabbed her face with it. "I had to read it twice before it actually sunk in."

She thrust a piece of paper under Mavis's nose. Mavis took it and perched her reading glasses on her face. As she read, her eyebrows worried into a V. Me and Attalee peeked over her shoulder.

The press release headlined, "Super Saver Dollar Store to Locate on Mule Pen Road in Cayboo Creek, South Carolina."

"Four checkout lines with over three thousand items in inventory," Mavis said. "Oh my lord."

"Super Saver expects to bring twelve jobs to Cayboo Creek," I read.

"The fastest-growing retailer in the Southeast with average monthly earnings of approximately $444.6 million." Attalee clawed at her chest. "If this is true the Bottom Dollar Emporium has less chance than a kerosene cat in hell."

I shot Attalee a stern look and then turned to Birdie. "You got any idea when's this supposed to happen, ma'am?" I asked.

"Not a clue. In the next few months, I'd imagine," Birdie said.

The paper shook in Mavis's hands and her voice sounded high-pitched, like she'd just inhaled a lungful of helium. "I only have fifteen hundred items and one checkout line," she said. "Cayboo Creek isn't big enough to support two dollar stores."

"Wait a minute, now." I laid a steadying hand on her shoulder. "Cayboo Creek may be small, but our customers are a loyal bunch. I don't think they'll abandon us for this new store just because they can choose from three different kinds of dishwashing soap instead of two."

"That's not so," Mavis said. Her voice squeaked with panic. "Remember when Goody's opened up? It ran the Vickery Family Clothiers right into the ground. And I was a party to that. Once Goody's opened, I never again stepped foot into Vickery's."

I wrinkled my nose. "Yes, but that's because Vickery's was so stuffy."

When I was a little girl, I remembered Mello Vickery sticking her nose in the dressing room when I was trying on one of their overpriced party dresses. She'd said, "Don't fidget so much, Elizabeth Polk, or you'll get that party dress all sweaty and I'll have to put it on the markdown table."

"They were even snooty about their underwear," Attalee said with a nod. "Calling them foundations instead of bras and panties."

Birdie sighed. "I'm sorry to be the one to deliver this news, Mavis. But I felt you needed to know immediately so that you could develop a plan of action."

She peered at her watch. "I need to be scooting, gals. The elementary school is having their fall festival and I've got to be there to cover it. The city councilmen are taking turns in the dunking booth. Good-bye, all."

Birdie's heels clicked out the door and the three of us sat slumped in our chairs, the weight of her news pinning us down.

"'Plan of action,' she says," Mavis said. "What plan of action? I'd be hard pressed to add one more register in here, much less three more. And forget about all that extra inventory; we're bursting at the seams as it is."

The three of us fell into a grim silence, interrupted only by the drip from the coffee maker and hum of the oscillating fan. Mavis's normally smooth complexion looked as rumpled as a much used bed sheet.

"I've got it!" Attalee bolted from her chair. "We undercut the Super Saver Dollar Store by a nickel. Instead of being the Bottom Dollar Emporium, we change our name to the 95-Cent Emporium."

"Sorry, Attalee," said Mavis. "There's no way I can undercut the Super Saver. They got so many stores that they have tons of bargaining power with their suppliers. I've got enough trouble keeping most items priced at a dollar."

"There must be something we can do," I said. "It isn't right for a rich corporation to swoop into town and swallow up the business that you've broken your back to get."

Mavis cast her glance to the floor. "That's the way it goes all over this country. Only in the Bible, it seems, is David able to beat Goliath."

"That sounds like a fancy excuse to give up," I said.

Mavis trained her tired, gray eyes on me. "I'm not giving up, Elizabeth. I'm just facing facts. A minute ago, you were talking about the loyal folks in Cayboo Creek. I suspect some of them will stick with us. 'Specially our little group who comes in every day to shoot the breeze. But the odds and ends they purchase won't even be able to pay the electricity bill. Truth is, most people in town will take their trade to a newer, bigger store."

"We're just going to have to figure out some way to keep them here," I said. "We have to fight this. I know how important this business is to you, Mavis."

Not six months ago, Mavis had bought a tidy cottage on Persimmon Road after having lived for years in a double-wide in an aging trailer court by the creek. I knew that she counted on the profits from the Bottom Dollar to make her mortgage payments.

"To think how many years I scrimped and saved to buy this business," Mavis said. "And now it's going to be gone. Just like that." She snapped her fingers.

I jumped to my feet. "Not if I have anything to say about it," I said. "I'm the manager here after all. I have a selfish interest in keeping this place afloat."

Last year Mavis had named me manager and Attalee assistant manager of the Bottom Dollar Emporium. There wasn't anybody below us to manage, seeing as how we were the only employees, but we appreciated the gesture. Our pictures had appeared in the "Up and Coming" section of the *Cayboo Creek Crier* and Mavis had presented us with new name tags.

"That's sweet, darling," Mavis said, trying to conjure up a smile on her pallid face. "But I don't know what you can possibly do."

Two

If Love were Oil, I'd be a Quart Low

~ Selection B-7 on the jukebox at the Tuff Luck Tavern

The news about the Super Saver Dollar Store spread, and as the day wore on, the Bottom Dollar Emporium got as busy as a Lotto vendor on the night before a Powerball drawing. People came by to gossip, to declare their loyalty, or even to drop by food. Hank Bryson from the hardware store (who I know is sweet on Mavis, though she pooh-poohs it) brought by a pot of his special medicinal chili, so-called because he pours two cans of Budweiser in the mix. My meemaw stormed in, her gray hair crackling in the dry air.

"I'll be darned, Mavis," she said, plunking down a chess pie. "If that upstart store thinks they can strut into town without facing a tussle, they've got another think coming."

Mavis shook her head sadly. "I keep hoping it's all a bad dream."

Meemaw patted Mavis's arm. "Don't fret, Mavis. There's bound to be an answer to this."

Her shiny, dark eyes trained on me like a crow to a silver piece. "Elizabeth! What do you have to say for yourself? You're the manager. Shouldn't you be throwing yourself in front of a bulldozer or something? What are you going to do to stop this foolishness?"

I kissed her wrinkled cheek and took in her clinging scent of BenGay and Pall Mall unfiltered. "Hey, Meemaw. Nice to see you, too." When I touched her wrist, her pulse jumped beneath her skin. "Did you take your blood-pressure pill today?"

Meemaw pushed her dark eyeglasses up on her nose and addressed Mavis. "That's the trouble with granddaughters. They turn saucy on you." She harrumphed. "As if a grown woman has to be hounded to take a silly little pill."

Her deflection made me strongly suspect she'd neglected her medication. Meemaw was leery of most doctors, except for her podiatrist. She'd limp into Dr. Bales's office at the first sign of a corn.

"I don't mean to lecture—" I said.

"Then don't," Meemaw snapped. "I'm too worked up about this new dollar store to worry about pharmaceutical fiddle-faddle. What am I going to do without the Bottom Dollar Emporium?"

Mavis sat in the corner grimly shredding a tissue. "What does this town need with a creaky-floored hole-in-the-wall when they can have four checkout lanes, piped-in Muzak, and three thousand items to choose from?"

"I need you, Mavis," Meemaw insisted. "Who special orders canning supplies for me every summer? Do you think a big corporate dollar store will care whether or not I have enough jars for my watermelon-rind relish?"

Mavis smiled weakly. "I truly appreciate your support, Glenda. Everybody's been so wonderful."

Attalee came in from the storeroom toting a shipment of decorative birdhouses. When she saw Meemaw, she clenched her jaw and said, "Glenda," and then made her way to the front of the store.

"Attalee," Meemaw said with a curt nod of her head. Meemaw and Attalee were fierce bingo rivals. They played every Wednesday night at the Senior Center.

"Do you know she's taken to bringing an air horn to bingo games every week?" Meemaw said in a low voice. "After she hollers out 'Bingo,' she gives out three blasts on the air horn. She's deliberately trying to ruin my concentration."

"I heard that!" Attalee said. She stomped over to where Meemaw was standing. "What about you? Humming 'Luck Be a Lady Tonight,' loud enough for the whole table to hear. Off key, I might add."

"The soft humming of a show tune is nothing compared to the racket of that horn," Meemaw said, her face turning red. "I missed a diagonal bingo last week because of that contraption."

"You know that Dixon is deaf as a post," Attalee retorted. "Twice he didn't hear me call out over the sound of the bingo blower. And don't blame your missteps on me, Glenda. Face it. You just can't handle so many cards anymore."

"Are you saying that my mind is failing?" Meemaw demanded shrilly.

"If the orthopedic shoe fits," Attalee said with a smirk.

"Meemaw. Attalee. Enough!" I said, stepping in between the two women. I glanced over at Mavis, who was staring blankly into space. "Now's not the time."

Meemaw hitched her pocketbook up to her shoulder. "I need to get going anyway. Mavis, don't fret so. We'll figure something out. You'll see."

She left the store under Attalee's frigid gaze. I continued my work of shelving canned goods. Just as I got a good rhythm going, my best friend, Chiffon, came in with a jar of scuppernong jam and a dozen biscuits wrapped in a dishtowel. While she poured herself a cup of coffee in the break area, her two kids weaved in and out of the aisles, wielding plastic squirt guns. They nearly toppled a rack of plus-size housedresses.

Chiffon, who had ten years on me, had won first runner-up in the Miss South Carolina pageant several years back. She used to be the most beautiful girl in Aiken County, but fifteen years and two little ones had puffed her up some, a condition Chiffon lamented as she studied her reflection in the teaspoon she'd used to stir sugar into her coffee.

"My face looks like a Moon Pie," she groaned. "I can't even find my cheekbones anymore."

"You're gorgeous," I said. And it was true. Chiffon may have gotten fuzzier around the edges, but she still had eyes the color of sparkling pool water and long, blond hair that licked her shoulder blades.

"You always say the right thing," Chiffon said.

"This is no time to be worrying about your weight," I said. Last week Chiffon had told me she thought she might be pregnant. "You should see the infant socks we got in last week. They're no bigger than your thumb and trimmed in lace and ribbons."

Chiffon patted my knee. "You're the one who needs to be having a baby. You're crazy about kids."

I let out a snort. "I best find me a husband first."

"I'm telling you. Lonnie works with some single fellows at the NutraSweet plant. Nice boys with steady incomes. We could set you up just fine."

I shook my head. "It's only been two months since Clip and I busted up. I'm just not ready yet."

Not ready. Not ready. The words pulsed in my ears as I pushed open the door to go home. The day, though dying, still dazzled. Sunlight clung to the front window of the store like honey in a jar and the air was sharp with the smell of burning leaves.

I strolled down Main Street, passing by Darling Do's, the new beauty parlor. I waved to Boomer of Boomer's Butcher Shop, who was just locking up.

"If you talk to your meemaw, tell her I've got some goat in for her," Boomer said.

Boomer was my grandmother's on-again, off-again beau.

"Are you and Meemaw fussing again?" I said.

Boomer nodded. "I sent her a dozen carnations and they all came back to me with their heads cut off."

"Ouch," I winced. "I'll tell her what you said. There's nothing like some goat to get back in Meemaw's good graces."

Meemaw was a fool for goat meat. She made kid goat stew, leg of goat, and even a dish called Hawaiian goat mini-kabobs. The thought of all that goat made my stomach grumble as I passed the Chat 'N' Chew and waved at Jewel Turner, the owner, through the window.

Across from the Chat 'N' Chew was the Rock of Ages Baptist Church. Reverend Hozey had lettered his church-front sign, "Where do you want to spend eternity? In smoking or nonsmoking?"

I traveled a block west from Main Street onto my street, Scuffle Road, which was lined with one-story mill houses, one room wide, with asphalt roofs and rusty tin awnings shading the porches. The shadow of the old Braun Brothers mill, shuttered since 1987, swallowed all the houses surrounding it.

I picked my way to my front door through a fleet of rusting Piggy Wiggly shopping carts. My next-door neighbor Burris had swiped them from the parking lot before the Pig went belly-up.

Just as I was about to turn the key, a truck drove by and I heard a snatch of the song "She Thinks My Tractor Is Sexy" by Kenny Chesney. Clip darkened my mind like an eclipse, blocking out everything, including the fall-cured breeze and the weakening sun. Right away, I was plopped back into a booth at the Tuff Luck Tavern, the "tractor" song playing on the jukebox. I could almost feel Clip's blue-jeaned thigh pressed up against my own and his warm breath stirring the downy hairs of my cheek. Spangles of light from the mirrored disco ball floated by like silver moons while Clip's low rumbling voice sang along in my ear.

How could he have sung to me so tenderly one week and then kicked me to the curb the next? Ever since we'd broken up, my mind worked overtime on that question. But I still hadn't come up with a decent solution. A half a dozen or more times I'd thought about calling him, but luckily my finger froze up before I punched in the last number.

I reasoned that if Clip was willing to throw me away like I was an empty bag of chips, I didn't have any business calling him. Let him come to me, knee-walking, with flowers, chocolate candies, and a tortured expression.

And when he did come to his senses, as I felt sure he would, I'd make him sweat it out for a while. Then, and only then, would I decide if he was worthy enough to come back into my life.

I savored the image of Clip holding a huge bouquet of sweetheart roses, calling out my name from parched lips. The picture made me smile for the first time that day.

ℭhree

Don't give up; Moses was once a basket case
~ Notice in the *Methodist Church Bulletin*

The mood the next morning at the Bottom Dollar Emporium was about as festive as an autopsy. Mavis ignored her mug of coffee as well as the pecan Danish I'd picked up from the Chat 'N' Chew. She stared straight ahead at the dust motes swirling around the plastic funeral flowers at the front of the store.

"Last night I called my sister up in Onida, South Dakota,' Mavis said quietly. "Her husband passed on last year and she says I'm welcome to her spare bedroom, should it come to that."

"South Dakota?" Attalee said, biting into her second Danish of the morning. The news about the Super Saver hadn't affected her appetite one whit. "Why would you move all the way up there?"

"It may be my only choice if I have to sell the house," Mavis said. "I'm not going back to the trailer court and I'm too old to get me another job. Madge has a little hobby shop up there called the Craft Coop. She said she'd take me on as a clerk."

I had the ledger spread out on my lap and was squinting at the figures written in Mavis's precise handwriting.

"Goodness, Mavis, I don't want to hear any talk about you leaving Cayboo Creek. We'll think up a way out of this," I said, hoping my voice held the right amount of conviction. According to the ledger figures, Mavis would be in a world of trouble if business dropped off more than a little.

"What do folks do in a godforsaken place like South Dakota?" Attalee asked.

"Madge loves it up there," Mavis said. "She darts around in her very own snowmobile. And she's chairperson for Onida's Annual Lutefisk Feed."

"Lutefisk?" Attalee said, raising an eyebrow.

"Lutefisk is dried cod treated with lye," Mavis said glumly. "Madge says it's very tasty."

"Enough!" I slammed the ledger shut. "The only fish you'll be eating, Mavis, is fried catfish right here in Cayboo Creek. We're going to fight this thing and we're going to win."

"Well, I know I can't afford to lose me this job," Attalee said, giving her curls a shake. "I just started making payments on my satellite dish. I pick up three HBOs and seven Showtimes and I ain't willing to give 'em up."

"You won't have to, Attalee," I said. "I've talked with some of the other business owners in town and they're upset about this too. I'm going to organize a meeting to see if we can't figure something out."

Attalee was no longer listening. Something outside had caught her attention. "Jonelle Jasper and her little girl Kimbro are crossing the street and coming this way," she announced. "Empty-handed," she added with a sniff. Attalee had been enjoying all the bounty that had come our way since we'd heard about the Super Saver.

"We ain't going to have us a catfight are we, Elizabeth?" Attalee teased.

"'Course not," I said, defensively. The rumor around town was that my ex-fiancé Clip had been stepping out with Jonelle the past couple of weeks. Chiffon, who waitresses at the Wagon Wheel, saw Clip feeding Jonelle a T-bone steak.

That burned me up, because whenever we went to the Wagon Wheel he'd always steered me in the direction of the chopped steak special. A few other folks had seen Jonelle in the cab of Clip's brand-new pickup truck.

Still, I didn't consider Jonelle a serious rival. She was something of a floozie and I didn't think she could hold Clip's attention for long.

I got up from my chair and looked out the window. Jonelle was tugging the arm of six-year-old Kimbro, who was grinding her Mary Janes on the asphalt. Jonelle gave Kimbro a sound smack on the back of her blue chenille, rhinestone-studded dress.

"That Jonelle must paint her blue jeans on with a roller," Attalee said with a snort. "And she dresses that child up like a Christmas tree."

Jonelle pushed open the glass door and waggled her hot pink fingernails at us. Kimbro trailed behind, her lower lip pooched out, sniffing back tears.

"Hey, Bottom Dollar girls. How y'all doing today?" Jonelle said, her voice as thick and sweet as Aunt Jemima syrup.

"Fine, Jonelle," Mavis said. She knelt down to speak with Kimbro. "Hey there, sweetcakes. Why the long face?"

"Oh she's got her Underoos all twisted in a knot, because we entered the Miss Dimple Darling pageant and she didn't even place," Jonelle said. She glared at her daughter. "It was her own fault. Little Miss Kimbro didn't want any Vaseline on her teeth. 'Vaseline tastes icky.' Well, it sure cost her a bunch of congeniality points when her smile muscles seized up."

Mavis tsked. "Well, maybe a Pixy Stix would help dry those tears? Can she, Jonelle?"

Jonelle shook her head. "Kimbro's off of sugar right now. She weighed in a little heavy at her last doctor's appointment. But you may pick yourself out a coloring book, Kimbro, as long as you don't dirty your dress."

Kimbro skipped to the toy department, holding up the corners of her pageant dress. Her brunette bouffant was coated with enough hair spray to qualify as a fire hazard. Jonelle raked her fingers through her dark mop of curls, which weren't teased or sprayed up high like Kimbro's. Instead, Jonelle had a just-crawled-out-of-bed look. She wore a tight, black blouse with a peek-a-boo back and her eyes were rimmed with dark blue eyeliner.

"What can we do for you today, Jonelle?" asked Mavis.

"Well, I didn't come here to market," Jonelle said. She turned in profile toward the door. I got a wee bit of satisfaction when I noticed her rear end revealed a strong resemblance to the hot side of a flat iron.

"Nothing personal," Jonelle continued. "I'm just so finicky when it comes to what I buy and y'all sell so many strange off-brands."

She picked up a can of peas and scrutinized the label. "I mean, who ever heard of Findley Farm Peas, for pity's sake? I won't touch peas to my lips unless they're LeSueurs."

"And I bet when you let loose a toot, it smells like designer perfume, Jonelle," Attalee said.

"Attalee," Mavis said.

Jonelle twisted her face into a scowl and narrowed her eyes at Attalee. Then she said, "Actually, I came here to see *you*, Elizabeth. I thought you should be one of the first to know." She paused dramatically. "Me and Clip Jenkins are now engaged."

"What?" I asked.

"Clip asked me to marry him last night." Jonelle smiled sweetly. "I felt compelled to do the Christian thing and tell you myself, so you wouldn't have to hear it on the streets."

The Duchess honey bun I was nibbling on suddenly tasted like a wad of sawdust.

"This is certainly a surprise," I said in a raspy voice.

Jonelle flashed a 150-watt grin. "It's been a whirlwind romance. And I do believe Clip will make a wonderful stepdaddy for Kimbro."

"That's enough." Attalee stomped over to Jonelle and stuck a finger in her face. "You didn't come here to be Christian. You came here to gloat. Round up your young'un and get on out of here, since you ain't buying nothing."

A red flush crawled up Jonelle's neck. "Mavis, you hear what she said to me?"

"Maybe you'd better just leave, Jonelle," Mavis said. She slid a protective arm around my waist. "You all right, Elizabeth?"

"Mummy! Look what I found!" Kimbro said. She ran to her mama with a package in her hand. Jonelle snatched it. "Fingernail tattoos? Well, that's just t-a-c-k-y. Come on, baby. I'll take you to Kaybee Toys in the Augusta Mall where they have quality merchandise."

I lifted my chin and looked Jonelle in the eye.

"Congratulations, Jonelle. I'm sure you'll be very happy. Clip's a fine fellow."

"He is fine folks, unlike some people I know," Jonelle said, sticking her tongue out at Attalee. "We're leaving now."

We watched her storm across the parking lot, dragging her little beauty queen.

"What a hateful girl," Mavis said. "I hope you weren't too hurt by her news, Elizabeth."

"I'd like to slap the taste out of that boy's mouth," Attalee said. "Leaving you a note with no explanation. And right after your engagement party. Furthermore, I should have pulled Jonelle's perm right out of her roots for sashaying in here with that announcement."

"You want to know what's the worst of it?" I asked, with a sniff. "It's not so much losing Clip, though that did hurt like nobody's business. It's the uncertainty. I haven't seen him since the night of our engagement party. I haven't the foggiest idea why he broke things off."

Mavis kneaded my shoulder. "Maybe it was just a case of cold feet."

I tried to squeeze back the tears, but they dribbled down my cheeks. "Then why aren't his feet cold with Jonelle?" I asked.

Mavis stooped down in front of my chair and stroked my cheek. "Oh, lamb, they just got engaged. Wait until they announce a date and she picks out a gown, then his feet will probably freeze up like Eskimos Pies. Or at least they ought to. That Jonelle is one scary woman."

Attalee was still staring after Jonelle.

"And that Clip is full of mysteries," she said. "First he breaks off his engagement with you. And then, right afterward, everyone sees him tooling around Cayboo Creek in that expensive truck."

I wiped a tear from my cheek.

"It's got everything on it: Nerf bar, KC Lights, and mud flaps customized with the Rebel flag," I said in between sniffs. "That was Clip's dream truck when we were dating. It costs thirty thousand dollars. There's no way he can afford that truck just delivering RC Colas."

Mavis rose from the floor. "I've heard rumors about him going around town flashing a big wad of bills. I wonder what that boy's gotten himself mixed up with."

"Whatever mess Clip might have gotten into isn't my problem anymore," I said in a ragged voice. "It's Jonelle's. And maybe she did me a favor coming in here and telling me about her engagement. Now I know there's no point in pining over him anymore."

"That's right!" Attalee said. "Out with the old, in with the new."

Of course we all knew that was easier said than done. With a population of just under six thousand, Cayboo Creek wasn't exactly spilling over with eligible bachelors. Folks could hardly blame Jonelle for snapping up Clip. Good-looking single men didn't have a long shelf life in these parts.

"Orson at the bait shop isn't a bad sort," Mavis mused. "Course, he's missing his thumb on his left hand from that firecracker accident a couple of years back."

Attalee snapped her fingers. "What about Garnell Walker? He might not be the prettiest fellow in South Carolina what with his overbite and all, but he's got seniority out at that kaolin company across the river—"

"Attalee!" Mavis said. "Garnell Walker is fifty-two. He's way too old for Elizabeth, plus he's keeping company with Effie Stykes."

"That's not so old," Attalee said with a pout. "And Effie has that big birthmark on her cheek. Looks like someone hit her on the side of her face with a tomato."

I held up my hand. "Stop. Both of y'all. I don't need to be rushing into anything."

"That sounds very sensible, Elizabeth," Mavis said. "Young women are much more independent nowadays. My goodness, it's gotten so a woman don't even need a man to have a baby. She can just run out to one of those banks and withdraw her some sperm."

Attalee made a face. "That don't sound like a whole lot of fun."

Mavis clapped her hands together. "Why don't we break out Elizabeth's birthday cake that Birdie dropped by?" she said. "There's nothing like a slice of red velvet cake to cheer a person and I think everyone in here could use a lift in spirits. What do you say, Elizabeth?"

"My birthday isn't until tomorrow." I glanced at my watch. "And it's only 8:30 in the morning."

"That's what makes it so naughty," Mavis said. "Let's live a little."

"I'm game," Attalee said. "Slice me off a big hunk. I need the energy. I was up all night with a twitching leg."

I rubbed a hand across the soft bulge of my belly. Maybe Clip had left me because I was too plump for his tastes. Certainly Jonelle wasn't toting any extra flesh.

"I don't think I want a piece. Y'all go ahead," I said.

"But red velvet's your favorite," Mavis said. Concern shined in her eyes.

"It would just get all caught up in my throat right now," I said. I hiccupped. "Will y'all excuse me for a minute?"

I didn't wait for an answer, but instead fled to the small bathroom in the back so I could cry in private.

Jonelle's news proved the idiocy of any reunion fantasies I may have had. Clip was really gone from my life and my silly wishes would never bring him back. He probably didn't think about me at all anymore.

As I caught a glance at my swollen face in the mirror, I got angry with myself. I had spilled enough tears over Clip Jenkins. If he could attach himself so quickly to another female—particularly one as sleazy and conniving as Jonelle Jasper—he didn't deserve even one teaspoon of my salty tears.

I splashed water on my face and blew my nose. I just didn't have time to be mooning over an ex-fiancé, not with the Bottom Dollar Emporium hanging by a thread and Mavis threatening to move to South Dakota.

I simply could not let that happen. Mavis was a Southern gal, born and bred. She should be surrounded by magnolias, not moose. And South Dakota was so far away it might as well be Jupiter. I'd probably never see her again if she moved.

One way or the other, I was going to fight this thing with the Super Saver.

Four

*Nothing is less important that what fork you use.
Etiquette is the science of living.*

~ Grace Tobias's favorite quote from Emily Post

"Here comes Gracie Tobias, pulling up in her big, white Caddie," Attalee hollered out. Her rag squeaked as she wiped down the glass window out front. Mavis and I were in the break area, nibbling on the remains of Birdie's cake. I'd turned twenty-six today.

Mavis went to the window for her own peek. We were all curious about Mrs. Tobias because she wasn't our typical Bottom Dollar Emporium customer. Her Southern accent was clipped and polished like a freshly groomed poodle, and she lived across the Savannah River in a rich area of Augusta, Georgia, called The Hill.

"Hello, ladies," Mrs. Tobias trilled as she swept through the door. She peeled off her little white driving gloves. She wore a tailored pink suit with gold buttons and pumps with matching pink bows. "Mavis, Attalee..." Her eyes searched the store until she spotted me behind a display of Krack-O-Pop Party Mix. "Elizabeth, there you are. Happy birthday, dear!"

"Hey, Mrs. Tobias," I said, sucking frosting from my thumb. "I can't believe you remembered."

Mrs. Tobias's nose wrinkled up like she smelled something funky.

"What did I say?"I asked.

"Elizabeth," she said, arching an eyebrow. "What have I said 'hey' is for?"

I blushed. "Horses. Sorry, Mrs. Tobias, I forgot myself."

I was accustomed to Mrs. Tobias's corrections of my English, and her gentle manner took the sting out.

"Of course I remembered your birthday," she said. "October fifteenth is a red-letter day. In fact, I even have a gift for you."

She pulled a long, slim box from her crocodile bag and handed it to me.

"Why, Mrs. Tobias. Thank you."

I removed the lid and saw a gold locket lying on a bed of cotton. I spread the necklace across my forearm. It was a little slip of a thing, delicate as a whisper. I guessed it wouldn't turn my neck green like most of my jewelry.

"Here, let me," Mrs. Tobias said. I held up my bush of dirty-blond hair. Mrs. Tobias draped the chain around my neck and fastened the clasp. The links felt cool and watery as they brushed up against my skin and the locket nestled at the base of my throat. She stood in front of me, beaming. I felt like a ship being christened.

Mrs. Tobias expelled a sigh. "You look lovely, Elizabeth. The necklace is brand new, but the locket belonged to me when I was a very young woman. Unfortunately, the latch has been stuck for several years and it doesn't open."

"This is a family heirloom?" I gingerly touched the locket. "Mrs. Tobias, I can't accept such a precious gift."

"Nonsense!" Mrs. Tobias said. "It's a simple trinket. Show the others how lovely it looks on your neck."

I hesitated, but the resolute look on Mrs. Tobias's face made me slowly turn to Mavis and Attalee. "Look, y'all, at the necklace Mrs. Tobias gave me. It's the prettiest thing I've ever worn."

Attalee fingered the chain. "Lord, goodness," she said. "That's a fine piece of jewelry. I'll bet you could get a nice sack of change for it at the pawn shop." She glanced up at Mrs. Tobias and cupped a hand to her lips. "As an insurance policy for the hard times ahead."

"I would never dream of hocking this, ever," I said quickly. I patted the necklace protectively. "And hard times aren't coming."

Mrs. Tobias fluffed her caramel-colored curls. "What's this talk about hard times?" she asked.

Mavis winced, and she abruptly turned her back on me to wipe down an empty shelf. This Super Saver business was taking its toll on her.

"Well, there's a new dollar store coming to Cayboo Creek a few blocks away," I said in a low voice. "It's going to be bigger and fancier than the Bottom Dollar and we're all a little worried—"

"Doomed is what we are, Mrs. Tobias," Attalee boomed. Her bad eye flickered rapidly behind the lens of her glasses. "That Super Saver Dollar Store will sink the Bottom Dollar Emporium like it's the Titanic."

"Let's not hear that kind of talk," I whispered. "You'll upset Mavis."

"She's got a reason to be upset," Attalee wailed. "This is even worse than when that opossum died in the air vent last fall and stunk up the store for weeks. And poor, puny Elizabeth thinks she's going to save us, single-handedly."

"It's not impossible," I said, squaring my shoulders.

"Oh yeah?" Attalee said. "Tell Mrs. Tobias about your latest bright idea. The dead Indian scheme."

"Well, I admit that didn't pan out," I said. "But I think my reasoning was sound."

Mrs. Tobias's hand drifted to her lace collar. "What's this about dead Indians?" she said.

"I did some research on the Internet yesterday," I explained. "I discovered that over in Arizona some folks opposed the opening of a new Wal-Mart because the store site was going to be on the ruins of a pre-Columbian village. Even though it was a long shot, I decided to research the Super Saver's plat of land, hoping for something historical underneath—like Indian burial grounds. Unfortunately, I didn't find anything like that."

"All that running around to the Augusta library and the county seat, and she didn't unearth one dead Indian," Attalee sniffed.

"That's true," I said. "But I did find out something interesting. Cayboo Creek used to be the asparagus capital of the whole world back in the 1930s, which is pretty exciting when you think about it. People in exotic locales like New York or maybe even Sydney, Australia, dined on asparagus from right here in Cayboo Creek."

"Oh my," said Mrs. Tobias.

I shook my head sadly. "As fascinating as that is, I wished I'd found something to save the Bottom Dollar instead."

Mrs. Tobias pursed her lips. Her pink lipstick matched the suit she was wearing to a T.

"What a shame!" she said. "These mammoth stores are always nudging out the smaller ones. It seems dreadfully unfair. I'm so sorry, Mavis."

Mavis turned to Mrs. Tobias and responded with a quick nod.

"Thank you, ma'am," she said curtly. "Attalee, I got some boxes in the back that need opening and I'll be requiring an extra pair of hands."

Attalee trailed behind Mavis as they both trudged to the stockroom.

"I'm sorry," I said to Mrs. Tobias. "I didn't mean to be heaping our troubles on your shoulders. Is there anything I can help you with today?"

"I believe I'm just going to browse a bit," Mrs. Tobias said. She hoisted a plastic basket on her arm and then paused.

"Elizabeth, I don't mean to be forward, but just how is it that the opening of the Super Saver is your affair? It couldn't be so difficult for you to get another job. If not here in Cayboo Creek, surely Aiken and Augusta are ripe with possibilities."

"I suppose I could, Mrs. Tobias, but I've been working at the Bottom Dollar since high school."

I could have stopped there, but decided to confide further. "Back then, I was in FCA, which stands for Future Cosmetologists of America. I had big dreams of opening my own hair salon one day. But then, on the third day of cosmetology class, my dreams were dashed."

Mrs. Tobias's eyes widened. "Oh dear. What happened?"

"I flunked pin curling," I said with a sad shake of my head. "I just couldn't get the hang of it even though I practiced on my mannequin late into the night. Mrs. Tippet, the cosmetology teacher, said pin curling always separates the wheat from the chaff. I could rattle off all the parts of a hair follicle and I was a whiz at skull anatomy, but I was chaff all around when it came to actually doing hair."

"I see," Mrs. Tobias said.

"Luckily, I saw a 'Help Wanted' sign in the Bottom Dollar that very day coming home from school. I marched inside and began my new career in retail sales working part-time. Since then, I've been promoted to manager and I've been here now going on ten years. It's not just a job to me. Mavis and Attalee are like family."

Mrs. Tobias glanced nervously at the back room. "I just wondered if you ever wanted something... more," she said. "You're still young and clearly quite bright. College, perhaps?"

"College?" I shook my head. "Oh no, Mrs. Tobias, that's not for me. We Polks don't do college. We're a hands-on people. Now, I have thought of taking a bookkeeping course or two out at Kerr Business College in Augusta so I could streamline Mavis's accounting system. But a place like the University is out of my league."

"Well, I declare," she said. "I've never heard such a thing." She seized random items off the shelves. "Not going to the University just because none of your people have." Into her basket she tossed scouring pads, pigskin work gloves, and a tin of Lick Your Whiskers cat food.

"I didn't know you had a cat, Mrs. Tobias," I said.

She inspected the can. "Land, I thought this was tuna."

She replaced it on the shelf. "I almost forgot. I also came in here today to ask you a favor, Elizabeth. Did I ever mention to you that I have a grandson about your age?"

"No ma'am."

"His name is Timothy, Timothy Hollingsworth, and he'll be

moving to Augusta from San Diego, California, in a matter of days. He's going to take my son-in-law's place at Hollingsworth Inc.," said Mrs. Tobias.

Mrs. Tobias's son-in-law Bettis Hollingsworth had died a couple of months ago. He got struck by lightning on the sixteenth hole of the Augusta National. He'd refused to leave the golf course, despite the lightning warnings, because he was five under par. It had been all over the newspaper, seeing how the Hollingsworths owned the paper cup factory in Augusta.

"Timothy's been away from his friends so long that he's lost touch," Mrs. Tobias continued. "I thought you might like to go out with him a time or two, on a friendly basis. Both of you are the same age and I think some company would do him a world of good."

"Oh, Mrs. Tobias, I just don't know." I toyed with my locket. "I'm not getting out a lot these days."

Her voice sharpened. "Don't tell me you're still pining over that soda salesman?"

"No! I mean..." I rocked on the balls of my feet. "Well, maybe just a little."

Mrs. Tobias had met Clip a time or two and hadn't been particularly impressed with him.

"I just don't think I'd be the best of company for your grandson," I continued.

"I see." Mrs. Tobias's lips were pressed together tightly like a woman's compact. Her blue eyes glittered during the silence between us. "And you couldn't set aside your feelings for just an evening or two to help me out in a pinch?"

"Mrs. Tobias, I wouldn't have the faintest idea as to what to say to a fellow from a big place like California. I'm sure I'd bore your grandson to pieces."

"Nonsense. Timothy is..." Her hand fluttered around her face like a moth. "Well, let's just say he's... different. And I'm convinced the two of you would get along famously. But if it's too much of a bother—"

"It's not a bother, it's just that—" I sighed. I knew when I was licked.

"I'll be glad to show him around town, Mrs. Tobias," I finally said.

She smiled. "Wonderful. I'll bring him by to meet you."

Mavis and Attalee returned from the stockroom and Mrs. Tobias brought her purchases to the checkout for Attalee to ring up. As Mrs. Tobias went out the door with a merry wave of her hand, Attalee watched her saunter to her car.

"That woman has the best skin I've ever seen," Attalee said. She tugged at the turkey wattle below her chin. "I've used Oil of Old Lady religiously for twenty years and my face looks like a stick of beef jerky. What do you suppose she puts on her face?"

"Oh, probably lots of those fancy department store face creams that cost fifty dollars for a tiny pot," Mavis said. "And she's likely had a nip and a tuck or two. Those rich women from The Hill go to their plastic surgeons so often, the doctors need to install revolving doors."

Attalee shook her head. "And I'll never figure out why she drives that Cadillac of hers all the way from Augusta to Cayboo Creek just to come to the Bottom Dollar Emporium."

Mavis looked up from the broom she was pushing across the floor. "She tells me we have the best deals on cleaning supplies in the whole area," she said. "But it does seem odd that she'd drive twenty minutes every week or so to save a nickel or two on a box of Brillo pads or a bottle of floor wax. Besides, there must be a half a dozen dollar stores in a city the size of Augusta."

Mavis glanced at me. "Mrs. Tobias comes in here because of you, Elizabeth. She dotes on you."

I shrugged. "I can't imagine why. It's not like I'm anyone special."

Five

My aim is to keep this bathroom clean. Your aim will help.
~ Cross-stitch sampler in Taffy Polk's powder room

On the night of my birthday, I drove to Augusta to visit my daddy. My half-brother Lanier had just been released from jail after serving six months for stealing a Camaro, so we Polks were throwing a celebration supper.

My daddy lives in a gated community called Brandywine. The place is on the swanky side of Augusta, but he's no blue blood. For years after my mama died, he was a no-account drifter. He worked every now and then in the mills or the granite mines until my granddaddy passed on and left a little furniture store on the Aiken-Augusta Highway, which runs outside of Cayboo Creek.

It wasn't much of a business then, just a collection of dusty dinette sets and ugly plaid sofas that my granddaddy sold to folks on a fixed income. But when my daddy got hold of the store, he turned it into a rent-to-own place called the Bargain Bonanza.

He had a grand re-opening and bought a slew of television spots making himself the spokesperson. He called himself "Insane Dwayne," and he'd blow something up in every commercial. His slogan was "Get on down to the Bargain Bonanza, where the savings are explosive." He'd even talked me into appearing in some of them.

I regretted that decision, because his commercials were the most obnoxious ones on the airwaves and too often I was recognized on the street as being the daughter of Insane Dwayne. But the TV ads sure did lure in the customers. Business got so good he had to move to a big warehouse up the road. He even added televisions, stereos, and DVD players to his inventory. And though I was glad that he'd finally done well for himself, I hated that his business robbed folks silly. A TV console that would normally cost a person about a five hundred dollars ended up costing them three times as much when they got done with Bargain Bonanza's rent-to-own plan.

Soon as my daddy got his first platinum American Express card in the mail, a gal named Taffy beamed into his life, just like on *Star Trek*. Two weeks after he met her at the Tuff Luck Tavern on karaoke night, he was saying "I do" in front of an Aiken County justice of the peace.

My stepmother Taffy doesn't talk much about her past, and I guess she's got her reasons. Meemaw's boyfriend, Boomer, swears that she looks a lot like one of the exotic dancers in the girlie clubs in Augusta he used to frequent. Boomer says if a body has a name like Taffy, she's either a stripper or a horse.

I don't know about that, but I do know that as soon as Taffy got the diamond on her finger, she insisted my daddy buy a house in Brandywine. It was a move my daddy would never have made on his own. Dwayne Polk might have the bank account of a doctor or a lawyer, but he has the soul of a South Carolina redneck. The sight of him sitting in their patio home on one of those velvet-padded chairs that Taffy bought from Ethan Allen looks stranger than a bulldog wearing a tiara.

I drove up to the gate at Brandywine and gave the security guard my name. Taffy's in charge of calling the gate when company comes, and she always manages to forget when I visit.

"What was the name again?" The man wiped his forehead with his sleeve. Even though it was mid-October, the thermometer read 80 degrees and he was cooped up in a gatehouse with no air conditioning.

"Elizabeth Polk. I'm kin to Dwayne Polk, who lives on Cordial Court." All the streets in Brandywine were named for after-dinner drinks.

He squinted at his list. "Wait a minute. I have a Betty Delores Polk. Would that be you?"

"Yessir."

He handed me the cardboard pass to hang on my rearview mirror and I drove on through. That Taffy. No matter how many times I tell her that my name is Elizabeth, she calls me "Betty D."

I poked my elbow out of the car window and drove over the sloping roads of Brandywine, admiring the way the landscapers managed to get the shrubs into shapes so perfect they looked like they'd jumped off the pages of an elementary school math textbook.

It had been so long since I'd visited, I almost took a wrong turn onto Grand Marnier Place. We Polks aren't a getting-together family; usually someone has to die, or in this case, get paroled.

I pulled up and parked on the street in front of their patio home. Taffy didn't like living in the patio-home section of Brandywine, which was called Phase III. She wanted one of those estate-type houses in Phase I or, at the very least, a big colonial house in Phase II. My daddy, who grew up in a mobile home made of little more than particle board and nails, said he wasn't spending that kind of cash just for a place to hang his hat.

Daddy's truck was in the driveway with his gun rack on the back, and so was Taffy's candy-apple-colored Trans Am. I walked up the sidewalk and mashed the doorbell. It played the song "I Got Friends in Low Places." Taffy's something of a catalog nut, and she's always buying doodads like musical doorbells or toilet paper that's got jokes written all over it.

As I stood by the door, my nose prickled at the delicious smell coming from behind it. Taffy is one heck of a Southern cook. She pounds out biscuits that are as light and buttery as croissants, and her flour gravy feels like silk on the tongue. Daddy always says that just about anyone can pull off decent fried chicken or black-eyed peas, but the true test of a country cook lies in her biscuits and gravy.

Taffy answered the door wearing a dress gleaming with a dozen or more brass buttons. She liked clothes with lots of buttons and braid trim, almost as if she'd been a bellhop in another life.

"Betty D. Glad you came. Happy birthday." She turned her back to me and hollered into the house. "Dwayne, your daughter is here!"

Taffy was forty-four years old, almost twenty years older than me, but she didn't look it. Her bland, baby-doll face seemed untouched by time.

"Damn, Taffy, I'm right behind you."

As my daddy rounded the corner, I saw his lip curled beneath his mustache. He was meaning to grin, but his expression came out looking like a sneer. My daddy is fifty-five, and he looks every second of it and then some. You can see the two-packs-a-day Benson and Hedges habit in the hollows of his cheeks, and his nose is battered with broken blood vessels from swilling Old Milwaukee every night.

From what I've heard, my daddy used to be one of the best-looking fellows in Aiken County, ever. My meemaw said he couldn't walk two feet without some girl throwing herself in his path.

"Hey there, who's my baby girl?" he said. His eyes looked as dark and rich as root beer in a mug and he was hiding something behind his back.

"Hi Daddy, Lanier here yet?"

"Lizzie. You didn't answer my question," my daddy said.

My finger traced the flocked fleurs-de-lis pattern on the wallpaper in the foyer. Meemaw had sweet tea coming out of her nose when I told her Daddy and Taffy had flocked wallpaper.

She howled, "I've lived in Cayboo Creek all my life and even I know that flocked wallpaper is tackier than sin."

"Daddy, please," I said. It was a game that he'd played with me ever since I was a little girl. He'd say, "Who's my baby girl?" and I was supposed to run into his arms and say, "I am, Daddy, I am." I was getting a little old for such silliness.

"Come on, Lizzie. Who's my baby girl?"

"The Queen of Sheba. Where's Lanier?"

"I sent Earl after him." Earl was Daddy's best friend and fetch boy.

"Happy birthday, Sugar," my daddy said. He brushed my cheek with his lips. Then he handed me a plastic bag. "Hope you like your gift."

I opened the bag and found I was the proud owner of a tool called the Ding King.

"It pops dents right out of your car," Daddy said. "They claim it'll pop out a dent the size of a grapefruit."

"Thanks, Daddy. I'm sure this will come in handy." I turned to Taffy. "Something sure smells good. Can I give you a hand in the kitchen?"

"Why don't you sit with your daddy in the library and keep him company while I cook," Taffy said.

The "library" was a den that contained over a hundred Harlequin Temptations paperbacks and a collection of back copies of the *National Enquirer*.

My daddy and I were strolling toward the library when the front door opened and Earl stuck in his gray head. "I got that boy of yours, Dwayne."

"Darn it, Earl," Taffy hollered from the kitchen, "I told you a million times you need to knock first. This ain't a boarding house. What if I was in my panties?"

"You heard the lady, Earl," Daddy said with a wink.

"Boy, get yourself in here." Daddy grabbed the knob of the door and opened it. My half-brother was crouching behind it.

"Shoot, Daddy, I was gonna surprise you." Lanier stood up tall and jammed his hands into the pockets of his blue jeans.

"Taffy, Lanier's here. Get out here and hug this boy's neck," my daddy said.

Taffy came streaming down the hall, her bracelets clanging together as she ran. She reached Lanier and gave him a big lip-smacking kiss, leaving a red splotch on his cheek.

Daddy cuffed Lanier on the shoulder every few seconds. It was obvious he wanted to wrap his arms around his boy and hug him, but the Polk men didn't get mushy with one another.

My daddy glanced at Earl, who was standing in the corner rubbing the bill of his John Deere cap.

"I'd ask you to stay, Earl, but this is kind of a family dinner. Understand?" my daddy said.

Earl nodded dumbly and slipped out the front door. Taffy grabbed a strand of Lanier's long, brown hair and fingered it. "Look at all the hair on this boy, Dwayne. I think you favor Keith Urban. Anyone tell you that you favor him, Lanier?"

Lanier wore his hair long in the back and cut close on the sides. The style had the unfortunate effect of making his narrow face look as skinny as a weasel's. Lanier didn't inherit Daddy's good looks or his sleazy brand of charm. My half-brother's complexion was the color of meat gone gray, and he held his mouth loosely like a toddler who lets his strained vegetables slip from his lips.

"Made your favorite dessert, Lanier. Peach cobbler," Taffy crooned.

"Just when is supper going to be on the table?" my daddy snapped.

Two spots of color bloomed high in Taffy's cheeks, but she knew better than to sass my daddy back in front of his boy.

"Come on, Betty D. We'll let the boys get reacquainted," said Taffy.

Lanier's head jerked in my direction as if seeing me for the first time."Hey, Sis."

"Hey Lanier," I said. I barely knew my half-brother. He was five years younger than me, and the product of a short affair my daddy had with a frizzy-haired woman named Nadine.

I tagged behind Taffy, knowing she wouldn't let me touch anything in her kitchen. I hopped up on one of the swivel bar stools while Taffy chopped onions on a butcher board on the kitchen island with a faux marble finish.

"Your daddy dotes on that boy. Some men dote on their daughters, but not Dwayne. The sun rises and sets on Lanier." Taffy was chopping so hard that her helmet of hair bounced on her shoulders. She glanced at me quickly.

"Sorry. Guess that wasn't a very nice thing to say."

I swiveled my chair back and forth. "It doesn't matter."

"How's things at the Bottom of the Barrel?"

"Things are fine at the *Bottom Dollar.*" I wasn't up to telling her about the Super Saver store coming to Cayboo Creek.

"You need to get out some over here in Augusta. It's not healthy for a girl to be cooped up in her house every night in a hick town with a mutt dog. 'Specially now that you're getting up there in years. Hell, by the time I was your age, I'd already run through two husbands. And you haven't snared you a one. When's the last time you've been out with a man?"

"One of my customers is setting me up with her grandson soon," I said, hoping she'd let me be.

Taffy leaned down to get the biscuits out of the oven and I felt my stomach rumbling. Just one biscuit, I vowed. My blue jeans had lately been cutting into my midsection.

"Who is he?" Taffy brushed the tops of the biscuits with butter.

"His name is Timothy Hollingsworth."

Taffy dropped the brush she was holding and gave me a surprised look. "Did you say Hollingsworth? As in Hollingsworth Paper Cups?"

I wanted to grab a biscuit and take a nibble, but instead I sat on my hands, inhaling the luscious aroma.

"Yeah, that's the one." I didn't like the way Taffy was staring at me. She had a blue vein that throbbed in her temple when she held her head real still.

Taffy flung open the door of the pantry. "Can't be. Can't be the same family. Why would a Hollingsworth date a girl from the Creek? Besides, a grandmother of a Hollingsworth wouldn't trade at a hole-in-the-wall place like that dollar store of yours."

"Grace Tobias thinks thrift is a virtue and she says that the

Bottom Dollar is just brimming with bargains," I said.

"Dwayne," Taffy said. "Get yourself in here!"

My daddy strode into the kitchen with Lanier behind him. His face was cloudy. "Is that any way to call a man to the supper table?"

"The heck with eating for a minute. You will not believe what your daughter told me right here in this kitchen. Go on. Tell your daddy what you just said."

All of their eyes were fixed on me. I wasn't used to being the center of attention in my family. I tugged on the hangnail on my index finger. "I'm going out on a date with Timothy Hollingsworth, is all."

Taffy clicked her fingernails on the counter. They were shiny and hard as billiard balls. "Timothy Hollingsworth. Son of that fellow who went belly-up on the golf course, owner of Hollingsworth Paper Cups."

"Well, imagine that. Our Elizabeth, doing the town with the son of a millionaire," Daddy said.

"That family is the richest one in Augusta," said Taffy.

Lanier looked bewildered at having lost his spot in the limelight. "When are we going to eat? I'm hungry," he whined.

"We will eat directly, Lanier," Taffy said. She shook her head sadly. "Elizabeth, you're a sweet girl but you aren't exactly high society. You won't have a clue about how to behave around a fancy pants like Timothy Hollingsworth."

"I'm sure I'll muddle through somehow," I said quietly.

Taffy lifted her chin and smiled brightly. "Luckily for you, I know a thing or two about how the other half lives. I'd be glad to give you some pointers before your date."

Daddy chuckled. "What do you know about the lives of rich folks, Taffy?"

"From reading books, Dwayne," Taffy huffed. "I have read every single word that Jackie Collins has ever written and those books are crawling with rich people. Or the 'jet set,' as they like to call themselves."

Taffy put her hands on her hips and looked me up and down.

"Your outfit just screams Kmart. You're definitely going to need some wardrobe advice."

My daddy flipped off the top of his beer. "Taffy, you've got more clothes that you need. Let her borrow some outfits of yours."

"Don't you have eyes? She doesn't got my figure. She's got nothing on top and a mite too much on the bottom," Taffy said. "However, I will let you borrow my faux zebra coat as long as you don't move around too much in it. It has a tendency to shed."

I scratched a mosquito bite on my ankle. "Thank you, Taffy. But I think I'll do fine with my own clothes."

"It *has* been a tad humid for the zebra," Taffy mused. "Listen here, if he takes you to a fancy restaurant and they set a little bowl with a lemon floating it in, don't drink it. It's to dunk your hands in. Rich people have all kinds of peculiar eating rules."

"Taffy, I know how to behave at the supper table," I said.

"Dinner!" Taffy said with a shake of her stiff hair. "People with class call it 'dinner.'"

"Tell me when you and Elizabeth stop your hen talk," my daddy said. "Me and the boy are hungry." He stole a gherkin from a cut glass dish and walked out of the kitchen. Lanier wandered behind him.

Taffy vigorously stirred a skillet of flour gravy on the stove. "There are so many things to remember. Don't spit chicken grizzle into your napkin. Don't sop your bread in the gravy." She turned her back on me to reach for some pepper in the cupboard. I probably had only a few seconds before she would whirl around with some other advice, so I took my chances and stole one of the biscuits from the cookie sheet and slipped it into my pocket book.

"Are you listening to me, Elizabeth?"

I nodded and hopped down from my perch at the bar. "Excuse me, Taffy, while I go to the powder room."

"I'll make a list," Taffy said. "That's what I'll do, and you can study on it before your date."

I walked down the hall on the copper-colored carpet that led to the powder room. Then I made myself comfy on the lid of the commode, retrieved the biscuit from my purse, and bit off a mouthful.

I thought about last Sunday's sermon at the Methodist Church. Reverend Matilda had quoted Mother Teresa's lesson about Jesus appearing in all of his distressing disguises. I thought of Jesus with blond hair, saline breasts, and blood-red nails. He surely would be hard to recognize. But he showed a glimpse of himself with the biscuits. As always, they were the best I'd ever tasted.

Six

Change is inevitable, except from a vending machine.

~ Handwritten sign on the Coca-Cola machine outside Bryson's
Hardware

Birdie tapped her gavel on a can of kidney beans. I'd asked her to chair the first meeting of SOB (Save Our Businesses) at the Bottom Dollar Emporium since she knew parliamentary procedure. "Order, please, order," she said in her high, sure voice. "Social hour is over. It's time to call our meeting to order."

The small group, who were huddled over a bowl of caramel corn, wandered over to the semicircle of folding chairs. Hank Bryson stuffed one last handful in his mouth and ambled to his seat.

As acting secretary, I noted everyone in attendance. Jerry Sweeny of the Stuff and Mount Taxidermy Shop was chewing on a piece of red licorice like it was a toothpick. He eyed Reeky Flynn with obvious interest.

Reeky, owner of the Book Nook on Main, had her nose in a copy of *Homeopathy, Healing and You.* Her curtain of long, brown hair obscured her face so that you could see only the glint of her granny glasses and the point of her sharp nose.

Orson from the Bait Box and Tanning Salon scooted his chair next to mine and tipped the brim of his hat in greeting. Jewel Turner, owner of the Chat 'N' Chew, had taken off one of her shoes and was massaging her stockinged foot. Boomer from the butcher shop wanted to come, but he had to attend a meat cutter's convention. That was everyone, besides Mavis, Attalee, and me.

"I want to thank all of you for coming out this evening," Birdie said. "I know everyone here sympathizes with Mavis's plight. And I'm sure she appreciates your support."

Mavis nodded, twisting her hands nervously in her lap.

"I'd like to turn the floor over to Elizabeth," Birdie said. "She's the one who called this meeting."

"Thank you, Madam Chairperson," I said softly. I cleared my throat. "I know y'all are here because you care about Mavis and you don't want her business to go under. But this is really more than Mavis's problem. Our whole town is being threatened."

With everyone's eyes on me, I felt my palms getting slick.

"This is about huge companies coming here with their corporate backing and their big bank accounts and knocking aside the little guys. This is about losing Cayboo Creek's character as a town. It started with Goody's wiping out Vickery's Family Clothiers. Now I know some of us here aren't too keen on Mello Vickery—"

"Her nose is so high in the air it oughta be on her forehead," Attalee remarked.

"Speaking of which, did you know that Goody's is having a big old sale on all their Dockers?" Jewel asked, twirling a strand of her red hair around her finger. "Twenty-nine dollars a pair. Sag Harbor's being marked down too."

Reeky glanced up from her book and consulted her watch. "Do they stay open to nine on weekdays?"

"Excuse me, Jewel, Attalee, and Reeky," Birdie said. "You've not been recognized." She nodded for me to continue.

"Thank you," I said. "Then of course, there's that new Winn-Dixie coming to town. Now I realize we desperately need a new grocery store, but—"

"Do we ever!" Attalee said. "I've heard there's going to be a deli, video rental, and an in-store ATM."

"Is there going to be a seafood department?" Jewel asked. "Or is that just a rumor?"

"Ladies," Birdie warned. "The chair doesn't—"

"There's been talk of an in-store coffee shop and restaurant," I said loudly. "They'll probably serve the same sort of things you do at the Chat 'N' Chew restaurant, Jewel."

"What?"Jewel gasped.

"And they may even have a whole aisle filled with paperbacks and bestsellers, Reeky."

"They wouldn't," Reeky breathed.

"Gosh, Elizabeth," Jerry said, in a nervous voice. "You don't suppose they'll have an on-premises taxidermist too?"

"No, Jerry," I said. "I think you're safe. You too, Orson. I've not seen live bait in many grocery stores. But what I've been trying to say is, this isn't just Mavis's problem. It's all of our problems and if we don't start addressing it now, some or all of us could be out of business one day."

Hank put up his hand. "Can I be recognized, Madam Chairman?"

Birdie nodded.

"Elizabeth has a real point here and nobody knows that more than me, being in the hardware business," Hank said. "Thanks to those big warehouse hardware stores popping up all over the country, family-owned hardware stores are as scarce as hen's teeth."

"Is a new hardware store coming into town?" Orson asked.

"Not that I know of," I said. "But it could happen. That's why I called this meeting. We need to prepare for those kinds of eventualities."

"I never even thought about that new Winn-Dixie carrying books," Reeky said in a panicky voice. "Right now the Book Nook is the only place in town that carries reading materials. I've had to add knickknacks to my inventory just to limp by. People in Cayboo Creek don't appreciate good literature."

Reeky had moved here from Columbia, S.C., two years ago to look after her ailing mother. She'd been a secretary in the English department at the University and we all got the impression that most Creek folk were a tad backward for her tastes.

Jerry grinned at Reeky. "I love to read. You carry Louis L'Amour in that shop of yours?"

"No," Reeky said, quickly.

"How about *Taxidermy Today*," he asked. "I read that every month."

"Magazines extolling the killing of innocent animals?" Reeky said. "I'd sooner carry *Soldier of Fortune.*"

"That's one heck of a magazine, too," Jerry said. "I'll have to come visit this shop of yours."

"Order, please," Birdie said with a bang of her gavel.

Jewel waved her hand. "Elizabeth, what can we do about this? I don't want Cayboo Creek to be taken over by big businesses. I like our town the way it is."

Everyone nodded, even Reeky.

"I do have some ideas," I said. "I visited a Web site called Sprawl-Busters that says towns can pass zoning changes that favor local businesses and keep out big old stores like Wal-Mart and Home Depot."

"Can those zoning laws be retroactive? Could we stop the Winn-Dixie or the Super Saver from coming here?" Mavis asked.

"It would be much harder to keep out businesses whose zoning have already been approved," I said. "Besides, I don't think we'd get support in town for keep the Winn-Dixie out. Folks are getting tired of driving twenty miles to Augusta for their groceries."

"My Fudge Swirl ice cream is soup by the time I get it home," Attalee said. "'Specially in summertime."

"As far as the Winn-Dixie is concerned, if it threatens any of our local businesspeople like Reeky and Jewel, we could start a campaign to discourage folks from buying books there or other items that take away from local businesses," I said.

"I don't know if that will work too well," Orson said, leaning back in his chair. "People might do it for a spell and then they'd slack off."

"I know," I said. "But there's no sense going off the deep end until we find out exactly what threat the Winn-Dixie will pose. A couple of phone calls should clear that up."

"I'd be glad to call corporate headquarters, Elizabeth," Birdie said. "I was planning to do a story in the *Crier* anyway, so I can find out what amenities the new Winn-Dixie will offer."

"Great, Birdie," I said. "Now I think it's time to turn our attention to the Bottom Dollar Emporium. What can we do to help save it?"

Hank squirmed in his chair. Jerry fumbled in his shirt pocket for his chewing tobacco. A couple of people coughed. The brainstorming session wasn't going the way I'd planned.

After a long moment, Jewel said, "How about offering trading stamps? I remember when I was a little girl, me and my mama always made a point to go to the grocery stores that gave away S&H trading stamps."

"I got a four-slice toaster with ten books of trading stamps. I had a green tongue for days," Birdie remarked.

"Offer the customer incentives," I said, writing on my notepad. "Good thinking, Jewel. We'll look into that. Anything else?"

"Why don't we write a letter telling the Super Saver not to come?" Attalee said. "Tell them we already have a dollar store here and one is plenty."

Everyone chuckled. Mavis shook her head and patted Attalee's shoulder.

"I wish it were that simple, dearie," she said.

"Wait a minute," I said, suddenly inspired. "It might just *be* that simple. Suppose we *do* write a letter to the top brass of the Super Saver saying they're not welcome here? But along with the letter we enclose a petition signed by the townspeople saying they won't patronize the Super Saver if it opens here."

Hank slapped his ample thigh. "You know, Elizabeth, you might just have something there."

After some discussion it was decided that everyone in attendance would keep a petition in their businesses urging customers to sign. Other petitions would be distributed to all the businesses on Main and Mule Pen Road. Birdie would write an article in the *Crier* about our campaign and all of us would try and get as many signatures as possible.

Everyone seemed encouraged except Mavis, whose face was awash with uncertainty.

"I called Madge last night," she said softly. "She says Onida has five inches of snow on the ground. Can you imagine? And here it is only October." She pulled her sweater tightly around her and shuddered.

"Don't you worry, Mavis," I said. "This next October you'll be wearing your summer nightie and sleeping under the ceiling fan as you've done every October of your life."

"I wish I could be as sure of that as you, Elizabeth," she said.

"Don't worry so, Mavis," Birdie said. "I do believe we've made some accomplishments this evening. And this is just the beginning." Birdie gave one final tap of the gavel. "Meeting adjourned."

Seven

Heck is where people go who don't believe in gosh.
~ Sign outside the Rock of Ages Baptist Church

The first time I laid eyes on Timothy Hollingsworth, he was wearing a sheet. Not a Klan sheet with a hood, mind you, but more like something you'd pull off a Sealy Posturepedic. It was all bunched up on one side, leaving one of his shoulders bare. Not only that, his head was as smooth as a doorknob.

"Elizabeth, may I present my grandson, Timothy Hollingsworth." Mrs. Tobias beamed at him so hard her face nearly cracked.

"How are you?" I said. I laid down my price gun and extended my hand, which he shook with one abrupt jerk. He didn't say "hey" back.

Mavis and Attalee, who'd been stocking bottles of Shur Fine Hot Sauce, stopped in their tracks.

"I've told Timothy all about you, Elizabeth," Mrs. Tobias said. "He's been anxious to meet you."

Timothy's expression was blank, trancelike. He nodded and kept nodding, like one of those bobble-head puppy dogs that folks stick on their dashboards.

"I'll be only a minute here, Timothy. Why don't you wait in the car for me?" Mrs. Tobias said. She kissed him on the cheek and he swept out of the store like a big, white bird.

"Who was that, Jesus H. Christ?" Attalee demanded.

Mrs. Tobias smiled, beneficently. "I knew all of you would be curious about Timothy's robe. It's what he always wears. He's a Buddhist."

None of us could think of anything nice to say, so we didn't say anything at all. Mavis patted the slight brush of a mustache above her upper lip, like she always does when she's nervous.

"I'm so sorry, ma'am. And I don't be meaning to tell you what to do, but there are deprogrammers who can wipe clean all that garbage cults cram into young people's minds. I saw it on *60 Minutes,*" Mavis said.

"Buddhism is not a cult," Mrs. Tobias replied curtly.

"She's right, Mavis." I didn't have much formal learning, but I read a lot. "I've heard about Buddhism. Buddhists like to sit real still, and keep their minds blank, like an Etch A Sketch after it's been shook up. It's called meditation."

"Sounds like brainwashing," Attalee remarked.

"It's utterly harmless," Mrs. Tobias said.

"All the same, you'd better keep that young'un away from Kool-Aid," Attalee said.

Mrs. Tobias touched me lightly on the shoulder. "What did you think of Timothy, Elizabeth?"

"He's very handsome," I said. "Although he does seem a little shy."

"He's not used to being in the real world," Mrs. Tobias said. "And Elizabeth, I believe you're just the person to get him re-acclimated."

"That's a dear thing to say," I said. "I'll be glad to help."

"Good," Mrs. Tobias said. She pulled on her driving gloves. "I'll have him contact you as soon as his vow of silence is over."

A week later I decided to give my dog, Maybelline, a flea dip. (I named her Maybelline because she's slick, black, and streaky, like mascara.) I was wrestling with her when the phone rang. It distracted me a minute, giving her a chance to slip out of my arms and hop up on the bed and rub flea dip all over my brand-new bedspread. I nearly shouted "hello" because I was so aggravated with Maybelline, and the line went quiet.

"Hello, hello," I demanded.

"May I speak with Elizabeth Polk?"

I am nobody's fool. I know when folks use your full name on the phone, they are generally trying to sell you something.

"Now, mister, I know that you're hard at work in your cubicle, trying to scratch out a living, and I respect that. But the fact is, if I want to buy something, I go to the store and get it. I don't like to be pestered in my home. Besides, if you knew how few nickels I have to rub together, you wouldn't waste your time trying to sell me replacement windows or a cruise to the Caribbean."

The line remained silent. The caller wasn't much of a telemarketer. The good ones usually squeak in their sales pitch the second a person pauses to take a breath.

"This is Timothy Hollingsworth. My grandmother..."

A blush heated up my cheeks. "My goodness, am I ever sorry. Mrs. Tobias told me that you'd be calling. I didn't mean to be rude, but Maybelline escaped and was rubbing her dirty belly all over my nice, new bedclothes. And I thought you were one of those telemarketers."

"Maybelline?"

"She's my dog. She's a good dog most of the time, except when she pees the bed."

Timothy didn't have much to say about that, or anything else, for that matter. He was stingy with his words like he was paying for every syllable, but I figured he was just out of practice. And, if the truth were known, some people are a bit too talky anyway.

He asked me if I'd join him for a mineral water the next night. He said he drank only water, because he was following something called "precepts," which meant he couldn't ingest substances like coffee or alcohol. After he asked for directions to my house, he told me he'd be picking me up around five o'clock since he went to bed very early. I said that it all sounded fine to me, only I was a little worried about the mineral water. Most places around here get their water straight out of the tap.

Feeling nervous about going out with a near stranger, I hung up the phone. I noticed a wet, black nose sticking out from under the dust ruffle of my bed. Armed with a bath towel, I called Maybelline. She crept out on her belly and looked up at me with pleading, dark eyes. Her tail made one cautious thump on the braided bedside rug.

"Get over here, girl," I said in a soothing voice. She darted across the floor and just before she reached me, she shook herself, sending a flurry of hair and water droplets into the air. I gathered her up in the towel like she was a baby and started drying her.

My gaze settled on my open closet, reminding me I didn't have much to wear for an evening out. I willed my eyes to skip over the pristine wedding dress encased in plastic. No luck there.

I set Maybelline down and went to inspect the dress. I unzipped the plastic bag and put the silky fabric next to my cheek as I had done on and off for two months, ever since Clip broke off our engagement. I closed my eyes, imagining Clip squeezing me close and whispering into my ear how much he loved me and how he'd stay with me forever.

The image used to be so vivid to me—all of Clip's features crisp and clear, like a glossy photograph on a magazine cover. But now, although I remembered parts of him—eyes dark like plums, a sharp, stubborn chin—I couldn't put them together in my mind anymore. I had brought out his memory so often that it was wearing out, like a design on a T-shirt that fades with too many washings.

I picked up the dress and studied it. It didn't even look like my sort of style anymore. The neckline was tight and prissy and the skirt had too many layers. It was time for the dress to go up into the attic.

Eight

I Still Miss You Baby, But My Aim is Getting Better
~ Selection F-7 on the jukebox at the Tuff Luck Tavern

The knock at the door was so soft I might have missed it altogether if Maybelline hadn't barked.

I flung open the door and there stood Timothy Hollingsworth, dressed not in his flowing robe, but wearing a robin's-egg blue button-down shirt and a freshly pressed pair of khakis. I noticed his scalp was no longer completely bald. Little bristles of growth made his head looked like a hard-boiled egg covered in pepper.

"Hey there. Come on in," I said with a grin.

He took his time wiping his feet on the doormat, although his loafers looked clean and the ground was dry.

He looked up at me with nervous, blinking eyes, but stood stock still. He had a square jaw and a large Adam's apple that rested above the top button of his shirt.

I gave him wide berth to come in the house and he took one baby step inside. Maybelline chose that moment to streak past me and hump Timothy's leg.

"Stop that right now, Maybelline! You hear me? Get down. You are a nasty young lady!"

Maybelline reluctantly let loose her prize. She plopped on her back and lolled on the carpet like a Playboy bunny. Timothy went pale, expect for the tips of his ears, which turned bright red.

"Excuse my dog. She doesn't have a lot of manners."

He swayed like he might topple over headfirst onto the carpet.

I scooped up Maybelline and stashed her in the bedroom. "Are you all right? Can I get you some water?"

Timothy didn't reply. Instead he glanced around the room. His eyes swept over the glass shoe collection on my knickknack shelf, which had been passed down to me by my mama. He took in the two-toned shag carpet and my big ugly couch—the color of orange marmalade—that I'd bought at the Rock of Ages Baptist Church's annual attic sale.

"It's not much, I know, but it's home to me," I said.

His eyes abruptly dropped to his shoes and he stood in the middle of my room as motionless as a magnolia tree.

"Did you have a mind of what you wanted to do?" I asked, slipping into a light jacket. "I can't think of anyplace around here that has mineral water."

He was breathing slowly and deliberately.

"We could eat," he finally said in a voice barely louder than a whisper.

"There's the Wagon Wheel just a few blocks from here. We could walk even," I suggested.

"A wagon wheel," he repeated, like I'd said something in a foreign language.

"It's a steak restaurant, but it's also home of the fifteen-foot Mega Bar."

He glanced up from his shoes. "When I was in San Diego, sometimes I would eat only a bowl of rice, the entire day. I would sit and chew each grain. It would take hours."

It was the longest string of words I'd ever heard him speak. He looked winded from the effort.

"They got rice at the Wagon Wheel," I said. "Well, rice and gravy."

He didn't reply. He strode to the door and I followed behind him, down the rickety wooden steps. Out on the sidewalk, Timothy was still breathing heavily, like he could use a snort from an asthma inhaler.

"You okay? Sounds like the ragweed might be getting to you," I asked.

"I'm just keeping track of my breathing," he replied.

Far as I knew, breathing was one of the few things in this world we didn't have to keep up with. But I wasn't arguing with him. We walked a little farther in silence. It wasn't an easy, friendly silence. It was like a big plate glass window. You just wanted to pick up a rock and break it.

"I know that Buddhists meditate, but what do you meditate about?" I said.

Timothy stopped for a moment, as if stymied by the challenge of talking and walking at the same time.

"I often meditate on my own impermanence. I imagine my flesh pulling back from my cheeks to reveal my skull. I see my skin rotting away and my bones turning to dust."

I was beginning to think that silence wasn't such a terrible thing, after all.

"You deliberately think about stuff like that?"

"Yes, humans are like dead plant matter." He toed a pile of leaves with his shoe. "We have our season and then we perish."

We started walking again. I looked up at the pine trees. Hundreds of chattering birds rose from the branches in a dark wave.

My shoes made a hollow sound on the pavement. I decided to cut through Hank Bryson's yard when I remembered too late that he lived one house over from Jonelle. On the clothesline in Jonelle's yard hung tiny black lace panties for all the world to see. They twitched in the breeze like frilly little flags. I flinched at the mental pictures they brought to mind.

"When I was a little girl I thought death would show me a loophole," I said. "I was sure it wasn't going to happen to me. Does meditating on death make it less scary?"

"Fear is just a mind state," Timothy replied curtly.

"Buddhism must be some kind of powerful religion if the people who believe in it never get scared."

He strode slightly ahead of me, his arms as stiff as planks. He glanced back at me and said, "It isn't that you aren't scared of anything anymore, it's just when your fear arises, you observe the nature of it, thereby robbing it of its power. My teacher had us practice with troublesome mind states like fear."

I quickened my pace to keep up with his long legs. "What kind of things did he have you do?"

"I've always feared the dark, so he made me meditate amongst the tombstones in a nearby cemetery."

"That's awful. Weren't you scared?"

Timothy stopped walking again. "Maybe a little. But I impersonally watched my fear. It started out like the distant rumbling of thunder. If something would rustle in the leaves or I thought I heard approaching footsteps, it built to this enormous crescendo, beseeching me to become caught up in its maelstrom, but I was like the Buddha under the Bodhi tree; I resisted. Finally it disappeared."

Timothy's eyes flashed as he spoke; talking about Buddhism made him come alive. He was nice company, as long as he didn't talk any more about his skin rotting off.

The breeze picked up, causing a piece of my hair to fly into my mouth. Dried-out leaves scraped across the pavement.

"The Wagon Wheel is just around the corner." I gestured with my head.

Cayboo Creek's commercial area consisted of Main Street and Mule Pen Road, which was home to the vacant Pig. Next to the empty Pig was a patch of field (soon to be the site of the dreaded Super Saver Dollar Store), the diner called the Chat 'N' Chew, the bowling alley, the Tuff Luck Tavern, Dun Woo's House of Noodles, and the Wagon Wheel. As Timothy and I crossed Mule Pen Road, several cars honked and I waved in response.

When we walked inside the restaurant, Hank Williams Junior was crooning "I Got a Tear in My Beer" on the jukebox.

We filled our plates at the Mega Bar. I took a slab of meatloaf, some fried onion rings, a square of cornbread, and a piece of corn on the cob, dripping with butter. Timothy seemed stymied by all the choices, but eventually settled for some plain rice, vegetables, and a helping of salad. I steered him away from the okra (Maynard, the head cook, boils it too long and it has a tendency to be slimy) and talked him into a made-from-scratch helping of peach cobbler. With our plates heaped high (mine considerably higher than his), we sat down at a red, padded booth. Our waitress was Chiffon. She wore a button pinned to her uniform that said, "Ask me about our all-you-can-eat catfish nuggets."

"Hey there, Elizabeth. How's your meemaw?" She cut her eyes at Timothy and I knew she was dying to know who he was.

"Feisty as ever. How's the young'uns and Lonnie?" I asked, even though I'd just talked to her on the phone two hours ago.

"Emily stuck a pinto bean up her nose just before I was leaving for work, but luckily she sneezed it right out," Chiffon answered. She jotted our drink orders on her pad. "Y'all need anything else?" she asked.

"That ought to do it," I said, knowing that Chiffon would see to it that everyone in Cayboo Creek knew that I'd been spotted in the Wagon Wheel with a mysterious man with hardly any hair.

Chiffon brought ice water for Timothy and sweet tea for me and then left the table. Timothy leaned forward and said in a low voice, "There is something that scares me and meditation isn't helping."

"What's that?"

He whispered, "Surfing."

"Shoot, I don't blame you for that. Those big waves? Maybe getting bitten clean in half by a shark? It's pretty terrifying. Did you have a bad scare out there in California?"

Timothy smiled. At first it looked something like a scowl, as if his muscles were out of practice, but then the corners of his mouth turned up into a full-fledged grin.

"Actually, I was talking about surfing the Internet."

I snickered. "Of course. I guess since you came from California, I thought you meant..."

He was still smiling, and then he let loose a dry bark that sounded like he was either choking on a chicken bone or trying to laugh.

"I'm sorry. It's been a long time since I've been amused. Zen Buddhists don't laugh much."

"Well, I guess it's hard to laugh when you sit around thinking of rotting and dying all day," I said.

Timothy shook his head. "I apologize. I've made Buddhism sound grim when it really isn't. It can actually be quite joyful at times."

He paused to squeeze some lemon into his water. "But it also kept me away from the modern world. For the last ten years, I've begged for alms, chopped wood, and meditated. I haven't been on a computer in years. I start a computer skills course next week, but when I report to work at my family's company, I won't even know how to look up our Web site."

"Shoot. I have a PC at home. I could give you a few lessons after we eat."

Timothy leaned back into the booth. "Would you do that for me?"

"Of course."

He balanced his fork on the edge of his plate. "I'm a little nervous about going to work tomorrow. The employees are bound to think I'm odd. My mother says I should tell everyone I've been in the Peace Corps. She says people in Augusta won't understand about my being Buddhist."

"She might have a point. There're really only two accepted religions around here, Baptist and NASCAR." I chuckled at my own joke.

Timothy's face went blank. "NASCAR?"

"Lord, you *have* been away from the real world."

He swiped at his mouth with his napkin. "I learned more from watching my teacher chop carrots than I could learn from a hundred books or sermons."

I was pleased to see Timothy relaxing a little. He wasn't panting like a dog anymore and he was talking louder.

"So you learned something from a man just by watching him chop carrots, did you?" I asked.

I was reminded of my old Sunday-school teacher, Miss Dolynick, who I thought was an angel in disguise because her lips were as shiny as a Red Delicious apple, and she smelled like honeysuckle. She led us in the song "Jesus Loves the Little Children," and her big blue eyes would fill with tears of love for Christ. Then one day after Sunday school, I was in the church parking lot and I saw her scratch her key along a brand-new Honda Civic. She didn't know I'd seen her do it. Later I found out the Honda belonged to Sonny Hotchkiss, her ex-boyfriend. I, too, learned a lot from Miss Dolynick that day.

"My teacher was an amazing man," Timothy said in between bites of coleslaw. "If it weren't for him, I'd have turned right around after a week of sleeping on the ground and walking barefoot on the cold cobblestones. But then I met him, and just by looking at him, I could see there was a whole other way to be."

Timothy's eyes were as lively as flames in a gas burner. "Those years in the monastery were the most content I've ever known," he said.

"Then why did you leave?"

Timothy ran his finger along the rim of his water glass.

"As you probably know, my father died a few months ago. After the funeral, my mother expected me to come home. I'm ashamed to say that I didn't want to return to Augusta, but my teacher gave me no choice. He said I belonged with my family. He feared I was using the monastery as a refuge."

We were silent for a moment. Chiffon padded over to our table in white shoes with spongy bottoms. She filled my tea glass to the brim and asked Timothy if he wanted some more water, which he turned down.

After she left, Timothy inhaled sharply. "So now instead of

solving koans, I'll be running a company and learning to live all over again. The biggest koan of all."

"Koans? What are koans? Buddhist Bible verses?" I asked.

Timothy chuckled.

"Koans are puzzles that Zen students try to solve. But they aren't intellectual exercises, like algebra problems or riddles. Two students can give the same answer to a koan and yet the teacher may say that only one of them has given the correct answer."

"I'm pretty decent at the Jumble in the newspaper. Give me a koan."

Timothy stared me down. "I'm warning you, a koan is not like the Jumble. But if you insist, I'll give you my first koan."

I rummaged through my bag for a pen and a scrap of paper. I found a deposit slip from the bank and poised my pen over it.

"Go ahead, shoot."

"All right then, Elizabeth. Here it comes: What was your true face before you were born?"

I wrote down what Timothy said. "Okay, I got it. What was my face before I was born? Go on."

"That's all. That's the koan."

My left eyebrow arched. "Well, how in the world am I supposed to figure this out? It doesn't even make sense. I didn't have a face before I was born. Give me another one. An easy one."

"I'm telling you, Elizabeth. Koans aren't ordinary puzzles like the one about the rooster laying an egg on a barn. You won't figure it out using logic. You must meditate on the answer. However, I'll give you another one. Ready?"

"Let me have it."

"What is the sound of one hand clapping?"

I dropped my pen on the table. "Now I know you're flat making this up. I have my own koan for you. 'Whose leg do you think you're trying to pull?' Now give me a real one. Don't underestimate me, Timothy Hollingsworth. I got a lot of common sense."

"I would never underestimate you, Elizabeth." His eyes were

teasing, and I liked hearing him say my name. For a minute it was almost as if he were a regular guy flirting with a girl.

"By the way, Timothy Hollingsworth," I said in a sly voice. "Roosters don't lay eggs."

After we finished eating, we ambled to the checkout. Timothy completely ignored the toothpick dispenser, which I thought was classy. Clip always zoned in on it, like a dog taking to a fire hydrant. I smiled at Timothy and he returned the grin, but this time it came easily for him.

As he smiled, I noticed what a nice, full bottom lip he had and I briefly wondered what it might be like to kiss him. But then I decided that was silly. The two of us came from completely different worlds. Also, even though Timothy had opened up to me some, it was obvious that he was so shy that if he even thought about kissing a girl, he'd probably have a heart attack.

Still, I thought he might be a nice fellow to have as a friend.

Nine

Warning! In case of rapture this car will be unmanned.
~ Bumper sticker on Reverend Hozey's Chevy Lumina

"That a new dress?" Attalee asked me. She'd forgotten to pencil in her eyebrows, so her forehead appeared to occupy three-quarters of her face.

"It isn't new." I shook out a nylon nightie and slid it on a hanger. I'd just finished putting out a new shipment of sleep-wear.

"Is so," Attalee jutted out her bottom lip. "You never wore it before, and I've seen you nearly every day for the last ten years. I could sit here and tell you everything you got hanging in your closet. The lilac sweater and skirt set that's all nubby around the hem and sleeves, that black dress with the empire waist that's torn underneath the armpit, that polyester shift that's either rust or burgundy—"

"It's just not brand-new," I said to hush her. "I got it at the Goodwill for five dollars. Nice bargain, huh?" I did a little twirl in front of her and then walked to the canned-goods aisle to take inventory.

Attalee swung around to address Mavis, who was in the break area reading *Us*. Her hand was tucked into a bag of pork rinds.

"You have a surly store manager here, Mavis," Attalee said. "Asked her if she had a new dress, and she said it ain't new, it's new to *her*. Well, la di dah, Missy, new to you means new." Attalee stuck her tongue out at me.

"Uh, huh," Mavis said reading her article. Mavis's mustache had an orange tint to it, so she must have bleached it recently.

"Did it ever occur to you that your wardrobe is all over the color wheel?" Attalee asked me. "You wear lilacs, blacks, reds, and pastels. You're supposed to stick to a season. My granddaughter Shawnee would rather be naked than put anything on her back that wasn't from the autumn family."

"Mavis, we're running out of Clover Valley soups," I said. "All we've got left is Cream of Celery and Vegetable Beef."

"And don't be trying to change the subject," Attalee shouted. "Which was...? Heavens to Betsy, what was the subject?"

Mavis put down the magazine. "I could go for years without reading one more thing about Miley Cyrus." She strode to the back of the store.

"I remember the subject!" Attalee interjected. "The subject is why Elizabeth is all of a sudden showing up in new things. Today a new dress. Yesterday a brand-new scarf; the day before a dolphin pin with a rhinestone eye."

"It's a whale pin," I remarked.

Attalee shrugged. "Dolphin. Whale. Do I look like Jacques Cousteau to you?"

"Attalee!" Mavis shouted. "If I've told you once, I've told you a hundred times, please don't leave your teeth lying around. I just ran across them in health and beauty and they like to have given me a stroke."

"Now you're changing the subject again, trying to confuse me," Attalee said. "Elizabeth is wearing fancy new things and lately when she gets a phone call, she ducks into one the aisles. Not that we can't tell that something is up because of all the giggling and carrying on and using big words trying to impress certain people. It's plain as the nose on my face—"

The door opened and Mrs. Tobias walked into the Bottom Dollar.

"—that our Elizabeth is smitten with that bald boy!"

Mrs. Tobias clutched her purse close to her side. "What's this

I'm hearing about Elizabeth?"

I felt the skin on my face turn all kinds of colors. I have delicate, paper-thin skin that shows my emotions just like one of them mood rings. I felt like giving Attalee's curls a good yank.

"Oh, it's just Attalee carrying on," I said.

"Well, if you're discussing Timothy and Elizabeth's friendship, I want you to know that I think it's just lovely," Mrs. Tobias said. "Ever since they've met that child's been like a new person. There's a new lilt in his step and I think Elizabeth deserves full credit. And thank goodness, he's once again growing a lovely head of hair."

"And staying away from airports, I hope," Attalee said.

"Attalee," I said, sounding a warning note that she couldn't have missed. But she ignored me and stalked over to Mrs. Tobias.

"Elizabeth's been acting loopy, too," she said. "I think she's setting her cap for your grandson. But it would never work. She was raised Baptist, and he's a Buddhist. What would the young'uns be, Booptists?"

I opened my mouth to speak, but nothing came out except a feeble exhale of air.

"Timothy was born a High Episcopalian, and he will be buried as a High Episcopalian." To punctuate her statement, Mrs. Tobias gestured like a cop stopping traffic, though the gumdrop diamond on her hand could have caused quite an accident. "This Buddhism business is clearly a stage," she added quickly.

"I'm glad Timothy's so chipper," I said. "But I'm sure it's not just because of our friendship."

I put the emphasis hard on the word "friendship," so Mrs. Tobias wouldn't think I was getting any outlandish ideas. Since our dinner at the Wagon Wheel and his lesson on the computer, Timothy and I had gone out for two lunches and a walk along the Savannah River. The most intimate Timothy had ever gotten with me was when he accidentally kicked my leg underneath the table at the Chat 'N' Chew.

"Mrs. Tobias, you want a cup of coffee?" I asked. "I made some fresh."

She crossed toward me with a warm smile on her face. At least she didn't seem concerned about Attalee's remarks. She took my hand and patted it. Her palm was cool and dry, as if she had dusted it with powder.

"I want you to know that I am tickled pink that you and Timothy have hit it off so well. He's my favorite grandchild and you're my favorite... well, you're my favorite young person, Elizabeth."

"Thank you, ma'am."

"Any more news about this dollar store that's supposed to be coming to Cayboo Creek?" Mrs. Tobias asked.

At the mention of the Super Saver, Mavis seized her coffee cup and strode to the stockroom.

"Nary a word," I said. "It's kind of a delicate subject around here, Mrs. Tobias," I whispered. "But I'm not putting my head in the sand. I rode over to the Small Business Development Center out in Augusta and got every pamphlet they had on marketing techniques. When and if they open up, I'll be ready for them." I also filled her in about the first meeting of SOB and asked her to sign the petition.

She signed with a flourish. Her handwriting was so pretty it almost looked like calligraphy. "Elizabeth, you really should look into attending the University," she said, tucking her fountain pen back into her purse. "They have night classes, you know, for more mature students. If it's a matter of finances, well, I'd be delighted to speak with my banker. I'll just bet he could find a student loan with an uncommonly low interest rate. And if not, why, I'd just lend you the money myself."

"I've told you before, Mrs. Tobias. I'm just not college material." I handed her a mug of coffee. "Besides, why would you want to lend me money?"

Mrs. Tobias smiled. "I just think it's important that young people have long-term goals," she said. "Besides, what am I going to do with all my money? Spend it on fussy little senior tours to peep at leaves? I should think not."

Just then Chiffon charged into the Bottom Dollar in her gingham waitress uniform. Her hair net was askew and she was out of breath.

"Elizabeth, we need you right away at the Wagon Wheel!" she shouted. "Alice Faye Pruitt clutched her chest and fell face first into the coleslaw bin. We think she may have had a heart attack."

I tossed my clipboard aside. "Did you call 911?"

"Yeah, they're on their way, but I knew you could get there quicker," Chiffon said.

"What's this all about?" Mrs. Tobias asked in a high, thin voice. "Why do they want you, Elizabeth?"

I didn't pause to answer, but as I was hustling out the door, I heard Attalee say, "Elizabeth was a lifeguard when she was in high school, so she knows CPR and that Hind-lick maneuver. She might save Alice Faye's life."

Chiffon and I tore across Mule Pen Road like our sneakers were on fire. We dashed inside the Wagon Wheel, where I saw a knot of folks kneeling by Alice Faye, who was laid flat out on the carpet by the Mega Bar.

"Move aside!" Chiffon hollered. "We got someone here who knows CPR."

People scattered like cue balls and I crouched beside Alice Faye, who looked gray as granite and still had matchstick carrots and mayonnaise all over her face from her dive in the coleslaw bin.

"Alice Faye, hang on in there. We'll fix you up."

I tilted her head back and listened for any sign of breathing. I didn't hear a sound, so I pinched her nose and blew into her mouth.

Still nothing. She was limp as a noodle and no breath came out of her blue lips.

"Come on, Alice Faye," I whispered. "Come on back to us."

I pressed down on Alice Faye's chest the way I'd done on the dummy during my last Red Cross class. Fifteen chest compressions and then two breaths, and it all had to be done quickly. Sweat from my brow dripped down on Alice Faye's paisley print dress as I continued with the chest compressions. Nothing seemed to be happening. I had no way of knowing if I was doing it right. There was no Red Cross lady looking over my shoulder to critique my technique.

"Any sign of the EMTs?" I yelled as I pushed on her chest. "Come on, Alice. Help me out here. Just breathe. You can do it."

Just then, I detected a slight exhale. Her breath was shallow at first, but grew steadier until there was no mistaking it. After a few good breaths, her red-rimmed eyes fluttered open. She jerked at the sight of me leaning over her and I said, "It's okay, Alice Faye. You're gonna be alright."

I nudged her to her side so she wouldn't choke on her own spit just as the EMTs sprinted in with a stretcher.

"Looks like she's breathing again," I said, as Josh Tucker knelt down to take Alice Faye's vital signs.

Chiffon crouched beside us and said, "Elizabeth jump-started her heart. That was amazing."

"You did good, girl," Josh said with a smile. He signaled for the other EMT to pick up Alice Faye's feet and they loaded her onto the stretcher.

I stood up with legs so weak I feared they'd splinter like toothpicks. Chiffon grabbed my arm to steady me, saying, "Lord, Elizabeth, watching you was like seeing an episode of *Baywatch* only without the beach."

Birdie weaved through the crowd of people that had gathered around us and snapped my picture with her old-fashioned flash camera.

"Elizabeth, you're a hero!" she cried out, as I blinked at the spots of the flash.

That's how I ended up on the front page of the *Cayboo Creek Crier,* my hair plastered to my head from perspiration, with the headline that read, "Dollar Store Girl Saves Dowager in Diner." (Birdie loved alliteration.)

Mavis bought ten copies and had one framed, which she displayed in the front of the store just above the shelves of Bunny bread.

Mrs. Tobias sent me a dozen pink roses and a card that said, "I've always known that you're a remarkable young woman." It was one of my proudest moments ever.

ᎢᎬᏁ

Timber! I'm Falling in Love
~ Selection C-10 on the jukebox at the Tuff Luck Tavern

Whenever Timothy and I had lunch plans, we would meet outside Hollingsworth Paper Cups, right under the gigantic cup made of Sheetrock. I liked to arrive early, because I enjoyed watching Timothy sprinting down the steps of the building in his dashing business ensemble. I was captivated by the idea of a man who got all spiffed up to go to work.

His shoes were as shiny and black as Maybelline's coat and the creases in his slacks were sharp enough to slice bread. His crisp, white shirts were monogrammed at the cuffs.

Timothy said his work clothes made him feel prickly. He continually fidgeted with the collar of his dress shirt and flung his tie over his shoulder as if it were the worst kind of nuisance. He confessed that when he was in the privacy of his office he would replace his stiff work shoes with sandals, and he often said how much he missed wearing his robe. I nodded sympathetically, but secretly favored his suit over his sheet.

Sometimes on weekends we'd have us a picnic along the banks of Cayboo Creek. We'd stretch out on a blanket to eat the lunch Timothy packed, dip elephant ears into the water, and listen to dragonflies hum as they slipped in and out of the knee-high rushes.

He got a kick out of bringing me foods he figured I hadn't tried before. Once he brought soft round cheeses about the size of half dollars that came in little mesh bags. Another time it was a big bottle of apple juice, all dolled up in foil so it looked like a bottle of champagne.

St. Thaddeus, the Episcopal church in downtown Augusta, featured performers during the lunch hour on Tuesdays. Since Tuesday was my day off, Timothy and I went every week.

I'd never seen such a variety of folks making music as I did at St. Thaddeus. I'm partial to country music—Clint Black, Faith Hill, and the like—but because of Timothy, I was starting to appreciate big band, blues, jazz, and even organ music.

Timothy listened during the concerts as if the world existed purely for the music. His attention was so fierce that it would pull me in when my own meandered, which was often.

I sat next to him on the pew, not touching him but close enough to feel his warmth. I would sneak glances at his profile out of the corner of my eye, because, given the setting, I was too shy for him to catch me looking at him. There was something very wifely about sitting next to a man in church.

St. Thaddeus had been Timothy's childhood church. One afternoon while we were waiting in line to get into the concert, I noticed some marble memorials on the wall in the church's entryway. I startled at the engraving "Lilly Tobias, Beloved Daughter and Sister, 1954-1975."

"Timothy, is this a relative of yours?"

Timothy nodded. "Yes. Lilly Tobias was my aunt. She died in a car accident before I was born. My grandmother says that my mother never really got over it. She and Lilly were identical twins."

I traced my finger over the letters, which were cold to the touch. "Mrs. Tobias never mentioned that she had a daughter who died."

"It was a terrible tragedy for all of them. She probably doesn't want to talk about it. Our family isn't one to discuss their pain."

I nodded and looked up at Timothy, who'd tucked his hands into his pockets. A November wind snatched up several leaves, which danced in front of us, as if alive. "You never mention your mother," I said. I could see puffs of my breath as I spoke.

Timothy shrugged. "Unfortunately, we aren't close. She doesn't even live here. Once I came home to look after the family business she flew off to the French Riviera, where she has a villa. As far as I know, she may stay there for good."

Timothy delivered this information matter-of-factly, but I thought I saw a twinge of sadness in his eyes, like he wished his mama was closer to him in more ways than one.

It was hard for me to imagine my family members scattered here and there like dandelion fluff. My own kin had always lived within hollering distance of one another in Cayboo Creek, until Daddy moved to Augusta when he married Taffy.

With his daddy gone and his mama an ocean away, I suspected Timothy sometimes felt all alone in the world. As the line started moving into the church, I touched Timothy's sleeve and smiled at him. I was glad that Mrs. Tobias had introduced us and that we were becoming such good friends.

One day Timothy and I were sitting on the bench by the creek, watching children pump their legs up and down on the playground swings a few hundred yards away.

"I remember doing that," I said. "Watching my legs fly out straight in front of me. Admiring the ways my knees wrinkled up. Thinking there was nothing as fine as legs that could snap out straight and bend at the hinges."

Timothy rubbed his chin. "You never seem to take anything for granted Elizabeth, not even knees. It reminds me of a poem by Whitman."

Then he recited an entire poem by heart. I'd never met anyone who could do such a trick—just fire off a poem as easily as pulling out a handkerchief from a jeans pocket. I loved the poem he recited; it talked about everyday things like a grain of sand and the egg of a wren.

"'And the narrowest hinge in my hand puts to scorn all machinery,'" Timothy said. He smiled. "That was the part that reminded me of what you said about your legs on the swing set, Elizabeth. I bet you didn't know that you think like a poet."

That poem made me hungry for others, and on our next meeting Timothy brought me a book full of some of the best poems in the world. I'd read one each night before I went to bed. I always thought poetry was only for college people or that you needed an English teacher to explain what they meant. But the more I read poems, the more I thought of them as word postcards to the reader. Like this: "Saw a chicken and a wheelbarrow. Wish you were here."

During one lunch hour, Timothy took me to the Morris Museum of Art in downtown Augusta. He taught me to notice the tiny strokes that made up the whole of a painting and to pay attention to the texture of the paint as it rose up from the canvas like frosting on a cupcake.

I stood in front of a painting of a river lined with live oaks, and I imagined pushing myself inside the canvas so I could feel the feathery brush of Spanish moss as it slithered down the trunks and smell the swampy water that splashed against the knuckled roots.

As much time as Timothy and I spent together, we weren't boyfriend and girlfriend, despite the winks I'd get from folks in Cayboo Creek as we walked down Main Street together. If his hand accidentally brushed mine, he'd quickly move it away. Friday and Saturday nights my phone stayed quiet, and my social calendar was as slow-moving as a glacier.

Sometimes when we were together, I felt Timothy studying me when he thought I didn't notice. As soon as I looked up, his eyes would jump to stare at the ground.

It got to the point that when I wasn't with Timothy, I thought about him—like how his newly grown hair licked his forehead and curved around his ears or his deep blue eyes that were really almost purple. Sometimes whole blocks of time would pass as I ran movies of Timothy in my mind. Soon enough I'd be rudely jolted out of my dream world when Maybelline barked or the oak tree outside my window scratched its branch across the screen.

Eleven

Snowmen fall from Heaven unassembled.
~ Message in the *Methodist Church Bulletin*

Fall withered into winter, and before I knew it the holiday season was upon us. Christmastime kept Mavis, Attalee, and me hopping at the store. It seemed just as soon as we put out the pumpkin pops and candy corn, it was time to replace them with marshmallow Peep snowmen and milk chocolate Santas wrapped in foil.

We were so busy, we didn't have time to stew over the impending opening of the Super Saver Dollar Store. Our group had collected almost two thousand signatures and sent it along with a letter to the corporate headquarters several weeks before, but we hadn't heard a word. There hadn't been any signs of progress on the vacant dirt lot since some surveyors had come around with their equipment in October. The neighborhood kids mostly used it to play dodge ball. I took this as a good omen. Maybe the Super Saver had decided to stay away from Cayboo Creek and just hadn't bothered to tell anyone.

The SOB group had lost some of its steam with the holidays looming. At our last meeting, Birdie reported that the new Winn-Dixie wasn't going to have a coffee shop after all. Nor would the store be much of a threat to Reeky, as they'd carry only a few paperbacks up front. Boomer's Butcher Shop would probably feel the pinch, but Boomer planned to add home delivery to give the

their money. SOB was also working with the
‿ng the zoning laws changed to keep out other
‿t that wouldn't help Mavis.
‿avis seemed too upset lately. With no stirrings from
‿   ‿er, she hadn't mentioned South Dakota in weeks. Plus
Mavi‿   ‿ real kick out of Christmas. She wore her candy-cane
earrings and sang "Rudolph the Red-Nosed Reindeer" in her
squeaky soprano voice as she hung tinsel from the ceiling.

Attalee had her "Merry Twistmas from Conway Twitty" album
playing on the boom box, and Santa Claus—who was actually Hank
Bryson from the hardware store—was scheduled to make an
appearance at the Bottom Dollar Emporium on Christmas Eve.

That afternoon Mavis closed up shop because she, Attalee, and
I were on the Christmas parade committee, which was meeting in
the break area of the store to finalize some last-minute details.

Hank Bryson scratched behind his ear with his pen and stared
at his clipboard. "Okay, so far in the parade we got the Pride of
Cayboo Creek marching band, the taxidermist shop, Miss Cayboo
Creek and her court of cuties, the Chat 'N' Chew who's going to
throw candy, yours truly as Santa, and—"

"About the taxidermist shop, Hank, do you know if Jerry plans
to display that mounted deer head on their float again?" asked
Reeky. "I personally found a dead deer wearing a Santa Claus hat
and a red nose a gruesome sight, and Lord knows what the children
thought."

Hank shifted uncomfortably in his seat, partially because his
girth wasn't meant to be stuffed into a $2.99 plastic chair, but also
because Reeky made him nervous. "I haven't checked with Jerry
over at the shop," he said. "But he's been doing that Rudolph thing
going on ten years now. Far as I know, the kids are crazy for it."

"'Traumatized' is surely the more accurate word," Reeky said.
Talking to Hank caused her smooth, pale complexion to prickle
with a rash.

"Well, Miz Flynn, Cayboo Creek is a hunting community," said
Hank in a patient voice. "When the young'uns around here see a

deer, they don't think Bambi, they think buckshot. Plus Jerry is one of our largest contributors when it comes to pitching in for Christmas decorations for Main Street."

More objections twitched on Reeky's lips, but she remained silent. Since her business was located on Main, she had a stake in seeing the street all gussied up for the holidays.

"I have a concern," said Birdie, who'd been recording the minutes of our meeting in her notebook. "Someone needs to approve the wardrobe choices for Miss Cayboo Creek and her court. Last year everyone was saying that they all looked like a bunch of hoochie-coochie mamas."

"I'm on that," Mavis said. "I told the girls they'd have to bring their gowns in here by the fifteenth for approval. By the way, Elizabeth, did you call the band director and tell him no more baton-throwing?"

"I did," I said.

Last year a stray baton had crashed through the window of the liquor store and nicked the ear of Prudee Phipps, who'd been purchasing sherry for some eggnog. When the baton broke the window, a group of women from the Rock of Ages Baptist Church had started shouting "Amen" and "Praise the Lord!" Prudee took it as a sign from God and had been a teetotaler ever since.

"I suggested that the students shake red and green pompoms instead of twirling batons, which I think will be more festive," I said.

"Anything else?" Hank asked.

We all shook our heads.

"Fine," Hank said. "Now the parade route will be the same, except we're going to go around Chickasaw Drive because of road repairs and—"

Chiffon's daughter, Emily, who was eight, burst through the front door.

Mavis rose from her chair. "Emily, we have a meeting going on here. We'll be opening back up in a few minutes."

"I know, Mrs. Loomis. But my mama told me to run over here

quick and tell you." The child's face was pink from the brisk weather. "We saw them. The cement truck. They're laying out the parking lot for that new dollar store."

We scrambled out of our seats without bothering with our jackets and followed Emily, who'd already torn out of the door in the direction of the vacant lot, her red scarf flying as she ran.

Our group trotted down Main and went one street over to Mule Pen Road, hugging our arms against the cool air. We crossed the road and heard the rumble of the cement truck before we saw it.

A sign had been erected on the site. "Future Site of the Super Saver Dollar Store," it read, over an artist's drawing of the finished store, complete with landscaping and cars in the parking lot.

"I'll be, Hank, that looks a lot like your truck in the drawing of that parking lot," said Attalee, her voice thick with accusation.

Hank glanced guiltily at Mavis. "Now Mavis, you know I wouldn't dream of trading anywhere but the Bottom Dollar."

We all stood there a moment, watching our breath cloud and listening to the churning of the cement truck.

Mavis broke the trance. "Come on. Let's go back. It's freezing out here." She looked forlornly at the Super Saver sign. "Although I suspect it's a whole lot colder in South Dakota. Last time I talked to Madge she said her mailman had to have the tip of his nose removed due to frostbite."

I wanted to buoy Mavis up. Tell her we couldn't throw in the towel, that we needed to prepare ourselves for a fight. But I could tell by the slouch in her shoulders and the shuffle in her walk that no matter what I said, she wouldn't be encouraged. Besides, I didn't know what to tell her. I was fresh out of ideas for saving the Bottom Dollar Emporium.

$\mathcal{T}$welve

I didn't fight my way to the top of the food chain to become a vegetarian.

~ Sign outside Boomer's Butcher Shop

On the afternoon of the Christmas parade, Timothy and I stood in front of Boomer's Butcher Shop watching a group of carolers traverse Main Street in a pickup truck decorated with holly and poinsettias. Boomer came out of his shop and saluted Timothy.

"So, Timothy," he said. "When are you going to make an honest woman of our little Elizabeth here?"

The tips of Timothy's ears turned bright red, and I dipped my head and studied the tufts of grass that grew out of the cracks in the sidewalk. Fortunately, at that very moment, Santa Hank appeared on his riding lawn mower with enough fanfare to deflect Boomer's question.

Timothy had taken to Cayboo Creek the way a water bug takes to a pond. He made small talk with the knot of men that hung outside Orson's Bait Box and Tanning Salon and folks around town were starting to call him by name. He'd even taken a few fishing trips with Chiffon's husband, Lonnie, saying that sitting in a bass boat waiting for a nibble was an excellent form of meditation. When he came in the store, both Attalee and Mavis teased Timothy about his easy acclimation to Cayboo Creek, saying he'd changed from Buddha to "Bubba" in under four months.

As Timothy watched Hank toss red hots and Smarties to the

kiddies, I made a rough head count for the parade committee. Clip and Jonelle were two among the crowd. I tried to move along, but Jonelle spotted me and made a show of clinging to Clip like a burr. When he saw me, Clip pulled up the collar of his jacket and ducked his head down like a turtle.

In spite of that personal dark moment, the parade went smoothly. The only off note came when Mello Vickery, who was marching in the parade as the Virgin Mary, tripped on her gown. The head of the doll she was carrying jarred loose from its body and rolled in the gutter, forcing Mello to finish out the route carrying a headless baby Jesus.

Regardless, Timothy said it was the nicest parade he'd ever attended. I sighed with relief when Miss Cayboo Creek and her court rode by, waving regally from their perches on the back of Ferrell Haines's pickup truck. The parade was finally over.

After the holidays, Mavis, Attalee, and I witnessed more progress with the Super Saver Dollar Store. The frame went up in January and by the end of the month, sheetrock was in place. Come February, the windows were in, the yellow Super Saver sign was erected, and a big banner announced "Grand Opening March 20."

Timothy Hollingsworth and I, on the other hand, were at a standstill. He spent almost all his free time in Cayboo Creek and although he was as sweet as he could be, I no longer anticipated him reaching across the table at the Wagon Wheel to stroke my hand. When he dropped me off at my house on Scuffle Road, I didn't linger in the passenger seat, thinking he might lean across the console of his Volvo and pull me in close for a kiss. And when I was alone, huddled beneath my comforter at night, I tried to blot out Timothy's blue eyes and his wavy, dark hair and replace it with the moon-shaped face of Orson Hobbs of Orson's Bait Box and Tanning Salon.

Orson had begun frequenting the Bottom Dollar Emporium on the pretense of being a customer, but we all suspected he was there to spark on me. As Attalee said, "It ain't humanly possible for a man to go through three boxes of Q-tips in one week."

On his visits to the store, he'd lean over the counter, wearing a T-shirt that said "Born to Fish; Forced to Work," and chat about how his bowling game was coming along. (He always kept his hand with the missing thumb discreetly hidden in the pocket of his Dickey work pants.)

Orson was a good-hearted man with an easy laugh. He lived in a brand-new double-wide trailer just on the banks of the creek and he didn't hang out at the Tuff Luck Tavern every night after work to toss back whiskey shooters. He also accompanied his mama to Rock of Ages Baptist Church every Sunday.

Fact was, Orson and I were a real logical match: dollar-store girl and bait-store boy. What could be more natural?

I'd made up my mind that if Orson got it in his mind to ask me out to the Wagon Wheel one evening, I was going to accept his invitation. I even told Mavis and Attalee that the next time Orson came in the store, they should prepare to see my eyelashes fluttering like palm fronds during a breeze. I was tired of spending every Saturday night alone watching Maybelline scratch fleas.

"What about Timothy?" Mavis asked. A crease of worry crossed her forehead. "Y'all make such a cute couple."

"He's clearly not interested in me as a girlfriend," I said with a flick of my hair. "Do you know that in all the months we've been keeping company he has not given me so much as a simple good-night kiss?"

Mavis and Attalee exchanged a look.

I slammed my price stamp down on a can of Tried and True Tuna. "He obviously doesn't find me attractive. Therefore, I think it's time to seek out greener pastures."

Mavis cleared her throat and touched me lightly on the shoulder. "I don't think that's true at all, Elizabeth," she said. "Why, when that boy is here, he can't take his eyes off of you. It's clear to everyone in town that he's smitten. I believe he just has a slower timetable than most fellows."

"Well, as everyone keeps reminding me, I'm not getting younger," I said with a sniff. "Maybe Timothy is just a little bit too leisurely for my tastes. Do you realize that it's two days before Valentine's Day and he hasn't even made a date?" I glanced over at Mavis. "Besides, you're the one who was pushing Orson on me before I met Timothy. I thought you'd be glad if we got together."

"A few months ago I would have been pleased," Mavis said in a soft voice. "But that was before I met Timothy and saw how good he is for you."

I planted my hands on my hips. "What do you mean?"

"Both Attalee and I have noticed how you've blossomed since you've met Timothy," said Mavis. She looked over at Attalee, who delivered an emphatic nod.

"It's almost like he's awakening the true Elizabeth in a way that poor, old Orson, bless his heart, never could," said Mavis.

"And you've been good for that boy," Attalee added. "He's stopped wearing bed sheets; he's filling out his dungarees some and he ain't nearly as peculiar as he used to be. Fact is, I've never seen two people in my life who were more suited for each other." She paused. "Well, except for me and Burl, of course. When Burl wasn't pie-eyed, he was as romantic as Burt Reynolds in *Smokey and the Bandit.*"

I leaned up against the checkout counter and sighed. "It may be true that Timothy and I are good together, but I could grow old and gray waiting to get a little sugar from him. And besides, I think y'all are wrong. I do believe Timothy Hollingsworth just thinks of me as a friend."

It was time for me to clock out, so I flounced over to get my jacket.

"Who knows? I might even stop by the bait shop on my way home and get me a little color in one of those tanning beds of Orson's," I said. "He said he'd be working there until 8 P.M."

"Elizabeth, you're not really going to throw yourself into the arms of Orson Hobbs, are you?" Mavis asked. "Can't you give Timothy just a little more time?"

"He's had four whole months!" I strode out the door, and let it slam with a noisy jingle. Then I plodded in the direction of the bait shop, with my hands in my pockets and my head ducked against the stinging wind.

Halfway to the Bait Box, my bravado evaporated in the frigid air and tears splashed my cheeks. I didn't really want to lean over the cooler filled with night crawlers and make calf eyes at Orson Hobbs.

Besides, it wasn't right to trifle with his affections when the only thing I really wanted to do was wrap my arms around Timothy Hollingsworth's neck and cover his face with soft kisses. Trouble was, I just didn't see that happening anytime soon, if ever.

I turned around and headed home. Everything in my life was catawampus. There was no solution in sight for the Bottom Dollar Emporium and my love life was about as titillating as G-rated movie.

As I wearily put my key in the lock, I could hear the phone ringing inside. I sprinted to answer it, nearly tripping over Maybelline, who was splayed out in front of the door.

To my surprise, Timothy was on the line. He sounded panicky.

"Elizabeth, I'm glad I caught you," he said.

I tried to calm Maybelline, who was repeatedly flinging herself against my leg.

"I just got home from work." I scooped up the dog, who immediately started bathing my face with her sandpaper tongue.

Timothy cleared his throat in a nervous manner. "I was looking at my calendar and I realized that this Saturday night is Valentine's Day. Did you have any idea it was coming up so quickly?"

"No," I lied. "I've not given it a single thought."

"Neither did I." His voice cracked slightly. "I was looking through my appointment book and the date just jumped out at me. I said to my secretary, 'Valentine's Day is two days away and I haven't even bothered to make dinner plans with my girlfriend.' She said I'd better go ahead and call you right away if I didn't want to be in the doghouse."

"Your girlfriend?" I asked softly.

"Yes, Elizabeth. That's what I said, 'my girlfriend,'" he said in a husky voice. "I hope it's not too late. Please tell me that you'll go with me and that you'll forgive me for not calling sooner."

My heart had stopped at the word "girlfriend." He'd never called me that before.

"What time will you pick me up?" I asked.

Thirteen

Why is there always so much month left at the end of the money?
~Sign tacked to the bulletin board in the Bottom Dollar Emporium

Mello Vickery stormed into the Bottom Dollar Emporium, spitting mad. She was wearing her fox pelt, and the beady eyes of the limp beast appeared to glare at me menacingly under the fluorescent lights of the store.

"Elizabeth, please get Mavis." She rapped her knuckles against the counter. "I have a bone to pick with her."

I was surprised to see Mello in the Bottom Dollar. She usually sent her ancient maid, Petunia, on her shopping errands. Mello lived in the biggest house in Cayboo Creek, a sagging, Victorian-style structure that had a yard choked with overgrown camellia bushes.

"Hi, Mello," I said. "Mavis is in the back office. Is there something I can help you with?"

Mello leaned over the counter. She smelled like mothballs and camphor. "No. I must speak with the person in charge."

I reluctantly walked back to Mavis's office. She'd been spending a lot of time in there lately, and I got the impression she wanted to be left alone.

"Mavis," I called outside the door. "Mello is here and she insists on seeing you."

The door cracked open and Mavis slipped out. Her eyes were puffy and red, like she'd been crying.

"Hey, Mello," Mavis said. "What can I do for you?"

Mello plunked a cellophane package of spoons down on the counter. "Petunia brought these home from your store Tuesday last week. What does this label say?"

Mavis held the package at an arm's length and squinted at the letters. "Fifty-one Pieces Heavy Duty Spoons," she read.

"Exactly," Mello said with a brisk nod of her head. "But imagine how I felt when I counted out the spoons and discovered there were only forty-eight. Forty-eight spoons! This package is three spoons short."

"Mello, I'm so sorry," Mavis said, clucking in sympathy.

"You should be," Mello said. "Every time I turn around someone's trying to cheat me. Why only last week a fellow called saying I'd won a free cruise to the Bahamas. All I had to do to hold my prize was give him my credit card number. I told that shyster that Mello Vickery wasn't born yesterday. The only way he'd get my American Express number was by prying the card out of my cold, dead hand."

"Good for you, Mello. You shouldn't let folks get the better of you," Mavis said. "I'll tell you what. I'll give you a refund on the spoons and I'll call the company who makes them and chew them out for shorting my customers. And for your trouble, why don't you pick out anything in the store with my compliments?"

Mello, who'd obviously been poised for a squabble, relaxed her face into a half smile. "Well, that's very nice of you, Mavis." She scanned the shelf near the checkout stand. "Since you offered, I believe I'll take this three-pack of fly swatters."

"Can't have enough fly swatters in the South," Mavis remarked. She opened the cash register and counted out a dollar and some change into Mello's outstretched palm. Mello rolled up the bag containing the fly swatters and tucked it under her arm. Her boxy black shoes clattered on the wood floor as she strode toward the exit.

"That woman is dotty," Attalee muttered after she'd left. "I heard she's taken to calling the psychic hotline nearly every day for spiritual guidance. Bert down at the post office says her phone bill is so thick it could choke a horse."

"Bert shouldn't be gossiping about other folks' mail," Mavis snapped. "And Mello hasn't always been so eccentric. It was only after she lost her business that she seemed to come unhinged. Who could blame her?"

It wasn't like Mavis to be so testy. I remembered how upset she looked when she came out of the office. Something must have happened.

"Mavis, what's wrong?" I asked softly.

She slumped into a chair. "I called the real estate agency today," she said in a thin voice. "They're going to put my house on the market next week."

"Oh, Mavis, no," I said.

"I should be grateful," Mavis said. "At least I have a family member to take me in during my time of need. Madge called last night. She said if I could get to South Dakota by the end of March, I'd still have a whole month or more to learn how to ice fish."

At the word "fish," Mavis's face crumbled. "Attalee, Elizabeth, what am I going to do?" she whispered. "Cold weather gives me chilblains. I don't want to live like an Eskimo."

Attalee and I rushed to Mavis's side.

"You could always move in with me at the Shady Elm," Attalee said, patting Mavis's hand. "I ain't supposed to have overnight guests, but we can sneak you past the front desk attendant while she plays solitaire on her computer."

I hugged her shoulder. "Please don't cry, Mavis. It's not over yet. You never know what might happen."

Although truthfully I, too, was beginning to feel defeated.

Mavis shook her head. "I'm sorry, Elizabeth. We've fought the good fight and we lost. Now it's time to cut my losses and move on."

I continued massaging Mavis's shoulder, wishing desperately that there was something I could do. The thought of my dearest friend moving so many miles away was too much to bear.

"I don't care what you say," I said. "I refuse to give up just yet."

Fourteen

Time may be a great healer, but it's a lousy beautician.
~Sign outside the Dazzling Do's Beauty Shop

On Valentine's Day I drove over to Meemaw's house to borrow my mama's fourteen-carat gold earrings for the evening. Meemaw lived about a mile away from me in a neighborhood called Dogwood Commons. A few months before, a practical joker had spray-painted an "F" over the "W" to make the welcome sign read "Dogfood Commons."

As I pulled up in her driveway, I noticed that her Christmas icicles were still dangling from the roof of her house. Meemaw had been fussing with Boomer for weeks to take them down, but obviously he hadn't gotten around to it.

I rang the doorbell and heard Pierre, Meemaw's miniature poodle, yipping inside and Meemaw's tobacco-cured voice grumbling a reply. My meemaw had been smoking Pall Mall unfiltereds for over forty years, yet with her cast-iron lungs she hardly ever coughed or cleared her throat.

She opened the door and peered out from behind the frames of her large glasses.

"Yeah?" she asked. She stood in the frame of the door and gave Pierre little pushes with her foot so he would stay back.

"It's me, Elizabeth. Let me in."

Meemaw opened the door wider and then took off her glasses

and rubbed the lenses on her slacks.

"Darn glasses. They're brand new and the optometrist must have ground the lenses wrong. You looked like one big blur standing on the step. Couldn't tell if you were the UPS man or a Jehovah's Witness." She squinted at me underneath eyebrows that looked like black, furry caterpillars.

"Whatever you do, don't ask me about Boomer, because I don't want to talk about that man," she said. She plucked a cigarette from the pocket of her oversized cardigan and stuck it in the corner of her mouth.

I followed her into the family room, where *Animal Planet* blared loud enough to make the windows vibrate. Meemaw turned down the volume a notch with the remote and flicked her ashes into an ashcan filled with sand, one of eight that she had bought from the municipal building after they went smoke-free. The heavy drapes and the thick carpets had soaked up years of tobacco smoke and the walls were the color of old piano keys. Even Pierre had a smoky, yellowish tinge.

"I won't tell you what he did. There's no point talking about him, because he's never coming back." She stubbed out her cigarette and immediately lit another.

"Was that the phone?" she demanded.

I shook my head. "It was just the television."

Meemaw plopped down on the sofa and folded her hands on her lap. She stared at the rings of smoke that hung in the air like a canopy. I sat down beside her.

"What happened?"

"I don't want to talk about it."

"What did he do this time?"

Meemaw shot up from the couch. Her fists curled into tight balls. "His mama called me a floozy to my face and he didn't say a word to defend me. He just sat there sucking on his teeth."

I forced back a laugh. Meemaw was as far away from being a floozy as I was from being an astronaut on Mars.

"Boomer's mama is just slipping. She's bumping up against

her ninetieth birthday," I said.

"Don't you believe it," Meemaw said. "I've seen her in action. That woman is a whiz at *Wheel of Fortune*."

The handset chirped in its phone and Meemaw lunged for it.

"Yeah?" She listened for a while and then said, "Yes, you just do that then."

She slammed down the handset on the phone and glanced up at me, thrusting her hands into the pockets of her cardigan.

"Boomer says he's coming by in an hour to take down those Christmas lights. I'll believe it when I see it." She paced across the floor. "I'm not letting him step foot in the house. Pierre will guard the door, won't you, Pierre?"

At the sound of his name, Pierre bared his gums. He was missing all of his teeth in his upper jaw.

"I won't be keeping you," I said. "I was just wondering if I could borrow my mama's gold earrings. I have a special occasion coming up."

Meemaw grunted and headed for the guest room, where she kept mama's things, and I trailed behind her.

The guest room used to be my mama's room when she was growing up and some of her possessions were still lying about. Meemaw kept the white dresser with gold trim and the four-poster bed that my mama had gotten when she was fourteen. On the dresser sat Mama's graduation picture in a large gilt frame, surrounded by smaller snapshots taken after she was married. Meemaw had cut my daddy out of them.

I picked up the photograph of my mama, taken about a year before she died of meningitis just shy of her twenty-first birthday. She was grinning like someone who's been given the keys to the world. Nothing in her face forecast that fate would soon whittle her down to no more than a stick.

I looked at the picture. My mama favored Meemaw, with her strong jaw and dark hair and eyebrows. I, on the other hand, had hair the color of cornmeal (thanks to monthly touch-ups with Nice 'n Easy), and my eyes and lips faded into my face if I didn't smear on a little color.

I returned the framed photo to the dresser. My mama died just before my first birthday, so whenever I looked at a photo of her, it was like staring into the eyes of a stranger. Although Meemaw had told me some details about her, trying to figure out what kind of person she'd been was like doing a dot-to-dot puzzle and not coming up with any picture at all.

From the top drawer of the dresser, Meemaw took out the blue velvet box that held Mama's earrings. My late granddaddy had bought them for my mama to wear on her wedding day. The last time I'd asked to wear the earrings was the night of Clip's and my engagement party.

That night, the moon had hung in the twilight like a big white thumbprint. Mavis had brought pink champagne, and it was a sight to see Clip's hunting buddies in their camouflage hats making toasts with plastic flutes and nibbling on cucumber sandwiches sliced as thin as tissue paper.

Clip had raised his glass in a toast and looked me in the eyes and said, "To the woman of my dreams."

I blinked to chase away the memory. How much time had passed since I'd last been sentimental about Clip?

Meemaw must have remembered, too, because she looked at me queerly and said, "Why did you say you wanted to borrow these?"

I hadn't said, as I had been waiting for her to ask.

"Just a date with a nice fellow," I said quickly.

Meemaw's eyes narrowed to dark, glittering slits. She had some Indian in her, and I swear sometimes she looked like she was sizing a person up for a scalping.

"You aren't getting near these until I hear all about this boy."

"Oh Meemaw, you'd really like him. He's so nice and polite. Real religious too," I said. 'Course I wasn't going to mention *what* religion, not just yet.

"Boomer mentioned you've been keeping company with a new fellow. Is he one of those boys from the Methodist Church?"

"No, he's not from the church," I said. "He's the grandson of one of my regular customers. And he's from California. He's moved to Augusta to work at the paper cup factory."

"Mmmm, California," Meemaw said. The corners of her mouth turned down. She harbored suspicions toward any place west of the Mississippi. "And he's a factory worker? On the line or a foreman?"

I twisted the hem of my blouse. "Actually, he's the chairman of the board of Hollingsworth Paper Cups. His daddy left it to him. His name is Timothy Hollingsworth."

Meemaw gripped a poster of the bed and sat down. "I just had me a flash of that daytime voodoo."

"You mean déjá vu?" I asked.

She nodded her head."Yes."

I plunked down on the bed beside her. "What do you mean?"

"I've never told you this, but your mama dated some rich fellow from Augusta." Her gray eyes darkened to black. "Never knew who he was. Darlene wouldn't bring him home to meet us. Instead she'd sneak around with him. I'm guessing she didn't think we were up to snuff for an introduction."

"I'm sure that's not true, Meemaw."

"I'm sure it is. Your granddaddy and me were as far away from being rich as a pigeon is from being a peacock. In the South, folks tend to stick with their own kind. But Darlene was at that age where she thought love could conquer all."

"Are you saying her story didn't have a happy ending?"

Meemaw didn't answer me, but rose from the bed and walked to the dresser and withdrew a small book.

"See for yourself. I found this in the bottom of a box when I was sorting through some of your mama's things. It's Darlene's diary."

"Have you read it?" I touched the cracked, leather cover.

"I looked through it. I thought you might want to have it, seeing how you're always asking me what she was like."

I opened it to the first page, with Mama's name on it in cursive with big, round loops.

"My mama's life, right here in this book?"

"A year or so of it, anyway." Meemaw wrinkled her nose. "It ain't a Danielle Steel novel, you know. Darlene wasn't a deep thinker."

"I don't care." I cradled the book in my arms. "This is a gift, Meemaw. Thank you for giving me this."

Meemaw fumbled in the pocket of her sweater for another cigarette. "So what's the story with this boy?"

"Nothing much." I tucked the diary in my purse. "Timothy and I are just buddies."

"Just buddies." She lit her cigarette with her Bic. "'Just buddies' does not borrow her mama's earrings when the last time she wore them was at her engagement party."

"Well, I'm not going to deny that I'm a little sweet on him."

"I'm not sure that Darlene ever got over her rich beau, whoever he was," Meemaw said in a forbidding voice. "Sometimes I think she pined for him until the day she died. Your daddy was her rebound man. Not one week after she and that rich boy parted ways, she took up with Dwayne and married him two weeks later."

I got up from the bed. "They married that quickly?"

"Land, yes. Dwayne was flat-out smitten with your mama at the time. She was a big step up for him. Dwayne's people were true 'crick' folks. Living like gypsies and spilling out of a rusty trailer parked up by the creek. Me and your granddaddy were hoity-toity folks, compared to Dwayne's kin." Her eyes narrowed again. "So am I going to be meeting this high-powered executive of yours? This fancy Augusta boy that has you running over here for your mama's earrings?"

"Of course, Meemaw. But he's not an uppity boy at all. You'll like him."

Meemaw snorted. "Let me be the judge of that."

Fifteen

Look at life through the windshield, not the rearview mirror.

~ Message in a fortune cookie from Dun Woo's House of Noodles

When I got home, Maybelline greeted me by jumping up and down and chasing her tail. As I leaned down to scratch her ears, I noticed a single Spaghetti O noodle in the middle of her nose, hard evidence that she had been rummaging through the trash again.

"Maybelline!" I yelled.

She knew that tone and scooted under the sofa. I went into the kitchen to survey the damage. Coffee grounds were strewn across the floor, and I found a pair of my underwear that she had dug out from the laundry basket. The crotch of the panties was chewed to bits.

When I'd set things in order, I sat at the wrought iron table in my kitchen, opened a bag of pretzels, and turned to the first page of my mama's diary. The crackling of the pretzel bag lured Maybelline from her hiding spot and she stood on her hind legs, begging. I groaned and tossed her a pretzel.

"You're just lucky they were my Hanes Everyday. If they'd been Victoria's Secret there'd have been hell to pay."

I opened the diary and started reading.

Dear Diary,

I was so excited when you showed up under the tree at Christmas. I need a confidant, someone I can confess my deepest

thoughts to without any judgments. I hope that you and I will be friends for life!

My hands tingled as I held the diary. Finally I would get some firsthand insight into the kind of person my mama had been. I eagerly turned the page.

The next dozen entries were disappointing. Instead of engaging in any heavy-duty unbosoming, my mama used the pages of her diary as a food journal in which she wrote down everything she ate and tried to estimate the calories.

I flipped through the pages. Although I was shocked to discover how many calories a Goo Goo Cluster had, I longed to read something more personal—something that would give me a clue about my mother's personality. As I flipped ahead a few pages, my eyes rested on an entry that was written in red ink.

The most exciting thing has happened to me. I met a wonderful man at the Tip Top Grill in Augusta, but I'm afraid to talk about him to anyone, even you diary, for fear that you will fall into the wrong hands. For now, I'll just call him "B."

From then on, my mama quit writing about food and focused all her attention on "B." "B" was the most sensitive, poetic man in the entire world. "B"'s kisses were so passionate that she could get lost in them forever. My mama had fallen hard for "B." I empathized with her as she described the giddy dizziness that came over her whenever she heard his voice.

Wherever "B" and I go out together, people stare and it makes both of us nervous. We spend most of the time in his car. Last night while we parked on the bank of the creek, we watched the moon and listened to the crickets. Before I knew it, it was almost midnight. Time disappears too quickly when I'm in in his arms.

Why, I wondered, did people stare at them? Was "B" much older than my mama? She mentioned he drove a BMW sports car and that didn't sound like the sort of automobile a high school boy would drive.

The diary went on to describe a blooming relationship

conducted increasingly in secret.

My mama wrote of receiving expensive gifts from "B" that she hid in a shoe box in the back of a closet. She never let "B" pick her up at her house; instead she met him places. In his car, they had long discussions about their future together.

"B" has decided that he's going to talk to his family about me tomorrow. We both fear their reactions. I hope they accept me, but we both know it isn't likely. "B" says he doesn't care what they say because he loves me.

The next few pages were brittle like they'd gotten wet, maybe with my mama's tears. Then there was this:

I haven't heard from "B" in over a week. When I try to reach him, he refuses to come to the phone. On top of all that, my period's late, and I'm always on time. I'm desperate to talk to "B."

My heart thudded hard in my chest and I quickly turned the page. There was no new entry. I went through all the remaining pages, but there was nothing. I couldn't believe it. How could she leave things hanging this way?

I knew my mama had gotten pregnant right after she'd married Dwayne. Was it possible that my real father was the mysterious "B" of her diary? Maybe Insane Dwayne wasn't my daddy after all. Maybe she just passed me off as his daughter. She was certainly in a hurry to marry my daddy. According to what Meemaw had said, they'd gone to the Justice of the Peace just two weeks after they'd started dating.

The trouble was, there was no way to find out "B"'s identity. The only person who knew his full name was my mama, and she'd been dead for over twenty years. And she hadn't even revealed his identity to her own diary.

Questions buzzed in my mind, but I knew it was useless to think about it now. Timothy was due to pick me up in an hour for our date and I hadn't even started getting ready.

I took a quick rinse in the shower and by the time Timothy knocked at the door, my face was pink from the warm water and I was spraying a little bit of Vanilla Fields on all of my pulse points.

Maybelline was barking and hurling herself at the door.

"Stop that, girl. It'll give you brain damage. If you haven't got it already." I walked in my stocking feet to the door and opened it.

Timothy was standing outside, wearing a sweater that picked up the color in his eyes. His khakis were freshly pressed and a shank of dark hair had fallen over his brow. I found myself holding my breath as he brushed the hair out of his eyes. All thoughts of "Who's my daddy?" scampered right out of my head.

"Look at you. Not even ready," he said, glancing at my feet. He took a step inside and as usual Maybelline offered up her white underbelly. Timothy obliged by scratching it.

"Let me slip into some clogs," I said.

I put on my shoes and we went downstairs and got into Timothy's Volvo. He dropped his keys twice before getting in, and he almost clipped a lamppost as he backed out of the driveway.

"Anything wrong, Timothy?"

He adjusted the visor against the brightness of the setting sun.

"Not a thing. Why do you ask?"

I crossed my arms over my chest. "I think you're telling me a fib, Timothy Hollingsworth."

He hunched his shoulders and his chin dipped to his chest. "I have something on my mind, Elizabeth, but I'll save it for after sushi."

I'd told Timothy that I'd been itching to try sushi, but now that the occasion had arrived, I was nervous. I was used to fried fish served with hush puppies.

We drove to a restaurant in Augusta called Ito's Hide-a-way. Timothy decided we'd sit at a table instead of the sushi bar.

"More private," he remarked.

The waitress led us past the sushi bar and glistening slabs of pink, orange, and red fish on the counter. My eyes also caught what looked like the arm of an octopus, studded with suction cups, stuffed beneath the glass.

The waitress, who was dressed in a gold kimono and had a set of chopsticks pushed through her dark bun, handed us menus with tiny origami paper pressed between the plastic covers. She disappeared behind a shower of beads and came back with rounded enamel bowls filled with a copper-colored broth that had rings of green onion drifting on the surface.

I opened the menu to read it, while Timothy grasped a stub of a pencil over a piece of paper that the waitress had given him.

He looked up and, seeing the menu in my hand, said, "Oh, you won't be needing that. It only has ordinary Japanese fare like tempura and chicken teriyaki on it. Let's just order from the sushi menu."

I shed the paper from my chopsticks.

"What's tempura?" I asked.

"It's seafood and vegetables that are lightly breaded and then fried."

"Sounds like how they do it at Captain D's," I said wistfully.

Timothy was making check marks on the sushi menu. "Let's see, we'll start off with some *unagi.*"

I didn't know the Japanese word for squid or octopus, but I wasn't taking any chances.

"Timothy, I can't."

He looked up. "Can't what?"

"Can't eat anything with arms and suction cups. I'd heave up—I know I would. I know I said I wanted to try sushi but I've lost my nerve."

Timothy smiled. "Don't worry. Octopus is for advanced sushi eaters. I'll order you some sushi starter food, like a California roll or a fried-shrimp roll."

"Fried shrimp?" Relief flooded my body. "Can I have tartar sauce with that too?"

"They have special sauces that you'll like even more. I promise. But we'll ask for tartar sauce, just in case." His forehead creased in thought. "Now, what to drink?"

"Iced tea with lemon is fine with me," I said.

"Tonight is special, so I'd like to order some Japanese wine."

"Wow, this *is* a special night."

Timothy dipped his spoon in the broth. "I'm not a Zen student anymore." He glanced up to look at me. "Things have changed."

"Like what?" I asked.

"I don't have to watch everything I eat or drink anymore. Even the Buddha believed in the Middle Way."

"The Middle Way?" I repeated.

"Moderation. Not too much, not too little," he replied.

I giggled. "I've seen statues of the Buddha in Chinese restaurants and I don't think he held back much when it came to food." I bit my lip. "Sorry, Timothy, I didn't mean to make fun of the Buddha."

Timothy chuckled. "I'm sure he wouldn't mind. He supposedly had a great sense of humor."

The waitress stopped by the table, and Timothy handed her our sushi order and requested some sake. While she was gone, Timothy busied himself with unfolding his napkin and pouring soy sauce into a small cup. I regretted undoing my napkin. It was folded to look like a geisha girl's hand fan.

We were served a carafe and two cups. Timothy poured the sake, explaining that it was a wine made from rice. I took a cautious sip and felt the liquid's warmth gradually spread from my throat to the tiniest veins in my fingertips.

We sipped the sake, looking at each other in a new, more intimate, way.

Timothy broke the silence.

"After living as a Zen student all those years, doing everything slowly and mindfully, I'd been used to taking my time with everything. Lately, it's come to my attention that maybe I've been too slow. Especially when it comes to matters of the heart."

I smiled shyly. "What do you mean?"

"I got a mysterious fax at work the other day," he said. He opened his wallet and showed me a folded piece of paper. He handed it to me and I instantly recognized the handwriting.

Beware: There's a fox lurking around your henhouse. Time's a' wasting. Valentine Day's around the corner. Take your best girl out and tell her how you feel about her.

My face turned the color of the business end of a baboon.

"I can't believe it. This is Attalee's doings."

Timothy laughed. "I thought it might be her."

"Oh, Lord, Timothy, I feel like crawling under this table."

He reached across to touch my hand.

"No, Elizabeth, this is a good thing. It's time that I told you what's in my heart. That is, if it isn't already obvious."

My pulse jumped in my hand. "What are you saying?"

He squeezed my hand and looked directly into my eyes. "Ever since I met you, I can't stop thinking about you."

"Me?" I squeaked.

"Before we met, I felt so isolated and cut off from my feelings, but then you came along—"

He licked his lips and studied me with his clear blue eyes. "Do you have any idea what I'm trying to say?"

I shook my head.

His voice came out raspy. "What I'm trying to say..." He lowered his eyelids. "I've fallen in love with you."

I swallowed hard. I haven't heard the word "love" too many times in my life. My family was as fond of sentiment as they were of sugar on their grits. My daddy reserved the word for things like hunting and professional wrestling. Meemaw only wrote it on birthday cards.

Even my fiancé, Clip, had stepped all around the word as if it were a pile of dog poop. He called it the "L" word and I played dumb, saying, "What 'L' word? Lima beans? Listerine? Louisiana?" until he was finally shamed into saying it out loud.

So when I heard the word coming from Timothy's mouth, in a restaurant with all kinds of people around, my whole body started shaking. It was as if I'd been waiting to hear that word from his lips my whole life and it didn't matter that I hadn't ever heard it in a proper way before.

"I love you too, Timothy," I said, putting a name to what I'd been feeling for him for the last few weeks.

The waitress brought our sushi order in a miniature wooden boat, but neither of us could eat a bite. Timothy asked for the check and after he paid, we went to his Volvo and clung to each other like shipwreck survivors. Then the moon slid out from the trees, a full yellow moon, and under its cool, healing light Timothy pressed his sweet lips against mine. I got a kiss from him that put to shame anything I might have imagined before.

Sixteen

If you're not the lead dog, the scenery never changes.
~ Graffiti in the men's bathroom at the Wagon Wheel

Hank snorted so loud in his sleep that he jolted himself awake. He jerked at the sight of me standing over him and knocked over a jarful of nails with his elbow.

"Hank Bryson, I could have robbed you blind while you were snoozing," I said.

Hank opened his mouth for a retort, but then the black rotary desk phone rang and he answered it, saying, "Bryson's Hardware."

I wandered around his store as he talked. It smelled like a mixture of sawdust and wet dog, although I didn't see any sign of Lance, Hank's black Lab mix, who was known to knock merchandise off the shelf with a sluggish wag of his tail. Flies buzzed lazily around the plastic feed bins near the cash register. I peered at the labels, printed in Hank's own hand: Knuckle purple hull, silver king corn, speckled butter peas, and Clemson spineless okra.

The store was a jumble of junk, with plastic worms displayed next to sharp-tooth saws and bins of bolts scattered over the scarred wooden floors. Mavis had offered to help organize Hank's stock into departments, but he said he liked things the way they were.

Maynard Gibbons, who was head cook at the Wagon Wheel,

shambled in, flustered to see a woman in what was obviously a man's domain. He mumbled something about wing nuts and swept past me.

"Hold up, Maynard. Take one of these and give them to folks at the restaurant." I handed him a stack of fliers. He rolled them up and shoved them in the pocket of his grease-splattered jacket.

Hank had since gotten off the phone. His feet were propped up on his desk and he was jawing a plug of Big Red gum. He'd given up dipping into his tin of Copenhagen snuff a couple of years ago when the habit had cost his uncle Jeb part of his tongue.

"What have you got there, Elizabeth?" Hank asked.

"Oh, it's an idea of mine to help the Bottom Dollar Emporium." I placed a flier on his desk. "You know the Super Saver is opening up in a week? Read it and see what you think."

Hank closed one eye and squinted at the paper with the other.

"Dear Friends and Neighbors of Cayboo Creek," he read. "Mavis Loomis and her employees at the Bottom Dollar Emporium want to thank you for being loyal patrons for the last twenty years. We hope you continue to be a part of our Bottom Dollar family in years to come. To show our appreciation for your business, bring this flier in for one dollar off of any of your purchases over ten dollars. Please support local businesses and the folks who run them."

He pushed the coupon across the desk. "That's real nice, Elizabeth. A strong sell, but not too pushy. But you're preaching to the choir bringing one to me. You know I'd come to the Bottom Dollar even if that Super Saver was giving away their merchandise."

"I know, Hank. But I thought you might pass these out to your customers for me."

"I'll do it." He flipped up the bill of his cap. "How's Mavis holding up?"

"She's trying to put up a brave front, Hank. But she's torn to shreds insides." I sighed. "She didn't even want to make up these fliers. She's convinced that the Super Saver will put her out of business. She's also put her sweet little house up for sale."

Hank nodded sadly. "I know. She told me. I'm sure going to miss that gal. I kinda wish..." He stopped short. "Well, I'm probably too old for that kind of nonsense."

I smiled knowingly. "Mavis loves that store, Hank. You should see how she frets over what's going to go in the display window. She had it all dolled up with hearts and cupids for Valentine's Day, and now she's putting up leprechauns and shamrocks."

Hank heaved himself up from his chair. "She's lucky she's got you, Elizabeth. I'll make sure anyone who comes in gets a coupon."

"Thanks, Hank." I left the hardware store, deciding where I should go next. I glanced up Main Street. The sign outside the Rock of Ages Baptist Church said, "The fires of hell await for people who sleep in late. Come to church on Sundays."

There was a hint of spring in the air. The ginkgo trees swayed in the warm breeze, and folks on the street were rolling up their sleeves and flinging back their heads to bask in the sun.

I poked my head into Boomer's Butcher Shop and was greeted by the dank stink of a leaky freezer. My neighbor Burris, whom Boomer had hired on as a clerk, was in the back of the store.

"Hey, Elizabeth!" he shouted, wiping his hands on his bloody apron. I didn't want to go in the back where the meat counter was located. There's certain parts of a pig I'd rather not see up close and personal.

"Boomer said I could leave some fliers for the Bottom Dollar here at the cash register," I said.

"I'll give them to everyone who comes in. By the way, we got a special today. Hot dogs are ninety-nine cents a pound," he responded. I glanced at the freezer by the door, which had a sale sticker on the glass. The hot dogs were the bright-red kind that always turned the cooking water pink.

"Maybe next time!" I left with a good-bye wave.

After I left Boomer's, I decided I'd check in with Matilda at the Methodist Church and see if she'd light a candle and start a prayer circle for the Bottom Dollar Emporium, come next Sunday. I'd grown up going to the Baptist Church, but as a little girl had been terrified of Reverend Hozey's hellfire-and-damnation sermons. As soon as I was old enough to choose, I started attending the Methodist Church, which had a charismatic black woman named Matilda Long as its pastor.

The Methodist Church was located at the end of Main Street in an empty brick building that used to be the apothecary. It had only been in Cayboo Creek for ten years or so and was still viewed with some suspicion by many townspeople because it was headed by a woman.

I opened the door and saw Matilda in the fellowship room folding a stack of baby blankets on top of the old soda fountain. The congregation had collected them for several months and we were going to distribute them next Sunday.

Matilda smiled at me. Her porcelain-like teeth seemed too fine for everyday jobs like biting into a Granny Smith apple or gnawing on a pork chop.

"How are you this beautiful spring day, Elizabeth Polk?"

Her cheekbones were so sharp they threatened to poke through her pecan-colored skin. If Matilda hadn't chosen the ministry as a vocation, she could have easily been a fashion model in her younger days.

Matilda noticed the fliers in my hand. "What have you got there?"

I told her about the coupons, and she agreed to light candles for the Bottom Dollar and have everyone pray next Sunday for the best outcome.

"There's also something I wanted to talk to you about," I said. "If you have a minute."

Matilda smiled. "I got time. How about sitting in the gardens? There's tea brewing. Would you like a cup?"

I declined, but Matilda went to the hot plate and poured herself some tea. We walked behind the church, where she was trying to coax a garden from the red clay. A skinny bush had sprouted with a few yellow flags, but neither the flower beds nor the two bony dogwoods she had planted showed any signs of life.

I gazed up at the Crayola-blue sky.

"Have you ever heard that saying about how a fish and a bird can fall in love but it's not practical, because they can't make a home together?" I asked, sitting down at the picnic table.

"Yes," Matilda said, with a nod.

"I've been seeing a man named Timothy who isn't anything like any of the fellows I've ever dated."

Matilda blew on her tea. "I've heard rumors that you've keeping company with someone new. There are no secrets in this town."

A wren rested on the lip of the birdbath, and Matilda and I watched it consider the possibility of a dip.

"I'm so in love with Timothy, I could care less about the differences between us," I said. I lowered my voice. "I just hope I'm not being too impractical. I'd hate to get my heart broken again."

"This fellow of yours. How is he so different from you?" she asked.

"It's mainly a background difference. His father was a bigwig and I'm the daughter of..."

Well, actually I wasn't exactly sure who I was the daughter of, but there was no point in pulling up that rug just then.

"I'm the daughter of a man who blows up ottomans on TV and who never misses a monster-truck rally," I continued. "Don't get me wrong. I'm not ashamed of my daddy or of how I grew up. I just know it was a lot different for Timothy when he was coming up."

"I know all about feelings of being born on the wrong side of the tracks," Matilda said. "I don't know if you know this, but my husband, Frank, came from a very wealthy family in Augusta, whereas I grew up here in Cayboo Creek. I fretted over marrying into such an intimidating family, but in the end I couldn't help myself. Our hearts were like compasses whose needles were pointing in the same direction. That's all that mattered in the long run." She paused to take a sip of her tea. "Does your Timothy seem troubled by the differences between you?" she asked.

I shook my head. "No, not a bit."

"Then I wouldn't worry." She took a luxurious inhale of spring air. "Although, I could read your tea leaves, if you like."

"Would you?" Matilda's tea-leaf readings were often chillingly accurate.

Matilda handed me a cup of tea. "Sip it slowly and think about Timothy."

I tasted the tea, tinged with honey and lemon, and pictured Timothy as he looked just before he leaned over to kiss me. I shivered, even though the tea was warm.

I handed the teacup back to Matilda, who swirled it clockwise three times and then peered into the cup.

Matilda read the leaves according to whatever shape or picture they took in the bottom of the cup. A sword meant an argument was on the horizon, whereas a cat indicated a false friend. Once Matilda had seen an open purse in Reeky's teacup, and the very next day Reeky won 250 dollars playing Red-Hot Cash in the South Carolina lottery.

"Oh Lord," Matilda said as she looked in the cup. "This is startling." Then she swiftly dumped the tea leaves on the ground.

"Why did you do that before I could look?" I asked. "You saw something terrible, didn't you?"

Two weeks ago Matilda had seen a witch in the bottom of Chiffon's cup, which meant she was in for a strange occurrence. And the very next day, a sleepy Chiffon accidentally brushed her teeth with Lonnie's hemorrhoid cream.

"No, not at all," said Matilda. She gave me a mysterious smile. "But there are certain things in life that should take you by surprise."

Seventeen

I'm in Love a Capital 'U'

~ Selection J-2 on the jukebox at the Tuff Luck Tavern

George Jones was holding a concert in my bedroom. He wore his signature tinted sunglasses and my seat was so good I could have reached out and touched the cleft in his chin as he sang my all-time favorite love song, "He Stopped Loving Her Today."

I jerked awake. Nobody was in my bedroom except Maybelline, who was snoring softly beside me. But I could still hear George "The Possum" singing, "Put a wreath upon his door and soon they'll carry him away."

My neighbor Burris must have his CD player up full blast, I thought, as I flicked bits of sleep from the corners of my eyes. I slid out of bed, pulled back the shade, and squinted in the darkness.

I pushed open the window and leaned out. A jasmine-scented breeze stirred the curtains. "Timothy? What are you doing out there with a boom box?"

"Elizabeth?" He yelled over the music.

I rushed to the front door, patting down my bed head on the way. There was Timothy, standing there under the yellow glow of the porch light. He cradled a bouquet of red roses in his arms and a hopeful smile trembled on his lips. "May I come in, please?"

"It's hard to turn down a fellow holding a dozen roses, even if it *is* after midnight." I took the flowers from him and set them on the coffee table.

"Two dozen, actually," Timothy said, as he perched on the couch. "There would have been more, but the Kroger in Augusta is the only place that sells flowers in the middle of the night and I cleaned out their cooler."

I sat down beside him and smoothed my gown over my knees, grateful I was wearing my white eyelet instead of my Betty Boop nightshirt. Timothy was biting his lip. The light in the room seemed incredibly bright, exposing us both.

"I know it's crazy, my coming here in the middle of the night, but ever since Valentine's Day, I haven't been myself. I'm just—" He shook his head. "Crazy."

I nodded. I knew exactly how he felt.

"That George Jones song is my all-time favorite," I said, after a moment. "It makes me cry."

Timothy looked up. "I know. I remember you telling me that. And your favorite candy is Baby Ruth." He glanced about. "I think I may have left the bag of candy I brought you in the car. Should I run out and get it?"

"That's okay. I generally don't eat sweets after 9 P.M."

Timothy swallowed. "I can hardly sleep or eat. I don't know what's happening to me, Elizabeth."

I nodded and took his hand. I'd been feeling exactly the same way since the night of our first kiss.

"My favorite candy, my favorite flowers, and my favorite song." I sought out his eyes, which looked naked with love. I felt like I was peering straight into his heart. "Brought to me by my favorite person," I whispered.

He groped in his pocket and extracted a small, blue box.

"I don't know your favorite stone. But I hope it's a diamond."

That night, as we drove to Edgefield, S.C., to get married in the Little Vegas Casino and Wedding Chapel, I knew that Matilda must have seen a ring in the bottom of my teacup.

Timothy and I said our vows to a woman named Sister Shelia, who was as wide as a love seat. We passed on the Lucky Seven

Package, which included the wedding ceremony and seven games of video poker. Instead we got the Precious Memory Package, which included a tape-recording of our wedding vows and a personalized license tag that read "Timothy and Elizabeth Forever," which Timothy screwed on the front of his Volvo following the ceremony. When it was over, we stopped by Timothy's house so he could pack a bag.

The next morning I woke up to the sound of rain on my roof.

I opened my eyes to see Timothy's dark curls on my pillow and I felt like dancing around the room in my nightie. He stirred, looked at the alarm clock, and bolted out of bed.

"Oh, no. I'm going to be late for work," he said, and bent to kiss my grinning face. "I don't know how I'm going to concentrate on business today."

I struggled to my feet. "I could make your lunch like a good wife is supposed to."

Timothy started dressing and I walked to the refrigerator and stuck my nose into it. "There's nothing in here but a pickled egg and a bowl of leftover coleslaw."

"That's okay." Timothy gave his suspenders a snap. "I've got to take a lunch meeting today." He fastened his top shirt button. "I guess you're going to break the news to everyone at work?"

I nodded. "They're going to pitch a fit that they weren't around to throw rice on me and scramble for my bouquet."

Timothy pecked my cheek. "We'll have a ceremony for our friends and families later. I just couldn't wait around that long."

"Me neither," I said knowingly. We exchanged glances and I knew I had to change the subject quick or neither of us would make it to work for a while.

"What about your mama?" I asked. "When are you going to tell her the news?"

Timothy stiffened slightly. "Whenever she comes back from France. I'd prefer to tell her in person."

"Your grandmother's at her time-share on Hilton Head. She won't be back for another week at least. Did you want to call her?"

"I think I'll wait until she gets back from her vacation." Timothy smoothed his tie. "I'm sure she'll be thrilled. Grandma Gracie thinks the world of you."

I sat cross-legged on the bed, inhaling the crisp scent of his aftershave. "I don't know. She likes me pretty well as a friend, but I'm not sure how she'll feel about me as a relative."

"She'll be ecstatic." He kissed my cheek. "Everything will be fine, you'll see."

Eighteen

Jesus is the quicker picker-upper.

~ Sign outside the Rock of Ages Baptist Church

Attalee was sitting in the break area, reading the newspaper and taking noisy slurps of her coffee when I walked out of the rain and into the Bottom Dollar Emporium.

"It says here in my horoscope that my day is going to be a five," she said to Mavis. "As I recollect, Scorpio has been stuck on five for near two weeks."

She glared at me as I fastened my name tag to my smock. "You're fifteen minutes late," she snapped.

"Sorry. Morning, Mavis." I noticed a wrapped package with a red satin bow on my break chair. "Who is this for?"

Attalee glanced back at her paper. "Today's the grand opening of the Winn-Dixie in the old Pig store. To celebrate they're offering spiral sliced ham for $2.99 a pound." She directed her comments at Mavis and refused to look at me.

"I'm sorry I was late, y'all, but you're hardly swamped with customers," I said.

Attalee's lips pulled into a pout. "Will you tell Miss Polk that when I got to the door this morning, the place was locked up tighter than a vault and that I had to wait an entire seven minutes in the rain?"

"I think she heard you pretty clearly, Attalee. I don't see any need to repeat it," Mavis said.

"I'm so sorry, Attalee. I thought Mavis would be here to let you in."

Mavis was uncharacteristically avoiding eye contact.

"You may want to tell our Miss Polk that this is the morning when you have your prayer breakfast at the church," Attalee said. "Also, why don't you tell Miss Polk what we were discussing before she breezed in here with her flimsy apology?"

Mavis was staring out at the rain that lashed the windows of the Bottom Dollar. "Well, it was more you, Attalee, than me. I listened, mostly."

Someone was definitely worked up about something.

"Mavis? Is there anything you'd like to say to me?" I asked.

"Maybe you'd like to ask her what's so special about today?" Attalee said.

Mavis whirled around. "Now, Attalee, it isn't that important. It's silly, really. It's just an anniversary. Don't you worry about it, Elizabeth."

My hand flew to my mouth. "Oh my gosh. How could I have forgotten? We've been working together for ten years today. Mavis, I am so sorry. It completely slipped my mind."

Mavis's gray eyes were downcast. "Who could blame you? You got yourself a new fellow. These things happen," she said.

I touched the gaily wrapped present on my chair. "I bet this beautiful gift is from you to me. May I open it?"

For the first time that morning, Mavis looked up at me. I could tell I'd been forgiven.

"It isn't much of anything. Just a little something that made me think, 'I bet Elizabeth could use that.'"

I put the package on my lap and tore the wrapping paper off a book called *Thirty Days to a Better Vocabulary.*

"Oh Mavis, thank you so much, you know how I love to learn new words."

Attalee stood on tiptoes for a look at the book. She looked like a wrinkled baby with her rain bonnet still tied under her chin.

"I was with her over at Reeky's place when she got it. It's a hardcover and she didn't even get if off the bargain table. She paid top-dollar."

"I can't wait to use it," I said.

"Why wait?" demanded Attalee. "Why not give us one of those thousand-dollar words right now?"

"That's an excellent idea." I opened the book and picked a page at random. "Ah, here's a good one. 'Iconoclast,'" I said.

Attalee's eye twitched. "What's that mean?"

"It means a person who doesn't bow to convention," I said.

"And what's that mean?" Attalee asked.

"Well, Attalee, you know when you go to your bingo game, and people have their good-luck charms all around them, like rabbit foots and fuzzy dice and their child's first baby tooth?" I said. "And how you refuse to do that because you think it looks stupid? Well, you're an iconoclast. You don't want to go along with the crowd."

"Well, I'll be a monkey's uncle." Attalee worked her jaw. "Only thing is lately I've been taking my lucky agate to bingo since my game's been off, but at least I ain't waving it around like I was some kind of witch doctor."

I leaned against the checkout counter and smiled at them both. "Look, I got something to tell you before any customers come in. It's really big news."

Mavis lowered herself into her chair with her coffee cup. Attalee's eyes narrowed.

I took a deep breath. "I don't know how to say this except to just spit it out. Timothy and I are now man and wife! We eloped last night." I stuck out my hand to show off my diamond ring.

"Eloped? My goodness, Elizabeth," Mavis said.

"You went off and got hitched and didn't even invite us, your nearest and your dearest?" Attalee asked. She grabbed my hand to get a closer look at the stone. "You could give someone a shiner with that rock."

"Timothy came over to my house last night at midnight and proposed," I said. My skin tingled as I recalled the scene. "Then he insisted we drive to Edgefield to get married right away. He'd brought over this beautiful ring that's been in his family for years. It was a whirlwind. I'm still trying to get used to the idea of being Elizabeth Hollingsworth."

"Oh, Elizabeth, I'm just in shock," Mavis said, fanning herself with a newspaper flier. "Our little Elizabeth, a Hollingsworth, of all things."

"Are y'all going to live here in Cayboo Creek?" Attalee asked.

"Yes. Timothy loves it here," I said. "He's going to move his things out of his condominium in Augusta and move in with me until we can find us a larger place."

"This is truly wonderful news," Mavis said. "You and Timothy are like biscuits and gravy; you belong together."

"Mrs. Tobias ought to be tickled about your news," Attalee said. "She's always been so sweet on you."

"I hope so. She's the one that got us together in the first place, but I don't imagine she expected we'd get married. She can be awful hard to read sometimes."

Meemaw, on the other hand, wasn't a bit hard to read. I stopped by after work to visit her and she started slamming cupboards in the kitchen when I told her the news.

"Timothy and I are going to have another ceremony so we can share the moment with all our friends and family. Maybe we could have it here," I said, knowing how Meemaw loved entertaining folks.

"Don't know how we could," Meemaw snapped. She banged a lid shut on the pot of stew simmering on the stove. "I don't have linen napkins and table runners and silverware with the coat of arms pressed into the handles."

"You're going to like Timothy so much, Meemaw." I followed her as she stomped out to the porch. "I know we should have waited and had a real ceremony with you there. It was just one of those crazy spur-of-the-moment things. Please forgive me."

She whirled around to face me. "What is it about this family and shotgun weddings? My daughter got married in the dusty office of a Justice of the Peace, but at least she invited me and your granddaddy. My granddaughter runs off to a gambling house to get married, not once thinking to pick up the phone so that her meemaw, who has raised her since she was tiny—" Her face turned red as a firecracker. "Oh, just go on with you. I'm too mad to talk now."

"I'm sorry, Meemaw. You're right. I should have made sure you were there."

"Scat!" She waved the spatula at me. I started slinking back to my car. "And you can tell that Mr. Hollingsworth of yours that he has already gotten off on the wrong foot with me," she hollered.

I continued to my car, knowing that once Meemaw stewed for a while, she'd come around.

"Have you told your no-good daddy this news?" Meemaw shouted after me.

Nineteen

Instant Redneck: Just Add Beer

~ Message on Dwayne Polk's T-shirt

I drove out to Taffy and Daddy's house after leaving Meemaw's. Just before I knocked at the door, I slipped my ring into my jeans pocket, out of habit mostly. There was a time in the Polk family when any jewelry would eventually end up behind the counter of a pawn shop.

Daddy and Taffy were enjoying their cocktail hour. Old Milwaukee for him and wine coolers for her. After I told them my news, Daddy's mouth twitched and Taffy went completely silent. She squinted at me, as if I were a road map that she was trying to read in poor light. "When's the baby due?"

"I'm going to be a granddaddy," my daddy said.

Taffy glared at him.

"There isn't going to be a baby," I said. "Because I'm not—"

Taffy held up her index finger. "Betty D. We weren't born yesterday. Were we, Dwayne?"

"Not the last time I looked," Daddy said with a husky laugh.

Taffy jumped up and circled my chair, clicking her nails on the kitchen table as she passed.

"You sign anything? Any kind of paper before you said your wedding vows?" She was behind me, close to my ear, and I could smell the fermented fruit scent on her breath.

"No, just the wedding license. And I'm not preg—"

She planted herself in front of me, so close that I could see the pink veins in the whites of her eyes.

"Then I suggest you get pregnant, quick like a rabbit, if you want to stay married. Once his kin gets wind of this, they'll wipe you out like a bathtub ring. But if you have a belly heavy with a grandchild, that's something else entirely," said Taffy. She was wearing a purple pantsuit that made her look like an eggplant.

My daddy squeezed his beer can and tossed it in the trash.

"Shoot, Taffy, I don't want to hear this talk about women's bellies."

"Go on in and watch your TV show," she said. "Your boy Lanier is in the den watching the Game Show Channel all day. See if he's still kicking."

As my daddy left the room, Taffy said under her breath, "Don't know why I married a man with children. First Lanier lounging around my house like a big smelly dog and now—"

I slid off my chair. "Well, I'm going home. I just wanted to tell you and Daddy about the marriage."

"Wait a minute, Betty D. Stay put for a minute," she said.

I stopped, feeling like a bug skewered by a straight pin.

A smile was toying at her lips. "To tell you the truth Betty D., I didn't think you had it in you. You've surprised me, girl."

"Taffy, it isn't what you think—"

"Shoot, Betty D., I mean... Elizabeth. We're both women here and since it's a man's world out there, we women gotta use what we got." She looked me up and down. "You got the stuff, Elizabeth, but I swear to the Lord, I never would have guessed that you knew how to use it. I underestimated you."

She looked at me with a creepy kind of admiration, the way a kid from the Little League stares at Chipper Jones. The gold chains on the breast pockets of her pantsuit jingled as she spoke. "I want to have y'all over for some supper sometime. We gotta meet this rich fellow of yours. You staying with him at his house?"

"No, he's staying with me for the time being."

She snorted. "Well, he isn't going to be lasting long in your hole-in-the-wall once he gets tired of hot- and cold-running fleas. You're gonna have to get rid of Estée Lauder." She hefted her wine cooler to her mouth and took a noisy swallow.

"Maybelline," I said, correcting her. "And why should I get rid of my dog? Timothy's crazy about her."

Actually, I was fibbing. Fact is, Maybelline was probably low on Timothy's list right now. There had been a fierce struggle over his sock this morning, a piddle stain on his side of the bed last night, and when we made love, Maybelline had stared at us from the corner of the room, eyes like spangles in the semi-darkness, a dark, panting, peeping Tom.

"The only kind of dogs rich folks have are the kind with pedicures, and your mutt doesn't got that," said Taffy.

"Pedicures?"

Taffy waggled her fingers impatiently. "Those fancy papers that says who the daddy is. You don't have any for her."

Or for myself, I thought. What would Timothy think of me if he knew his wife might not have a pedicure?

After I left my daddy's house, I stopped at the grand opening of the Winn-Dixie to pick up the makings for the first supper I would prepare as Mrs. Timothy Hollingsworth.

Outside the grocery store the Pepsi-Cola folks arranged a display of their cans to spell out "Welcome Shoppers." Freckles the Clown was inside making balloon animals and the high-school band booster club was out front selling boiled peanuts in rolled-up paper bags. Miss Cayboo Creek and her court were stationed throughout the store doling out free samples.

By the time I'd steered my buggy into the produce section, I'd sampled a Vienna sausage, a sweet-and-sour meatball, and a new kind of banana snack chip which I'd spat out in a napkin. In my opinion, there are certain places bananas don't belong.

I parked my buggy in front of the iceberg lettuce hoping to catch the thunder-and-lightning display I'd read about in the paper. Other folks had the same idea. Carts were lined up from the bins of corn-on-the-cob all the way down to the green peppers. Arnold Thorton, the produce manager, tried to break up a traffic jam near a Wishbone crouton display.

"The show's not for another ten minutes. Please keep your carts moving," he said in the overly bossy tones of newfound power.

I decided that if I was going to have supper on the table for Timothy, I'd better move along. I glanced at the recipe card Attalee had given me for "dump casserole." It didn't sound very appetizing, but she'd promised it was real simple. All you had to do was take a can of shoe-peg corn, a can of string beans, a can of cream-of-mushroom soup, and a jar of pimentos and dump them into a casserole dish. Shake some fried onions on top and you had a meal.

I was tooling my buggy down the canned-vegetable aisle when I heard someone calling my name. I turned around and saw Boomer and Meemaw standing behind me.

"Hey there, Toots. It's been a 'coon's age. Come and hug your Uncle Boomer's neck," Boomer said.

I parked my buggy and flung my arms around Boomer, who of course being Meemaw's beau wasn't any kin to me, but I didn't mind calling him uncle if it made him happy.

I went to hug Meemaw. Boomer, who was wearing a parrot-print shirt, said, "Watch out for that one. She's a real sourpuss today."

Meemaw felt about as cuddly as an ironing board in my arms. "I know," I said to Boomer, dropping my embrace. "We spoke only a couple of hours ago. So are you checking out the competition, Boomer?"

"What competition?" Boomer asked. "They don't even carry goat. What kind of meat department is that?"

"Not much of one," I remarked. "You'll still get all my business."

Boomer glanced at my purchases. "What's with all these cans? Are you trying to stock a bomb shelter?"

"I'm just picking up some odds and ends." I paused and looked at Meemaw. "I'm making my first supper for Timothy tonight."

"He won't be hanging around for long if you're serving him this kind of rubbish." Boomer put a big, soft hand on my shoulder. "Elizabeth, let me tell you a secret. Men marry women so they can *stop* eating out of cans. Do you think a fine young whelp like myself would have anything to do with your grizzled old granny if she didn't make the best chicken pot pie I've ever locked a lip on?"

"Hope you got a good memory because you aren't going to taste that pie for a while," Meemaw snapped.

Boomer scratched his bald head.

"She's also a great French kisser, but the only sugar I've gotten lately has been in my coffee."

"You better start checking it for hemlock."

Meemaw looked into my cart. "I hate to say it, Elizabeth, but Boomer's right. Opening a few cans isn't any kind of supper for newlyweds."

I twisted the ring on my finger. "But I don't know how to make much of anything else."

"You hardly need to know how to cook these days, what with all the convenience foods. Get you one of those roasted chickens in the deli. That will make a fine supper," Meemaw said.

"Maybe I'll do just that." I began replacing the cans on the shelf.

"And Elizabeth..." Meemaw's fingers ran up and down the buttons of her sweater. She seemed at a loss about what to do with her hands, seeing how she couldn't smoke in the grocery store.

"Yes, Meemaw."

"There isn't a thing to cooking." She blinked behind her glasses. "I could teach you a dish or two."

"I'd like that." I knew that Meemaw's offer was her way of forgiving me.

"It's settled, then. Come by this weekend, if you can tear yourself away from that husband of yours." Meemaw elbowed Boomer. "We need to get back."

Twenty

Bacteria is the only culture some people have.

~ Marcie Castlewood's favorite put-down

I was inhaling the homey scent of roasted chicken when I heard Timothy's key in the door, and I ran to greet him with a kiss. Unfortunately, it was one of those long, drawn-out smooches that gave Maybelline just enough time to hop up on the supper table and drag the chicken down to the floor. She was shaking it, like she wasn't sure if it was dead or not, when I walked into the kitchen.

I started boo-hooing right then and there, which isn't like me at all. It was as if my wedding ring gave me license to be silly and weepy, like Jane Fonda in *Barefoot in the Park*.

Timothy was the model husband. He wrestled the bird from Maybelline—after a *National Geographic-worthy* struggle— cleaned up the grease, murmured phrases like "there, there," and patted me gently on the back. Then he told me he wanted to take me out to a very fancy restaurant for supper so he could show off his brand-new, beautiful wife.

We drove to a restaurant in downtown Augusta called the Summit Club, a private dining room that's on the very top floor of the old First Atlanta Bank Building.

Full-length windows revealed the city lights, twinkling like a county fair. There was a man in the corner playing a big, black shiny piano. I'd only been in one restaurant with live entertainment before. Bobby's Barbecue on Highway One had a piano player who wore string ties and played "Turkey in the Straw." The fellow playing at the Summit Club wore a tuxedo, and it was my guess he wouldn't be playing any songs you could clap along to.

The dining room was hushed. A man in a dark suit spotted us in the doorway.

"Mr. Hollingsworth, how good to see you this evening. Will you be dining in your private room tonight?"

"No, Preston. My wife and I want to enjoy the view of the city."

I felt woozy at Timothy's use of the word "wife." It was still hard to believe we were married.

The Preston fellow pulled out my chair and then handed us both menus that looked like big books with tassels dangling from them. While we were opening the menus, a waiter wearing white gloves appeared at our table and filled our glasses from a silver pitcher beading with water droplets.

"Evening, Mr. Hollingsworth," said the elderly black man. His voice rumbled deep from his chest. "Will you need a minute to look over the menu, sir?"

"Yes, thank you, Gerald."

The waiter left and I leaned over the table and said, "How do you know these people?"

Timothy sighed. "This is where most of the board meetings are held during the day. Although we meet around the corridor in the Hollingsworth Room."

"You have a room in here all to yourself?" I asked.

"Yes. My father was a founding member of the Summit Club, so he had a private dining room dedicated to him. I've known Gerald, our waiter, since I was a kid." He lowered his voice. "I'd like a more casual atmosphere for business, but it's the way my father always conducted his affairs. People expect it from me as well."

"Well, it's very nice here," I said. My eyes took in the gleaming cutlery, the butter pressed into rosettes, and the sparkling city lights. "I feel like I'm in a movie."

"That's why I brought you here. I thought you'd enjoy the

view."

I folded my menu. "It's fantastic. I could sit here for hours. Just look at all those lights down there. It looks like everyone is scurrying around to prepare for a celebration. Just imagine if you were from another planet. Wouldn't you feel welcomed by all those lights? Wouldn't you want to hurry up and land your spaceship just so you could be a part of it all?"

He took my hand across the table and gave it a squeeze. "You're always helping me see how beautiful this world is."

Gerald appeared at my side and poured more water into my glass even though I'd only taken a couple of sips.

"Mr. Hollingsworth, have you decided?"

I stuck my nose in the menu. Fact was, there was a lot of strange-sounding food on it: potato and sorrel soup, pear and Gouda salad with pine nuts, mussels in white sauce with saffron. I was hoping Timothy would suggest something.

As if reading my mind, Timothy asked, "Do you like prime rib?"

"Lord, do I."

"She'll have the prime rib and I'll have the swordfish, Gerald."

After Gerald left, I eyed all my silverware, remembering how Mrs. Tobias had once told me that when faced with a mess of forks, I just had to work my way in.

In minutes, our salads arrived. The plates were heaped with odd-colored spiky lettuce that looked like yard clippings. Timothy started eating his portion and I poked at mine with my fork.

Suddenly a high-pitched voice carried across the Summit Club.

"Timothy? Timothy Hollingsworth? Is it really you?"

A woman hightailed it to our table. She had blond hair styled like a lion's mane, and she was wearing a black jumpsuit with gold chains around her waist. She was as skinny as a licorice whip.

Timothy squinted at the woman. "Marcie? Marcie Castlewood?"

"Yes!" the woman squealed. Timothy rose from his seat and she threw her arms around him.

"I don't believe it—"

"How long has it been?"

"Twelve, maybe eleven years. I think the last time was the Willinghams' barbecue, or was it the assembly dance?"

"The dance, I think. You were wearing that blue—"

Timothy suddenly looked at me, and so did Marcie for the first time. A tight smile flitted over her lips.

"Marcie, I'd like to introduce you to my wife, Elizabeth. We just got married," Timothy said.

Marcie's shoes were sharp and dangerous-looking, and they matched her cigar-shaped bag. I could sense her sizing me up. She looked at my flowered print dress and the navy blue pumps with the run-down heels. She took in the cubic zirconium bracelet that spelled out my name and my pantyhose that were suntan instead of nude, because the Bottom Dollar was out of size A in nude.

I'd thought I looked decent when I'd stepped out the door that night, but one glance from Marcie and I knew I was dressed all wrong.

"Timothy Hollingsworth married?" Her bright green eyes flashed at me. "This is a surprise."

"Marcie and I were neighbors. We also attended the same church," Timothy said.

"And went to the club pool together and to every party and tennis game and well, just about everywhere. We hung out together when Timothy came home from boarding school. Our friends called us Heckle and Jeckle, we were so close." Marcie's eyes narrowed. "You don't look familiar to me, Elizabeth. Are you new to Augusta?"

"I'm not from here," I said. "I live in Cayboo Creek."

"Oh, I see," Marcie said, not trying too hard to disguise her look of disdain. Many people in Augusta regarded Cayboo Creek as some kind of redneck backwater and called it "The Crick."

"What do you do out there in, uh, Cayboo Creek?" she asked.

"I work in a dollar store," I said softly.

"She's the manager of the dollar store," Timothy added quickly.

"That must be a *tremendous* responsibility," Marcie purred. "We have something in common then, Elizabeth. I'm a manager and I also work with dollars. I'm branch manager of Smith Barney Financial planners."

She opened her purse and took out a business card, which she handed to Timothy. "Now that the two of you are married I assume you'll be moving to Augusta. Timothy, I've heard that you've taken over the helm of Hollingsworth Paper Cups."

"You heard correctly, but Elizabeth and I won't be moving to Augusta," Timothy said, giving my hand a squeeze. "We'll be staying in Cayboo Creek."

Marcie's mouth flew open. "You're going to live in the Crick? Do they even have houses there?" She smiled sweetly. "I mean... other than all those clever manufactured homes?"

"Yes, Marcie, there are homes there, manufactured and otherwise," Timothy said. "Cayboo Creek is a charming community. You should drive over sometime."

"Yes, I'll have to do that," she said. She snapped her pocket-book shut. "I need to get back to my table. It was wonderful to see you again. Delighted to meet you, Elizabeth."

"She was pretty," I said, after she left.

"Pretty snobbish." He leaned to whisper across the table. "And I thought she looked like she'd just been released from a concentration camp. Why would a woman want to intentionally starve herself down to the width of a guitar string? I can't imagine it."

"I could tell she was underwhelmed by me."

"Then she has terrible taste in people," Timothy said, pouring more wine into my glass.

"She and I are day and night." I put down my fork. "Are you sure I'm the kind of woman that you want?"

Timothy was chewing a morsel of fish. He stopped in mid-bite and said, "You aren't jealous of Marcie?"

"Maybe a little." I took a stab at my meat with my fork. "I just don't want you to be ashamed of me."

Timothy's eyes glimmered in the soft lights of the candles. "Sweetie, girls like Marcie are as common in the South as kudzu. But there is only one genuine Elizabeth Polk Hollingsworth. Why do you think I took you here? I want everyone to know that you're my wife."

His face was so earnest that I believed every word he said.

"What is your mama going to say about you and I being married?" I asked.

Timothy leaned back in his chair and considered the ceiling.

"Actually, Elizabeth, I can't answer that, because I hardly know my mother. I attended boarding schools since first grade, and before that I had a full-time nanny. During the summer breaks I only spent a few weeks at home and then I was shipped off to camps. When I decided to join the monastery after my first year at Stanford, my parents cut almost all ties with me to register their disapproval. But it was hardly a severe punishment considering I'd never truly been a part of their lives."

He paused and shook his head sadly. "The only member of my family who's stayed in touch with me is my Grandma Gracie. As a matter of fact, the first time I saw my mother in ten years was at my father's funeral."

My fingers inched across the table to touch his hand and he seized one and kissed my knuckle.

"I used to think my parents ignored me most of my life because I was adopted," Timothy said.

"You're adopted? I didn't know that."

Timothy nodded. "I don't think my mother wanted to bother with the time and trouble of a pregnancy. Grandma Gracie says it's just the way my mother is. She says Mother keeps everyone at an arm's length."

"And your daddy?" I asked.

"My father, if anything, was more distant than my mother. He was a workaholic. He was always pleasant to me on the rare occasions that I saw him. Actually, neither of my parents were cold or unkind to me. They just didn't find me particularly...

compelling."

My heart ached, imagining Timothy as a little boy pining for his parents' attentions.

"I'm surprised you came back here at all," I said.

"At my father's funeral, my mother asked me to come to Augusta and learn the family business. I thought we'd work together and get to know each other." Timothy laughed, but there was no gaiety in the sound. "That wasn't the case at all. She'd already left for France by the time I arrived. She just wanted a warm body at the helm of the family company."

"But you stayed anyway."

"I stayed," he said. "You see, just as I was thinking about jumping back on a plane to see if I could regain my spot at the Zen center, I met this dollar-store femme fatale who bedazzled me so thoroughly on our first outing, I knew I was stuck here, as you might say, like a marshmallow on a fork."

"Really?" My cheeks warmed. "You stayed here because of me?"

"Yes, Elizabeth."

Timothy signaled to Gerald, who brought Champagne and popped the top right in front of us, just like in the movies.

Timothy lifted his glass for a toast. "To my wife. Who makes me feel like I've finally found a home."

I clinked my glass to his. "That makes two of us."

Twenty-One

Thanks to the Cathouse (I'm in the Doghouse with You)
~ Selection C-3 on the jukebox at the Tuff Luck Tavern

Back at the Bottom Dollar Emporium, a box of Uncle Ben's Long Grain Rice sailed through the air in a perfect arc. I ducked, but not quickly enough.

"Attalee, you're supposed to throw grains of rice, not the box!"Mavis said.

"Serves her right for not inviting us to the wedding. Besides, it wasn't going to hurt her." Attalee leaned down to pick up the box. "It's empty."

"What in the world?" I said.

I took in the white streamers hanging from the ceiling and the sound of "Here Comes the Bride" playing on the boom box. Crepe-paper wedding bells hung from the walls, and a single red rose stood in a vase in the break area.

"Happy Wedding Day!" shouted Mavis. She blew a stream of soap bubbles in my direction.

"Oh, my goodness, it's a party! Y'all are spoiling me," I said.

"Darn straight we are," said Attalee. "I told Mavis that you already got a hardcover book for your anniversary. It should be able to double as a wedding present. 'No,' Mavis says, 'Them's two separate occasions,' and next thing I know she's dragging me out to the party store for all this finery." Attalee stooped down to pick up an enormous wrapped package by her chair. "She even talked me into spending my bingo winnings on a present for you."

"Well, thank you, Attalee, I'm truly honored," I said, accepting the gift.

"Be careful with that wrapping paper because I want to reuse it," she warned. "Also, if you and Timothy bust up before the year's out, I want my present back."

"Attalee!" Mavis said.

I patted Attalee's cheek. "Never mind. It's the thought that counts."

"I wonder what it could be," I said, affecting a mysterious tone of voice. As I unwrapped the box, I found another box nesting inside.

"I think I know where this is going," I said. Sure enough, as I went along there were several more boxes to open. Attalee hooted every time I opened another box.

"Oh my goodness. I wonder if I'll ever get to the real present," I said.

"Who knows? It might take weeks!" Attalee was laughing so hard I was afraid she'd pee her pants. Which wasn't an idle worry. There'd been several times in the past when she'd gotten overexcited and had to go back home to change her britches.

"I think I've finally gotten to the genuine article," I said. I held up a battered Whitman's Sampler box in triumph. When I looked inside, I discovered a gift certificate.

"I am very touched, Attalee." I gave her speckled hand a squeeze. "Look, Mavis, Attalee has given me a full year's membership in Boomer's Meat Cut of the Month Club. This is the perfect gift for a bride. Thank you."

"March is beef shanks and April is whole fryers," Attalee said. She'd gotten hold of herself and was blowing her nose into a tissue.

"That's a very generous gift, Attalee," Mavis said. She reached behind her chair and withdrew a sack. "Here's another little something."

"Mavis, you're too kind," I said, beholding the two wrapped packages, decorated with foil wedding bells. The ribbons had been specially curled over a blade of scissors. Mavis always had such an attention to detail.

The first package held a bride and groom with bobbing heads and suction cups on their feet so that you could affix them to the dashboard of a car. Mavis blushed when I opened it. "Oh, that was just a gag gift. I didn't want you to open that first."

Attalee picked up the bride and groom. "I don't see anything funny about this at all. This is a dandy-looking knickknack."

"She's right, Mavis. It's precious."

Mavis flicked her hand at me. "Go on, open the other one. The next one is the real present."

I pulled off the top of the box and looked inside. There were two white guest towels. One was monogrammed with my initials in gold embroidery and the other was monogrammed with Timothy's initials.

"Would you look at this?" I exclaimed. "They make me feel so... I don't know... so married!" I held the towels up for Attalee to see.

"I had to call Timothy to find out what his middle initial was," Mavis said. "He almost didn't tell me. He seemed a little embarrassed about it."

I glanced at Timothy's towel. The initials were "THH."

"Can you believe it?" My hand went to my throat. "I don't even know Timothy's middle name. Is it Harold? Or maybe Herbert?"

"Horton? Horatio? Hagar?" Attalee guessed.

"Horace. His middle name is Horace," Mavis said.

"Horace? Horace." I slid backward into my chair. "My gosh, that's such a beautiful name."

"It's uglier than an army boot," Attalee said.

Mavis put a finger to her lips and said, "Shush," while I spread out the towel on my lap.

"Elizabeth Delores. Timothy Horace," I said, dreamily. "It's almost like our names rhyme. Oh Mavis, these towels are so wonderful." A tear rolled down my cheek and I hugged Mavis's neck.

"Twelve months of grade-A meat and not even a trickle of a tear. Two tiny little towels that wouldn't dry a midget's behind and the waterworks are on fall blast," Attalee muttered.

"Oh, Attalee, it's not about the towels. When folks are in love, every piddling thing makes them cry," Mavis said, rubbing my shoulders.

Attalee started warbling "Love Is a Many Splendored Thing," which was her all-time favorite song, except for "It Wasn't God Who Made Honky-Tonk Angels" by Kitty Wells. She had a decent voice, although a little shivery, as old ladies' voices tend to be.

As I listened to Attalee sing, "In the morning mist, two lovers kissed and the world stood still," I heard the jingle of the bell on the front door of the Bottom Dollar Emporium. I turned around and saw my ex-fiancé, Clip Jenkins, in the doorway. He took off his hat and stuffed it into the pocket of his jeans.

"Good morning, I'm looking for Liz. Is she here?" he rumbled in his deep, silky voice.

Attalee lunged at Clip, brandishing her price gun. Clip grasped her skinny arm. "What are you planning to do with this, Attalee? Give me sticker shock?"

He let her loose and Attalee shrank back into the corner of the room, snarling.

Mavis stepped forward. "Clip Jenkins, get on out of here. You're not welcome at the Bottom Dollar, boy. Ever."

Clip stayed rooted to his spot by the sunglass wheel. "I came here to see Liz, Ma'am. I need to talk with her."

I stole out from behind a pyramid of Dr. Topper Sodas.

"I'll handle this, Mavis, Attalee," I said softly.

At the sight of me, a grin spilled over Clip's face. "Liz, you're here," he said.

"That's right, Clip." My face was a stone mask. "I'm here. I've been here for the last few months. It's not like I'm hard to find."

I walked over to where Clip was standing. He hadn't changed much. Same reddish hair shot through with gold. Same way of standing with his hip cocked and his fingers pushed through his belt loops. He regarded me with dark brown eyes, the color of heart pine.

"Could we go out to the truck?" He jerked his head in the direction of the door.

I leaned up against the checkout counter and folded my arms across my chest. "Jonelle know you're here?"

"It isn't her business to know where I am." Clip shifted his weight to his other hip. "We've split up."

I sucked in my cheeks and nodded. He reached out to touch my elbow and I flinched.

His arm dropped to his side. "Liz, please come on out to the truck."

"No."

"Just for a minute," he said.

"Cain't you hear, hotshot? The lady said no," Attalee said.

I glared at Clip. "So you and Jonelle have broken up? Did she get real stationery for her 'Dear Jane' letter, or did you write it on the back of a fast-food bag like you did mine?"

Clip swallowed. "Look, Liz I never—"

"Wait a minute," I thumped the counter. "Why am I wasting these words? You couldn't ever understand how I felt when I found that note. How betrayed and hurt and confused I was."

He cleared his throat. "That's why we need to talk. There's things that need explaining."

"No, Clip. *You* need to listen and you need to look." I pointed at the white streamers on the ceiling and I thrust my left ring finger in his face.

A puzzled look crossed his face. "Liz?" he said.

"She's married, you ignoramus!" Attalee shouted.

Clip winced like he'd been slapped. "No. That can't be right," he said in a raspy voice.

I almost felt sorry for him. Here he'd swept into the Bottom Dollar Emporium thinking he could mend things with his cocked hip and his lazy smile, the way a child thinks Elmer's glue can fix a broken heart.

He hadn't changed a bit.

The only thing that had changed was the way I felt in his presence. He'd once made my heart burn in my chest like a sparkler on the Fourth of July, but now there were only cold ashes.

"Good-bye, Clip," I said.

Twenty-Two

Don't sweat the petty things and don't pet the sweaty things.
~ Message in a fortune cookie from Dun Woo's House of Noodles

I contemplated the pale, uncooked chicken lying on the cutting board. Meemaw was sucking on a Pall Mall. She pushed back a strand of gray hair from her forehead and poked the chicken with her finger.

"I thought we'd start with taking the innards out. Do you know if Timothy is partial to gizzards?" she asked.

"Don't we have time for a glass of iced tea first?" I wasn't in any hurry to be sticking my hand up a dead chicken.

"I expect we do." She grabbed the ceramic pitcher of tea from a shelf in the refrigerator. Meemaw prides herself on her iced tea. The only brand she uses is Luzianne, the leaves, not the bags, and she makes a special syrup from sugar and honey to sweeten it and garnishes it with bruised mint leaves.

"So what did you think of Timothy, Meemaw?" Timothy and I'd had dinner with Meemaw and Boomer the night before. She'd made her company meatloaf with ground sirloin and veal and she'd worn her sterling silver earring bobs for the occasion.

"I still don't think young folks should rush pell-mell into marriage." Meemaw turned around to face me. "But I do have to say that Timothy seems like good people. You'd never guess he comes from all that money."

"He was wild about your peach cobbler. I believe he had two helpings."

"Three," Meemaw said, with a smug smile. She couldn't resist a hearty eater.

Meemaw's kitchen is one of my favorite places. The bear cookie jar still sat on the same shelf it did when I was a girl. I knew without looking that its belly was filled with oatmeal-and-raisin cookies, just as I knew that her freezer was packed tight with bags of snap peas, string beans, and butter beans.

"Where's Boomer?" I asked as Meemaw poured some tea.

"Saturday is his day with his mama. He takes her to get a comb-out and a blow dry and then they go to the Chat 'N' Chew and have a cup of chicken noodle soup. They've been doing that now for thirty years, ever since Boomer's daddy died. Once the Chat 'N' Chew changed their Saturday soup from chicken noodle to split pea, and Boomer's mom made such a stink that they changed it right back."

For a moment we sat in silence, except for the clinking of the ice against our tea glasses.

Meemaw's dark eyebrows hung low on her forehead and she stared into her ashtray. "Is there anything you wanted to ask me about married life?" she asked. Her eyes were still fixed on the ashtray and her knuckles had turned white around her tea glass.

"No, Meemaw," I said quickly. "Not a thing."

She relaxed back into her chair and glanced through the kitchen window into the backyard.

"I see the Bradford pear tree is about to bloom. Seems it was just last week that I swept the last of the pollen off the screen porch and here spring's coming around again."

She squinted at something outside. "Oh, shoot. Here comes Patsy Ann. Headed straight for the back door."

Patsy Ann Dinkins had been Meemaw's neighbor ever since I could remember, and she was also my godmother. She worked as a baby nurse at the hospital in Augusta where I was born and was in the room when I was delivered.

The screen door squeaked as Patsy Ann pushed it open. "I got some black-eyed Susans for planting as well as some wisteria, and I thought I'd share the—" She spotted me and grinned. "Would you look here? I swear, Elizabeth Delores, you get prettier every time I see you."

She sauntered over to kiss my cheek and then looked at Meemaw.

"Isn't she a blond, blue-eyed vision? I saw this classified ad in the *Crier:* Models wanted for glamorous career opportunities in Atlanta. Contact the Spotlight Modeling Agency."

She snitched a Hershey's Kiss from Meemaw's candy bowl. "You ought to think about applying, Elizabeth."

"Maybe I will," I said, although at five-foot three inches and 125 pounds I wasn't anyone's idea of a fashion model.

Patsy Ann scraped a chair to the table.

"I can't believe you're having a visit with Elizabeth and didn't call me over. I never get to see my godchild anymore," she said, rapping her knuckles on the table. "I'll tell you the God's-honest truth, many babies have come through my nursery, but there's never been a baby that could hold a candle to our Elizabeth. Isn't that right, Glenda?"

"She was a sweet little thing," Meemaw said.

"I remember it like it was yesterday," Patsy Ann continued. "Not a hair on that scalp, but eyes so big, you were afraid you'd fall into them and—"

"Patsy Ann!"

It was Patsy Ann's husband, Edward. Edward had been frail and ailing for so many years I was surprised he was still alive.

"Patsy Ann!" he called again.

"Here I thought we could all have us a hen talk and—" Patsy Ann said.

"Patsy Ann!"

"Coming, Edward!" Patsy Ann screeched so loud that both Meemaw and I flinched.

"Lord, that man can't blink without me around. Elizabeth, it's a joy as always. Glenda, I left them plants outside the door."

When she left, Meemaw exhaled.

"God love her, but that Patsy Ann is something of a trial," Meemaw said. "She's always had a soft spot for you, though. The way she still talks about the day you were born, you'd think she was the one who gave birth to you."

"Speaking of which. The anniversary of mama's death is coming next week. Are you planning to go out to the cemetery?" I asked.

Meemaw squirted some lemon into her tea. "I don't know that I will. Darlene doesn't need me there and I don't get comfort from sitting by a headstone and talking to it."

"Something's been gnawing at me since I read her diary."

I watched Meemaw's face closely, a little afraid that I might be bringing up something she would just as soon see dead and buried. But she didn't seem at all upset. She just shook another cigarette from her pack and lit it. She exhaled, and watched a cloud of gray smoke hover near the ceiling fan.

"I thought you might ask. I was biding my time until you were ready."

I dipped my finger into the ring of moisture the tea glass had left on the table. "Are you saying that you know something?"

Meemaw shook her head. "Don't know a thing more than what that diary says."

"Oh."

"But I have my own ideas about what's written there."

"And what are they?"

Meemaw pointed her cigarette at me.

"Just hold your horses a minute, girl. This is serious. I'd be the last person to throw your daddy a life vest if he fell in the drink, but you've thought of him as your daddy as long as you've been alive. Are you sure you're ready for something that might change all that?"

I didn't answer.

She didn't say anything at first, just pulled her sweater on tighter and looked away. I could hear the whir of the ceiling fan and the clicking of Pierre's toenails on the linoleum as he paced underneath the table, hoping we'd drop some food on the floor.

Finally Meemaw looked at me. Her shoulders were hunched and she appeared small and dried-out in her oversized sweater, like something the wind could carry away.

"I have never once thought that weasel Dwayne was your father," she said finally.

Once she began, the words tumbled out like beans spilling from a bag. She said my mama had known Dwayne for a year. They'd both worked at the What-A-Burger near the mill, and my daddy had taken to slipping my mama notes into the pocket of her uniform and buying her cheese crackers and cans of root beer on her break. But she didn't give him a flicker of attention and had gone so far as to make fun of him, calling him Dwayne the Pain, even though all the other girls would have gladly peeled off their clothes and dived into the back seat of his Maverick at the snap of his fingers.

Besides, at the time, Meemaw said, my mama was keeping company with that mysterious "B" of her diary.

"Darlene was a talker, but she didn't want to say nothing about this one." Meemaw scratched her elbow, which was poking out of a hole in her sweater. "I can't tell you how long it went on. A month, maybe more. All I can tell you is when it ended."

"What happened?" I asked.

"One morning Darlene called in sick at her job. She didn't go to work or anywhere else for three days, just stayed locked in her room. I found a gold bracelet that "B" must have given her in the wastebasket. It was all twisted out of shape. I knew then what had happened.

"We'd decided to leave her be, your granddaddy and I, but on the afternoon of the third day I was going to make her come to supper that evening. Just before we sat down to eat, Dwayne came by the house, wondering why Darlene hadn't been at work the past few days. I told him she was ailing, but no sooner had the words come out of my mouth when your mama came breezing out of her room, wearing a fresh coat of lipstick and making a fuss over Dwayne as if he'd been away at war, instead of flipping burgers at the What-A-Burger. She took off with him and from that day forward, the two of them were hardly ever apart. It was as if there had never even been a boy with the initial "B."

Meemaw leaned across the table and her eyes narrowed.

"When she and Dwayne came to your granddaddy and me, telling us they were off to the courthouse to get married—after dating less than two weeks—I didn't even try to talk them out of it, because I knew a young'un was on the way. I just didn't know who was the true father of the young'un—Dwayne or that boy in the diary."

She stubbed out her cigarette, which she had smoked clean down to the filter. "But my money was on that 'B' fellow."

"Didn't you ever ask Mama about it?"

"Never." She got up from her chair and rinsed her tea glass in the sink. "And I didn't say a word when you were born eight months after they got married," she said over her shoulder. "You weighed eight pounds and five ounces, but I kept quiet."

I got up and stood behind her. "But why, Meemaw? Why didn't you ask?"

She turned around and leaned back against the sink. "If that other boy was your daddy, your mama went to a whole lot of trouble to make it seem like you were Dwayne's child. It just seemed best to leave things be."

We were silent. I took a sip of my tea and studied Meemaw, who had a fresh cigarette burning in her hand.

"All my life, I wanted a different kind of daddy," I said. "I used to wish for a daddy like Charles Ingalls on *Little House on the Prairie*. But I got Dwayne instead."

"A water moccasin would have made a better father," Meemaw said with a grunt.

"Maybe. Dwayne hasn't been the best of dads, but he has been a daddy, something that 'B' person hadn't ever been."

Meemaw folded her arms across her chest. "What are you saying?"

I swallowed hard. "I don't know. I guess I'm saying it doesn't matter so much one way or the other where I came from. Maybe it did when I was little, but it doesn't now."

Twenty-Three

Even Jesus had a fish story.

~ Sign outside the Bait Box and Tanning Salon

When I got home Timothy was sitting on the couch, reading and scratching Maybelline's belly. The dog was ecstatically thumping her leg on the couch. Timothy was so deeply absorbed that he didn't glance up until I'd shut the door behind me, just in time to see him shove his reading material behind the sofa cushion.

"Hi, Elizabeth, did you have a nice time at your grandmother's?" he asked.

He looked up at me in a completely innocent way, as if I hadn't caught him in the act of trying to hide something from me.

"I did."

I paused in the middle of the room, cradling my big container of soup to my chest. "What's going on?" I stared hard at the cushion.

"Nothing much. A little tummy rub is all. It took a while, but Maybelline and I have finally made our peace."

"Well, I'd still keep an eye on my boxers and socks if I was you. That dog would cozy up to the dogcatcher if she thought she'd get a belly scratching out of it."

I walked into the kitchen to put my soup in the refrigerator, wondering over Timothy's secretive behavior. I guessed he'd been reading one of them nudie magazines like *Playboy* or *Pent-house*.

Clip had kept stacks of them beside his waterbed and didn't even bother hiding them when I came over. I wouldn't have figured Timothy as the type to be looking at girlie pictures, but I could be wrong.

I heated up the soup for supper and when I served it, Timothy was so complimentary that I almost forgot his earlier sneakiness. He also insisted on helping with the dishes, which is a chore I had never seen any man do.

Over at Taffy and Daddy's house, me and Taffy would be in the kitchen after dinner scraping the dishes and loading the dishwasher while Daddy and Lanier were plopped in front of the television, gnawing on toothpicks.

It never even occurred to Taffy or me to ask them to pitch in. And if we had, my daddy would surely say that washing dishes was a job for pansies, which is what he said about most household chores, with the exceptions of weed-whacking, killing bugs, and slapping a coat of Turtle Wax on his pickup truck.

After the dishes, we took our coffee into the living room and Timothy asked me how I felt about going house-hunting this coming weekend.

"This place is cozy, but too small for the two of us," Timothy said. "I'd like a home with a study; you need a bigger kitchen; and I think Maybelline would enjoy a nice big, fenced yard where she could frolic, chase butterflies, and dig holes or whatever it is that dogs like to do."

Timothy wasn't going to get a whole lot of frolicking out of Maybelline—she was more the snoozing-on-the-couch and licking-her-bottom kind of pooch—but I was thrilled to bits at the idea of a house of our very own.

I wanted a place with a bathtub—a step up from my shower with its scummy tile floor covered with stick-on daisies that had been there so many years, they were brittle and black with mildew. I was imagining myself in the tub, with my hair piled high on my head like in those bath-bead ads, covered up all the way to my neck in bubbles and resting my head on one of those shell-shaped inflatable pillows, when I heard a voice outside my front door say, "Toughen up, Dwayne, there's just three steps. You act like we're climbing up the Empire State Building."

I felt like someone had dumped a Slushee down my back. The voice belonged to Taffy. Obviously she had dragged my daddy over here for a surprise visit. I felt like grabbing Timothy's hand and escaping out the back door, but unfortunately there was only one entrance to Casa Elizabeth.

"Knock, knock, Betty D. You got some visitors. Get yourself decent, if you ain't," Taffy said outside our door.

Timothy shot me a quizzical look and I whispered, "It's my daddy and his wife."

I opened the door and there they stood. Taffy must have told Daddy what to wear, because instead of his usual Dickey work pants and Budweiser T-shirt, he was wearing a golf shirt with a tiny little horse on the breast and a pair of khaki pants stiff enough to have come straight off a mannequin. Taffy, on the other hand, was wearing a bright red pantsuit with epaulets and elaborate gold braiding. The only thing she needed to top off her look was a matching pillbox hat.

"Betty D., I hope we weren't interrupting anything." Taffy's neck craned to see behind me, hoping to get a peek at Timothy. I noticed she was holding a package in her hand.

"No, we just finished up our supper. Y'all come in."

Maybelline chose that moment to shoot out from her spot under the coffee table. Her teeth bared and her chest hair ruffled as she growled at Taffy.

Taffy backed away, the blue vein in her forehead throbbing. "Lord, Betty D. Would you call off Revlon, for God sakes? Why does she always do that to me?"

My daddy picked Maybelline up by the scruff of her neck and said, "Shoot, this is more rat than dog." He let Maybelline loose, and she crawled back to her spot under the table, with her tail between her legs.

"Now a pit bull, that's a dog," he said, directing his comment to Timothy, who was standing by the couch, holding his coffee cup and staring at Taffy and my daddy, open-mouthed, as if rubbernecking at a traffic accident.

"Taffy and Dwayne Polk," I said. "This is Timothy Hollingsworth. My husband."

Whatever trance Timothy had been in, he immediately snapped out of it and dived right into all the social niceties.

"An honor to finally meet you, sir," he said, pumping my daddy's arm. "Mrs. Polk, so good to have the pleasure of your acquaintance. Please sit down and make yourself comfortable. Could we offer you a beverage? Coffee, perhaps?"

My daddy made a face, most likely because of the offer of coffee during his usual happy hour. He sprawled out on the sofa, spied the remote in between the cushions, turned the television on, and began flipping through the channels.

"Dwayne, what are you doing?" Taffy said.

"Looking for the motor cross races on ESPN. What do you think I'm doing? You a motor cross fan, son?" my daddy asked Timothy.

Timothy was standing in his stocking feet, shifting his weight from one foot to the other. "Uh, motor cross. I don't think—"

"Your cable is out." My daddy tossed the remote aside. "All I'm getting is a lot of fuzz and the local stations."

"Daddy, I don't have cable," I said.

My daddy looked shocked, as if I had told him that I didn't have indoor plumbing. He shoved his hands in his pockets and shot Taffy a stormy look.

"I bet now that they're newlyweds, they'll get cable. Maybe even a few of those premium channels too," Taffy said.

I nodded vaguely. No point telling them that neither Timothy or I had much use for television. It wasn't a notion they'd understand.

"Lordy, I nearly forgot," Taffy said. "The reason we busted in on you like this was we were hoping to meet you, Timothy, of course. But we also wanted to give the two of you a wedding gift."

She handed me the box and perched herself on the edge of a director's chair. By her stiff posture and the way she kept cutting her eyes in Timothy's direction, I could tell that she was nervous about meeting him.

I unwrapped what looked like a very small Crockpot, not even big enough to hold a couple of new potatoes, much less a side of beef.

"Taffy, this is very—"

"It's one of them pot-pourri burners," Taffy said, pronouncing the silent "t." "Open the lid, and there's a bag of pot-pourri. You plug it in and it will make your whole house smell like a country morning."

"What an original gift, Mrs. Polk," said Timothy. "I'm certain that Elizabeth and I will put it to good use."

Taffy beamed. "You're welcome, Tim. 'Course you can call me Taffy." Her glance dropped to the floor. "Or even Mama, since you're a member of the family now. Not that I'm old enough to be your mama, of course."

"No, it's obvious that you're not nearly old enough to be my mother." Timothy took a step toward the kitchen. "Now, does anyone want to take me up on that coffee? It's freshly brewed."

"I'd adore a cup. Just black though," Taffy said.

Timothy looked at my daddy, who put up his hand and said, "Pass."

Timothy walked into the kitchen and my daddy said, "What's wrong with you, girl? Your leg broken or something?"

"What do you mean, Daddy?"

"You got your husband fetching for you like he was Betty Crocker."

I made a shooing motion with my hand. "Daddy, where is it written that the woman is the one who is supposed to wait on everyone?" I asked.

"The Bible," he answered quickly.

I snorted. "Like you ever read the Bible. I read the Bible, Daddy, and nowhere does it—"

"Betty D. Don't disrespect your father," Taffy said. "He doesn't read the Bible. But he does watch *Hour of Power* with me sometimes, which is even better."

"Here's your coffee, Mrs.—I mean Taffy," Timothy said, coming back from the kitchen.

Taffy accepted the cup. "Why, thank you, Timothy. Did Betty D. tell you that Dwayne and I live out in Brandywine? We'd love to have the two of you over for supper sometime. Are you familiar with Brandywine, Timothy?" Taffy asked.

"Yes, I am. It's a very nice area. I work with a man named Pavey. Maybe you know him and his wife, George and Annette Pavey?"

"Let me think now..." Taffy put a finger to her temple. "Pavey, Pavey."

"Shoot, Taffy. They must live in Phase I. That's where all them big houses is," my daddy said. "We live in Phase III, the Brandywine ghetto. Only folks we ever spoke to was the ones down the street who called security on us because Lanier was making doughnuts in the driveway with his truck."

Taffy's face flushed. "I would hardly call a $350,000 patio home with vaulted ceilings a ghetto house, Dwayne."

My daddy crossed his ankle over his knee and jiggled his foot. "I've seen cardboard boxes that were built better. But Taffy had to live in a swanky neighborhood with a guard house and I can afford it."

He leaned forward to speak to Timothy. "I got a rent-to-own business. You may have seen my commercials. I'm Insane Dwayne of the Bargain Bonanza. By the way, if any of your kin needs a big-screen TV or a sectional sofa, I'd be glad to give them the family discount."

"Lord, Dwayne. You don't even know what you're talking about." Taffy was still smarting from his ghetto remark. "Timothy's kin wouldn't go to a rent-to-own place to buy furniture. Your place is for folks who are down on their luck."

"All folks, rich or poor, like to take advantage of a bargain,

Taffy," my daddy snapped. "That's how they stay rich, isn't it, Tim? I'll get you a few of my business cards to pass around."

"More coffee, anyone?" Timothy asked.

My daddy got up from the couch and plunged his hands deeply enough into the pockets of his khakis to reveal a narrow strip of beer belly.

"Now that Taffy's delivered her gift, we better be on our way," he said. He toed the brown shag carpet at his feet. "Speaking of houses, there's a few up for sale in Brandywine. I sure hope you got something better in mind for my daughter than this shotgun shack she's been living in all these years, seeing how you're this bigwig at the paper cup place."

"Daddy!" I gasped.

"I'm just speaking my piece." He looked on as Timothy gaped with astonishment. "You don't mind that, do you, son?"

"Daddy, Timothy and I are going to look for a house this weekend. We were talking about it just before you got here." I stepped in between the two of them, as if to shield Timothy from my daddy's crassness.

Timothy's eyes darted from my daddy to the floor. "Excuse me for a moment, please," he said in a hoarse whisper. He walked swiftly down the hall to the bathroom and shut the door behind him.

"Daddy!" I said. "Timothy, are you all right?" There was no response behind the bathroom door.

My daddy stuck a thumb in Timothy's direction and raised an eyebrow. "What's wrong with him?"

By this time Taffy had gotten up and was standing by the door with her purse tucked underneath her arm. "Betty D., your father just doesn't know how to act around quality people. That's why he chose Phase III. That's why I have to endure the sneers of those security guards every time I go by the gate house, because we live in the patio homes and not the real houses."

"Taffy," my daddy said in warning.

"You tell Timothy that I'm very pleased to meet his

acquaintance and that we will have that dinner one night, even though my dining room is so small I can't even put in the extra leaf, cause folks' heads would be bumping against the wall," Taffy said.

"Out to the car, Taff, now," Daddy said.

He lingered on the front landing. "Your boy is acting like a woman. You sure he ain't... you know." He made his wrist limp and stuck out his pinkie finger.

"Maybe you'd better go on home now," I said quietly.

He stood there rocking back and forth on the balls of his feet, jangling loose change in his pocket. His aftershave did little to mask the scorched smell of cigarette smoke that clung to his clothes.

"Well, give me some sugar before I take off."

I brushed my lips with his cheek.

"And who's my baby girl?" he asked in that sly tone of his.

Not me, most likely, I almost said, but I bit my lip and replied, "Cleopatra, the Queen of the Nile. You take care now." Then I shooed him out the door.

I dashed to the bathroom and started banging on the door. "Honey, are you all right?"

There was silence.

"Timothy?"

No response. I was getting alarmed. "Timothy, I'm really sorry about my daddy acting like that. That's just his way. He didn't mean it."

I jiggled the doorknob.

"Timothy!" Again there was no sign of life behind the door.

"All right now, you're starting to worry me. I'm just going to have to bust down this door. It's flimsy and I'm pretty sure I could do it. But I'll lose my security deposit, which is two hundred fifty dollars."

The door cracked open and Timothy slunk out, avoiding my eye.

"Well, thank goodness, Timothy. I was starting to get worried. You have to understand about daddy. When God was handing out social graces to folks, my daddy was outside taking a cigarette break."

"You must think I'm a loon." He tugged at his halo of dark curls. "I'm just ashamed of myself because something your father said made me realize that I've not been completely honest with you."

"Does this have anything to do with what you stashed behind the cushions when I walked in the door?"

He nodded, his hands tucked behind his back.

I reached behind the sofa cushion. After unearthing a petrified French fry, a plastic chew steak of Maybelline's, and the June issue of *Celebrity Hairstyles,* I found the book *The Angler's Almanac.* I looked at it, puzzled.

"Why were you hiding this from me?"

Timothy sunk down into a chair beside the sofa. He exhaled noisily. "I didn't want you to know I'm a failure."

"Why in the world would reading *The Angler's Almanac* make you a failure?"

"It's not the book. It's the reason that I'm reading it." He toyed with the zipper on one of the throw pillows. "There's no sense in hiding it any longer."

I folded my arms across my chest. "Go on. Spit it out."

Timothy's Adam's apple bobbed nervously. "I don't want to work at Hollingsworth Paper Cups. I can't stand being a corporate executive. I'm not even very good at it."

He looked so forlorn that I sat down beside him and gave him a hug.

"That's okay, sweetie," I crooned. "I'm not really that surprised. You've never seemed very happy over there. But I still don't understand what this has to do with bait."

He bit his lip and looked up at me, nervously. "Orson wants to sell his bait shop. He's moving to New Orleans to work on an oil rig. And I want to buy it, so I've been reading up on the different kinds of bait."

"You want to buy the bait shop?"

Timothy nodded. "I'm sorry I ducked out when your father

was here, Elizabeth. But he made me realize that you married me thinking I was this hotshot CEO of a big company when the only thing I really want to do is sell mealworms to fishermen."

I shook my head in disbelief. "The bait shop. Well, I'll be darned."

"Bait shop and tanning salon," Timothy said, correcting me. "Although I've never understood how the two go together. But Orson said the tanning salon has ended up being a nice little money-maker for him."

"My husband, the bait and tanning salon mogul," I said.

Timothy winced. "Are you terribly disappointed?"

I laughed. "Of course not. If selling worms to folks makes you happy, I couldn't be more tickled." I paused. "Just make sure you wash your hands real good before you come home."

Timothy threw his arms around me. "Elizabeth, I'm so glad you understand. I'm going to notify the board of directors as soon as I can work this deal out with Orson."

"Who are you going to get to replace you at Hollingsworth Paper Cups?" I asked.

"I don't know. I guess Mother will have to deal with that." He shuddered. "I don't want to even think about breaking the news to her."

"Well, don't put it off too long," I said.

"I won't, but there's no sense in calling her until everything is definite," Timothy said. "And Elizabeth, there's one other thing."

"What is it?" I asked.

Worry etched his forehead. "I do have a fairly generous trust fund that Grandma Grace set up for me and I'll be using part of that to buy the store. But bait store owners and CEOs of companies are in completely different income tax brackets. There will be less money coming in."

I smiled at my husband, trying to picture him doling out crickets to the local fishermen. "That'll suit me just fine. I'd rather have a content husband than a rich one."

He kissed my cheek. "We'll always have enough to get by. As a matter of fact, even with buying the bait shop, I'll still be able to treat you to a wonderful honeymoon. How would you feel about walking along the Seine or sailing the Greek Isles this summer?"

"You know I'd love that," I said. "But there's really only one thing that I hope we'll be able to afford to do, when the time's right."

"What's that?" Timothy asked.

"Babies," I replied coyly. "I was hoping that we'd have one or two of them someday."

"Babies?" He rolled the word in his mouth like a butterscotch drop. "Oh, that would be something, Elizabeth." His brow wrinkled. "Just one or two though?"

"To start."

"Babies," he said, breathing in the word. "I like the idea of that very much."

Twenty-Four

I'd been curious about Timothy's role in the operation of Hollingsworth Paper Cups, so with his permission, I poked around his briefcase and perused some of his P-and-L numbers. He found me the next morning sitting at the table and snoozing on a stack of quarterly statements.

"Morning, sweetie." He planted a kiss on my earlobe. "Did you fall asleep reading my papers? I'm not surprised. Deadly dull stuff, isn't it?"

I twisted my back to get rid of the crick I'd gotten in the night.

"It's fascinating to me. Accounting, marketing, operations, the whole tamale. You sure you want to leave this all behind?"

Timothy stood in the slant of sunlight, sipping his coffee. "You know, Elizabeth, if business is an interest of yours, you should consider taking an evening class or two at the University in Aiken."

I stifled a yawn. "You sound like your grandmother. I'll tell you what I told her. I'm not college material."

"Says who?" Timothy said, slathering some of Meemaw's marmalade on his bread.

"Mrs. Babb, the guidance counselor at Cayboo Creek High School. She wrote 'Vocational Tract' in big red letters across my records folder. Plus, none of my kin has ever gone on to college. Our minds just aren't wired right for higher learning."

Timothy's jaw fell open. "You can't possibly believe that."

"Sure, I do. It's what I've been told all my life. Daddy always said Polks work with their backs, not their brains." I picked up the butter knife. "Any of that marmalade left? And quit eye-balling me like I've grown a horn through my forehead."

"Elizabeth, you, like most people, are shortsighted when it comes to seeing yourself as others do. When I first met you, guess what sent me straight to the moon?" He kissed me on the top of my head and whispered. "It was your big, beautiful brain."

He thrust out his wrist so I could fasten his cufflink—just one of the little rituals of married life that was becoming so dear to me.

"The next time you're at the library, look in the reference section," Timothy said, as he slipped into a suit jacket. "See if they have any SAT practice guides. I want you to take the test the next time it's scheduled."

"Timothy, I'm telling you, I can't—"

Timothy put his finger up to quiet me. "Elizabeth, maybe it's true that you can't do it, although I seriously doubt that. But you should try at least."

"Timothy—"

His lips grazed my cheek. "Trust me on this, Elizabeth."

After he left, Maybelline barked, letting me know that the postman had shoved my mail through the slot.

I picked up the few pieces on the floor. There was a pizza flier, the electric bill, and a postcard that said "Greetings From Hilton Head" on a photograph of a stretch of sand, dotted with beach umbrellas. The postcard was from Mrs. Tobias, saying she would see me in a few days when she got back from her trip.

There was a knot of nervousness in my stomach at the thought of Mrs. Tobias's return. What would she think of me once she found out that I had gone and married her grandson?

I stuck Mrs. Tobias's postcard under a magnet on the refrigerator with all the rest of her postcards. Mrs. Tobias was a big traveler, and she'd sent me nine postcards in all. Everything from a tour of Williamsburg, Virginia, to a trip to see the geysers in Yellowstone Park.

I lolled the rest of the morning away, enjoying the luxury of my day off. About 11:45 A.M., my stomach growled. I decided to head over to Pick of the Chick for the Lickety Split special—a drumstick, a dinner roll, and a jalapeño pepper.

The Pick of the Chick was a drive-in restaurant dating back to my daddy's youth. Customers consulted billboard-sized menus with long-since-faded pictures of chicken and fixings, then placed their orders over loudspeakers.

Even though the landscaping was scraggly, the speakers crackled with static, and the waitresses moved like they had cement in their shoes, the Pick of the Chick bustled because it had the best chicken in Aiken County. A friend of mine who worked there one summer swore that the secret to Pick of the Chick's chicken was Wise potato chips crushed up into the batter. All I knew is once every couple of months, I had a fierce craving for a piece of their chicken, whatever the secret ingredient.

I hollered my order into the speaker and while I waited, I fiddled with the radio pre-set buttons. Timothy had last tuned it to Public Radio. I tried to listen, but I couldn't cozy up to the announcers. Their voices reminded me of the museum guards cautioning school kids on a field trip, "Please remain behind the velvet rope."

I turned the station to Big Sky Country WBEG and listened to a Dixie Chicks song, a Faith Hill ballad, and two used-car commercials before my food was trotted out by Eloise Jenkins, who's worked at Pick of the Chick for over twenty years and is also Clip's second cousin.

"Sorry, Elizabeth, about the wait. I dropped a bottle of Texas Pete on the floor and I had to get it up," she said, placing my order on the window tray.

"That's okay. Though I don't know why y'all call this the Lickety Split special. You ought to call it the Belated Bird."

Eloise laughed and stuffed her hands into the pockets of her uniform. The day was blustery and dogwood blossoms were scooting around the parking lot.

"Clip's been coming around here a lot lately. He's chewed my ear off, talking about you. Says he made a big mistake, letting you get away the way he did."

I made a face and reached for my food. "I don't care what that buzzard thinks. No offense. I know he's your kin, but he's not been my favorite person for a good while."

"And no one could blame you," Eloise said, raking her fingers through brown, fuzzy curls.

"I am a little curious about something though." I shook my jalapeño pepper from its paper wrapper. "How in heaven's name did Clip get that big, red truck he's been tooling around in?"

Eloise's pupils widened. She leaned over the window of my car and said, "You and everyone else in the family. His mama's scared to pieces that he's involved with the Mafia."

"The Mafia? There isn't any Mafia in Cayboo Creek," I said.

"Oh, Clip's mama thinks there is. She's suspicious of that restaurant called the Olive Haven that opened up a couple of months ago on Highway One. She thinks it might be their headquarters."

"What's Clip's explanation as to why he's suddenly got such an expensive truck?" I asked.

"He just says he bought it. He showed his mama the title, but he won't say where he got the money."

I dabbed at my face with a Wet One. "You mean he didn't even finance it?"

"That's right. And Clip refuses to discuss it any further. You want to know something else? He bought this truck the day after you and he split up. Now what do you think about that?"

"Well, I had nothing to do with it," I said. I was getting impatient with the conversation. I had enough troubles of my own without worrying if my ex-fiancé had turned into some kind of criminal.

"Of course you didn't. Clip's mama says you were the best thing that ever happened to him. According to her, you're a saint."

"Is that so?" I took a nibble of my drumstick. I was flattered. Not that Clip's mother was the most sophisticated woman in the world. She read supermarket tabloids cover to cover and was utterly convinced that Batboy was a real person.

"Eloise!" called the manager of the Pick of the Chick.

Eloise rolled her eyes. "Gotta go. Don't be a stranger now. I'd like to see you more often."

After eating, I drove to the Augusta Library and checked out a stack of books on marketing, as well as a book entitled *Ace the SAT*. Although I didn't think I had any chance of getting into the University, I decided to placate my husband.

I slid into my car and balanced a book on my knee, intending only to flip through it, but soon found myself engrossed in an account of Wells Fargo's corporate turnaround. But I couldn't keep my mind on the reading. I kept thinking about Mavis losing the Bottom Dollar Emporium and moving to South Dakota.

No one had made an offer on her house yet, but Mavis was talking about renting it out until it could be sold. She'd asked me and Timothy to serve as landlords while she was in South Dakota. She was also planning a liquidation sale of the Bottom Dollar shortly after the grand opening of the Super Saver. She was so resigned to moving that she'd bought seven pairs of long Johns during Goody's winter clearance sale. As I was trying imagine a world without Mavis and the Bottom Dollar Emporium, a knock sounded on my passenger window. Startled, I let loose a shriek.

I looked up and saw Clip's face looming through the glass. I cranked down the window.

"You like to have jarred the fillings right out of my teeth, Clip Jenkins," I said.

Clip wore his blue RC Cola work shirt. The breeze stirred his reddish-gold bangs.

"Good afternoon, Liz. Or should I call you Mrs. Hollingsworth now?"

"How'd you find out my new last name?"

Clip shrugged. "Cayboo Creek is a real small town, Liz." He stuck his head through the open window. I could smell his Mennen cologne, a musk blend of some sort. "Could you come out here? I need to talk to you."

I turned the key in the ignition. "I gotta go, Clip."

"Look, Liz." He cast his eyes downward. "Jonelle didn't mean nothing to me. That girl's got snakes in her hair." His fingers gripped the inside of the door. "It wasn't anything like what I had with you. What the two of us had meant something."

I looked into his familiar tanned face. I'd once counted the freckles on the bridge of his nose and traced the arch of his eyebrow with my finger. But now he just seemed a stranger to me.

"Move your fingers, Clip. I'm out of here."

"This marriage of yours, Liz. It's a rebound thing. We've been together since high school. You barely know this Timothy"

I started rolling up the window and revved the engine.

"You gotta hear me out, Liz. That family you married into—" His voice dropped to a ragged whisper. "They aren't right, I tell you."

I shook my head at him. "You're the one who's not right, Clip. I hear your mama is worried sick wondering where you got that fancy truck of yours."

He sighed wearily. "Worst decision of my life."

As he spoke, I noticed that there were dark splotches under his eyes, as if he hadn't been sleeping.

"But in a couple of days everything will come out in the open. And you and I can have another chance, Liz," he said softly.

I shook my head. "Clip, I'm married. Very happily married. I'm leaving now."

"But Liz—"

The window went up and Clip hastily backed away. I took off, and in my rearview mirror I saw Clip gazing forlornly after my departing car.

Twenty-Five

When down in the mouth, remember Jonah. He came out all right.
~ Message in the *Methodist Church Bulletin*

The Cayboo Creek Crier slapped down on the stoop of the Bottom Dollar Emporium. I waved at Birdie's grandson, Gordie, as he pedaled down Mule Pen Road, tossing papers, his red hair a flag of color in the pale morning sunlight. I scooped up the newspaper, knowing what the headline would read without even looking at it.

Once inside the store, Mavis noticed the paper in my hand. She held up her palm. "I don't even want to see that thing." She retreated into the storeroom with her coffee cup, saying, "If anyone asks for me, tell 'em I'm busy."

Hank plodded through the front door holding an African violet plant in his hand, followed by Birdie, who cradled a box of doughnuts.

"Where is she?" Hank said, scanning the store. Attalee had taken the paper from me and had it spread out, so we could all read the headline splashed across the front: "Super Saver Opens Today in Cayboo Creek."

"She's in the back, stewing," Attalee said. She thumped the paper. "Doggit, Birdie. This headline's so big it looks like an eye chart. Couldn't you have buried this in the back, with the lost pet notices?"

Birdie had opened the doughnut box. Her index finger hovered like a divining rod over the rows of doughnuts, finally zeroing in on a chocolate one with pink sprinkles.

"As much as I love Mavis, I'm first and foremost a journalist," she said, holding the doughnut delicately between her fingers. "This week the two biggest stories were the opening of the Super Saver Dollar Store or Reeky's cat Moonbeam catching fire after leaping over one of those aromatherapy candles. A grand opening will nudge a charred kitty off the front page every time."

Hank was sprawled out on a chair, drumming his fingers on his overall-covered belly. "Maybe I oughta go back and check on her." He craned his neck in the direction of the storeroom. "You think I should?"

"Let her be for a while, Hank," I said, gently. "I think part of her thought this day would never come."

Mavis emerged from the storeroom and was standing in the doorway, her broad forehead marred by grooves of distress.

"Mavis?" Hank said. "Are you all right?"

She shook her head. "I kept praying for a miracle, thinking that maybe God would smile on me. I even put an extra five dollars each week in the offering plate." She covered her face with her hands. "That was just plain foolishness."

Hank awkwardly patted her back with a pawlike hand.

Mavis removed a hankie from the pocket of her smock and blew her nose. "I'm truly a silly, old woman."

"No, Mavis," I said gently. "You're not a bit silly."

"I'm not just sad about this. I'm also angry," Mavis said. "How dare these people come into town with their bulging bank accounts and their buying power and not give a care who they're hurting! I've a half a mind to walk over there and give them what for."

"We *should* go over there," I said.

"Into enemy camp?" Hank asked. He'd helped himself to a powdered doughnut, and sugar trailed from his chin to the top button of his plaid shirt.

"Yes," I said. "Not to bless them out. But just so we can see what we're dealing with, once and for all. Maybe there's something we're missing."

"What's the point, Elizabeth?" Mavis said. "It's all over."

"Just humor me, Mavis," I said.

Mavis pressed her lips so tightly together they disappeared. Then she fumbled in her pocket and out came the silver flash of her cash-register key. "Attalee, will you mind things while we're gone? Nowadays, we can't afford to miss even a chewing-gum purchase."

Hank hitched up his overalls, while Birdie adjusted the brim of her basin-shaped hat. The three of them trudged behind me in a dejected line. I, on the other hand, felt a surge of hope urging me across the road.

Several cars were already parked in the Super Saver lot. None of them looked familiar except a bright, blue Volkswagen bug bumper-stickered "I break for butterflies."

As if on cue, Reeky came out of the store hugging a paper bag brimming with items, the head of a toilet brush peering out at a jaunty angle. At the sight of our little group, arrayed in a phalanx, she screeched and dropped her bag.

I stopped a cylinder of breath mints with my foot, while Hank crouched down to pick up the other fallen items. He shamefacedly ignored a box of Tampax that had flung open, sending a half a dozen or more rolling merrily down a grassy knoll on the edge of the parking lot.

"You scared me to pieces," Reeky said. "You shouldn't creep up on folks like that."

Hank had gathered up all of Reeky's things and handed them to her.

Reeky blinked rapidly. The whites of her eyes had a pinkish cast to them like that of a rabbit's. "I know this looks terrible. And I wouldn't have dreamt of setting foot in here. Except today I got this coupon in the mail. It's five dollars off every purchase of fifteen dollars or more. *Five dollars.* I swear that now that I've used the coupon, I'll never darken their door again."

She rummaged through her macramé bag and took out a piece of blue paper. "Here's what I received. Of course they already tore off the coupon part."

Mavis put on her reading glasses and read the paper aloud.

'Howdy, Neighbors! Super Saver Sam wants you to save a lot of dough at your neighborhood Super Saver Dollar Store.'

"If that isn't just the limit," she said. "This big corporation pretending to be our neighbor."

"Super Saver Sam"'s cartoon head was ridiculously oversized and he had an exaggerated cleft in his chin. Dollar signs danced in his eyes.

"Five-dollar savings," Mavis said with a shake of her head. "It makes our coupon look pathetic."

"Let's just see what's going on inside," I said, shooting Reeky a poisonous look.

Plate glass was strung with multicolored triangular flags. Just outside, a line of gleaming shopping carts with the Super Saver logo beckoned customers, while a sleek, coin-operated spaceship promised to entertain the little ones.

"Seventy-five cents for this dinky ride," Hank remarked. "That's a crime."

I was fixing to push the door, but it flung open on its own accord. A gale of icy air whooshed out, along with the stereo sounds of "Crystal Blue Persuasion."

A hush fell over our group as we took in all of the sights of the new Super Saver Dollar Store. The clerks at each register were garbed in matching navy-blue smocks with red piping. (I recognized them as local girls, just out of high school. They'd turn surly soon enough, but today they all wore toothy, customer-friendly grins.)

The cash registers made satisfying blips as items were scanned through the line. Red, white, and blue balloons swayed above each checkout. But it was the inventory that boggled the mind. Bottles of shampoos, organized by color, stretched out in endless rows. Towers of towels loomed on the shelves. I gaped open-mouthed at an entire back wall devoted just to laundry detergents.

Feenie Myers, a regular at the Bottom Dollar, ducked behind a display of potted meat when she saw me coming, but I was too spellbound to pay her any mind.

The store was as big as an airplane hangar. We drifted like sleepwalkers through the seemingly endless aisles. Finally, Mavis tugged my wrist in the automotive department. (Such a thing didn't exist at the Bottom Dollar.) "I've had enough. Let's head on back."

We exited to eager cries of, "Please come back and see us."

As soon as we got back to the Bottom Dollar Emporium, Mavis collapsed into a chair. Hank handed her the little silver flask he always carried in the pocket of his overalls. Mavis unscrewed the cap and took a big swallow, even though the only alcohol that generally passed her lips was in Birdie's Christmas rum cakes.

"Good Lord Almighty. It's even worse than I thought. We might as well board up the windows today. No one is going to shop at the Bottom Dollar after they see that place," Mavis said. Her cheeks were flushed from the alcohol.

"Now, dearie. Don't get overwrought," Birdie said, patting Mavis's hand.

Mavis leveled her gaze at me. "What do you think, Elizabeth? Are you finally convinced that there's no way to save the Bottom Dollar Emporium?"

Everyone waited for me to speak. Attalee, who was on a stepladder, dusting the tops of shelves, lowered her feather duster and peered down at me.

I cleared my throat. "After visiting the Super Saver, even I'm convinced that we don't have a prayer trying to compete with them. They're bigger and better than us. Going head to head with that place would be like a gnat trying to tussle with a killer bee."

"Cripes, Elizabeth," Attalee hissed. "You could try to soft-soap it some."

"No. I need to hear the unvarnished truth," Mavis said through colorless lips.

I smiled. "But in answer to your question, Mavis, yes, I think the Bottom Dollar Emporium can be saved. And I think I know exactly how to do it. Seeing the Super Saver up close has given me a wonderful idea. It's the most fantastic idea I've ever had."

"Well, what is it?" Birdie said. "Don't leave us in the dark."

"I'm not ready to share it yet," I said, quickly. "I need to do a little research first. Before I get my hopes up, I have to make sure that my plan is feasible."

I strode over to Mavis and slung my arm around her. "Tell you what, Mavis, give me twenty-four hours. That should be enough time if I take the rest of the day off. We'll all meet here tomorrow and then I'll tell you what I have in mind for the Bottom Dollar Emporium."

Twenty-Six

People are like tea bags. You gotta put them in hot water before you know how strong they are.

~ Note tacked on the bulletin board of the Bottom Dollar Emporium

Timothy and I strolled down Scuffle Road, which was canopied by rows of Japanese magnolia trees in the process of losing their heavy pink and white blossoms. The street was downwind of the Wagon Wheel and usually smelled of cooking grease, but today it was as fragrant as a harlot's bedchamber.

We passed by my neighbor Burris, who was sitting on his porch in his undershirt, smoking a cigarette and listening to a Clint Black song on a transistor radio.

"Hey there, Elizabeth," he said, twitching his propped-up feet to the music.

"Hi, Burris," I said. "What's new?"

"Everyone's talking about your top-secret plan to save the Bottom Dollar Emporium," he replied. "At least, that was the word at the Tuff Luck Tavern last night."

"Your secret is out," Timothy said, squeezing my hand.

"Is it true, Elizabeth?" Burris asked. "Or just tavern talk?"

"It's true," I said, with a mysterious smile, as Timothy and I continued down the street.

When we were out of Burris's earshot I said, "Maybe there's

something I've overlooked. Maybe my idea isn't so great after all."

"It's a brilliant plan, Elizabeth," Timothy said. "I don't know how it can miss."

"The main thing will be convincing Mavis. She might hate the whole idea."

"She'll love it," Timothy said in a reassuring voice.

As we turned the corner and reached Main Street, I noticed that the Bottom Dollar parking lot was almost empty, which was unheard of for a Saturday morning.

Just as the two of us started up the walk, Birdie came rushing out of the store.

"Oh, Elizabeth, it's terrible! Courtney Cooper is here and she's got an offer on Mavis's house," Birdie said, breathlessly.

"Oh Lord," I said, quickening my pace. Courtney Cooper was a ruthlessly aggressive real-estate agent who would sell the dress off her mother's back as long as she got her seven-percent commission. She'd paid to have an ad featuring her photograph inside each buggy at the Winn-Dixie, so everyone had to endure her perky, blonde visage as they stood in the checkout lines.

"She hasn't signed anything yet?" I asked.

"Not yet!" Birdie said. "But she's mighty close."

Timothy was on my heels as I flung open the door. I immediately spied Mavis poised over a document holding a gold pen as Courtney stood over her. A wide-eyed Attalee was watching in horror.

"Stop!" I shouted. "Mavis, don't sign those papers!"

"What in the world?" Courtney asked with a frown. "Mavis and I are trying to transact business here, so if you don't mind, sugar—"

"I do mind, Courtney," I said. "Mavis, I thought you were going to give me twenty-four hours."

Mavis rubbed her upper lip. "I know, Elizabeth, but look around. It's Saturday morning and this place is a ghost town. Every minute I stay open is like pouring money out the window."

"But I wish you'd listen to my marketing idea, Mavis," I pleaded. "I really think it could work."

Courtney took a step toward me in a pair of canary-yellow pumps.

"Excuse me, Elizabeth. I don't recall," she said. "Which university did you get your MBA from?"

"I don't have an MBA, Courtney. You know that," I said. "Mavis, all I'm asking for is—"

"Elizabeth Polk, this store isn't a lemonade stand. You don't know the first thing about business. Now if you'll excuse us, Mavis and I have a grown-up transaction to discuss. So shoo, will you?" she said with a wave of her hand.

Mavis's eyes were cast to the floor. "I think this is probably for the best, Elizabeth," she said, her voice on the verge of tears.

"It *is* for the best, Mavis," Courtney said. "As everyone says, Courtney Cooper cares about her clients."

"You mean Courtney Cooper cares about her commission," Attalee said. "But Elizabeth would take a bullet for you, Mavis. You need to let her say her piece."

I touched Mavis's shoulder. "Please, Mavis. Give me just a few minutes."

Mavis looked up. Her face was moist with tears. "I don't suppose a few minutes could hurt," she said in a small voice.

"Thank you, Mavis," I said. I flung my arms around her.

The first, shrill notes of "Dixie" pierced the air. Courtney fumbled in her pocketbook and snapped open her cell phone. She listened for a moment and then said, "I don't care if the termites are out on the porch having a wiener roast, you tell Hal I need that termite letter and I need it today."

She tucked the phone back into her purse. "I have an emergency to attend to. Mavis, call me later on when this love fest is over and you're ready to get down to business."

She plucked her gold pen from Mavis's hand and flounced out of the store.

"So what is this big plan of yours, Elizabeth?" Birdie asked. "We're all dying to know."

"Are you ready to hear, Mavis?" I asked.

Mavis smiled uncertainly and then nodded. Everyone took a seat in the break room, but I remained standing.

As I started to speak, my mouth was dry and my hands shook, but my heart soared with excitement.

"When folks shop at the Bottom Dollar Emporium they leave with a twenty-five-gallon trash can or a package of triple-A batteries, but that's not all they leave with when they walk out the door." I searched their faces. "What do we give them that they can't get at the Super Saver Dollar Store?"

"There's always a pot of coffee brewing," Birdie volunteered.

"Last winter, I gave DeEtta Jefferson that case of the flu when I coughed on her," Attalee offered.

"DeEtta is a good example," I said. "But not because you gave her the flu, Attalee. Remember when she came in here last week to buy that skein of baby-blue yarn? What did you say to her, Mavis?

Mavis shrugged. "I just asked her how her baby blanket was coming and if she was far enough along to finish it before her grandbaby's birth."

"Yes. And you ordered that color of yarn especially for DeEtta because we didn't carry it." I smiled.

Birdie's eyes gleamed and she held up a finger. "I do believe I know what Elizabeth is getting at. At the Bottom Dollar Emporium, there's a certain personal touch that will always be lacking at the Super Saver."

"Exactly," I said with a nod. "Along with a customer's purchases comes the pleasure of connecting with another human being who knows them and cares about them as a person. That's our strength. Old-fashioned service that you don't run into much anymore."

"I hear what you're saying, Elizabeth," Mavis said. "But sadly too many people will trade in the personal touch for stores with lower prices or bigger inventories."

"True," I said. "So I thought to myself, why stop at just old-fashioned service? Why not expand on that theme? Not just to our service, but to our inventory and even our facility. Let's make the

Bottom Dollar Emporium a community gathering place that offers things the Super Saver couldn't even dream of."

I pointed to the area near the cash registers. "We could have barrels of old-fashioned candy out front. Stuff you can't get just anywhere, like wax bottles filled with juice, Necco wafers, Black Jack gum, candy lipstick, Slo Poke suckers, candy buttons on paper tape, and clear jars of stick candy in all different flavors."

"Horehound candy used to be my favorite," Birdie said, dreamily.

"I was always partial to licorice laces," Attalee remarked.

I nodded. "We could carry things people don't come across that much anymore, like ice cream makers you turn with a crank. Or even whetstones, weather vanes, and corn-cob pipes. How about a collection of cast-iron cookware? Or maybe a line of old-fashioned toys like tiddlywinks, stick balls, and hobby horses."

I crossed to the back wall of the store, which was lined with mops, buckets, and brooms. "But the final touch would be an old-fashioned soda fountain with swivel stools. We'd serve ice cream sodas, phosphates, and—"

"Sarsaparillas!" Attalee shouted.

"Where would you get all of that old-timey merchandise?" Birdie asked.

I smiled. "There are wholesalers who sell those items. A store like the one I have in mind not only becomes a gathering place for local folks, but it also brings in tourist trade. We could post a billboard on the Aiken-Augusta highway to draw travelers."

I could almost see the sparks flying between Mavis's ears. But then a dark cloud crossed her face. "I'll just bet one of those old-fashioned soda fountains costs a fortune."

"That's the best part, Mavis!" I said, clasping one of her hands. "The building where the Methodist Church meets used to be the old apothecary. There's a used soda fountain that Matilda's been looking to get rid of. It would need to be smartened up some, but I know she'd let us have it for a song."

"I'd be glad to lend a hand with fixing it up," Timothy said.

I snapped my fingers. "See Mavis, everything's already falling into place. I honestly believe this was meant to be."

We all stared at Mavis. Her gray eyes darted as she thought things through.

"I think you may have something, Elizabeth," she said.

Twenty-Seven

Want to avoid burning? Use 'Son' block.

~ Sign outside the Rock of Ages Baptist Church

I was shaking Tabasco sauce on a mess of scrambled eggs in the skillet when Timothy's cell phone rang. Timothy was singing "My Girl" in the shower. I answered the phone and heard a male voice.

"This is Mrs. Bettis Hollingsworth's private secretary. May I speak with Mr. Timothy Hollingsworth?"

"He's unavailable at the moment," I said. "May I take a message?"

"Yes, please do. Tell Mr. Hollingsworth that his mother is flying in from Paris this afternoon. Her connection from Paris lands at the Augusta airport at 3 P.M. She requests his company for dinner at 7 P.M. at the Summit Club in the family's private dining room." The snippy-sounding voice paused. "Have you got all of that?"

"Yes, sir, I do. Seven o'clock at the Summit Club. I'll see that he gets this. Anything else?"

"That will be all. Thank you very much."

Timothy emerged from the bathroom in a cloud of steam, toweling his hair dry. I repeated the phone message.

"Why do you suppose your mama didn't call herself?" I asked.

Timothy shrugged. "My mother's a very impersonal woman. But you'll discover that quickly enough. You'll be meeting her tonight at the Summit Club."

"Tonight?" I dropped my spatula.

"Yes." He snitched a curl of bacon draining on a piece of paper towel. "There's no telling how long she'll stay. For all I know, she could be leaving the next day."

As soon as Timothy left for work, I ransacked my closet for a suitably impressive outfit. After a long search, I found the black dress that Meemaw had bought me to wear to my granddaddy's funeral. I'd clean forgotten about it because looking at it made me so sad.

Meemaw had picked it up at Ritzy Repeats, the secondhand store in Augusta where the society ladies took their castoffs. I glanced inside the dress at the label and sure enough, there was a designer name on the tag.

I pulled the dress over my head to make sure it still fit and when I leaned down to smooth it, I saw a thatch of mousy roots on the top of my head that would have put Madonna to shame.

Even if I wore pure mink to the Summit Club, I'd still look like white-trash, walking around with dark roots.

I seized the phone book, flipping through it to find one of those trendy hair places in downtown Augusta. No Nice 'n Easy for me this time. I wanted a classy cut and a first-rate dye job done with foils.

I ended up getting lucky. The first salon I called, a place called Viva La Coiffure, had a cancellation and could take me at three P.M. Then I called Mavis asking for permission to knock off early from work.

All morning long at the Bottom Dollar Emporium I kept peeking at my watch. The day seemed as long as a month of Sundays, even though we were busy marking down items for our "Everything Must Go Sale" so we could make room for the new merchandise we were ordering for our grand re-opening. I was headed for the stockroom when my elbow caught the edge of a shelf, knocking several packages of lime gelatin to the floor.

"Elizabeth, your mind ain't on your work today," said Attalee, who was marking down bedroom slippers. "A half hour ago, you like to have dropped a jumbo can of Mussleman's apple pie filling right on my foot. And me just recovering from last week's accident with that can of fancy whole-kernel corn." Attalee rubbed her leg.

Mavis glanced at her watch. "Elizabeth has big plans today, and I've told her she could leave early. You can go ahead and clock out now if you want, Elizabeth."

"Big plans? What are you up to now, Elizabeth?" Attalee asked.

"She's driving to Augusta to get her hair highlighted and cut in a fancy downtown salon," Mavis said.

Mavis emphasized the word "salon." She thought they were uppity places. She got her hair cut in Luna Pickens's converted carport.

"So, where are you meeting Timothy's mama? Is she coming to Cayboo Creek?" Attalee asked.

"No, to Augusta. We're going to the Summit Club," I said.

"I dined at the country club in Vidalia twenty-five years ago. It was so elegant. They served lamb chops dressed in white panties," Attalee said.

After I clocked out and shed my smock, I drove to Augusta to Viva La Coiffure. I eased my car into a parking lot on Telfair Street, where the salon was located.

It was one of those days when the light picks up every little sparkly thing that's stuck in the sidewalk, making it hard to see. I put on my sunglasses and tried to spot the salon. I'd been walking the length of Telfair and couldn't find it. So I decided to duck into a little sundry store called Wong's to see if anyone in there could tell me where it was.

When I opened the door, I almost collided into a hand truck full of six-packs of RC Cola. Unfortunately for me, Clip was the one who was pushing it.

"Liz! I tried to call you a while ago, but now here you are. It must be fate," Clip said. He lowered his aviator sunglasses on his nose.

I put a hand on my hip. "I don't believe in that fate nonsense."

"You were always the practical type. One of the many things I love about you."

"Whatever you say, Clip. Excuse me. I've got an appointment to keep." I swept by him.

"Wait. Don't you want to know why I was calling you?"

I turned my head to glance back at him.

"Not really. But from now on I'll let my husband answer the phone. I'm sure he'll be very interested in talking to you once I tell him that you refuse to let me be."

"I'll let you be, if that's what you really want." He slid a Kool cigarette from the pack in his shirt pocket and stuck it in the corner of his mouth. "But I do think there's a couple of things you should know about that snazzy new family of yours."

I snorted. "Clip, what could you possibly know about the Hollingsworth family?"

He struck a match on the sole of his shoe and said, "A lot more than you would guess. Why don't you meet me for a drink after your appointment? I'll fill you in on what I know about the Hollingsworths."

"I don't think so, Clip."

"There's a little sports bar about three blocks from here called Maurice's. I hear they serve the best onion rings in the area."

I shook my head in amazement. "Clip, when are you going to understand that I'm married now? I feel like I'm talking to the wind."

He pushed his hair behind his ears. "I'm accepting it. But I'm also telling you that there are certain things you should know about that family." He blew out a lopsided smoke ring. "Strange things."

"Heavens to Betsy, Clip. I don't have time for this." I glanced at my watch. "I'm going to be late for my hair appointment. You'll just have to entertain someone else with all your big mysteries about the Hollingsworth family."

Clip took a long draw on his cigarette. "She came to me. The older woman in the Cadillac. Wearing these white gloves like she'd just been to a fancy tea party. Of course at the time, I didn't know who she was or what she was up to."

I stopped short. "Grace Tobias came to see you? What for?"

His grin was wider than a slice of honeydew melon. He pointed his cigarette at me and said, "Meet me at Maurice's in an hour and I'll tell you all about it."

I shot him a dark look. My curiosity had gotten the better of me.

"Give me an hour and a half," I said.

I was surprised I even noticed the entrance to Viva La Coiffure, considering how distracted I was by Clip's claim that Mrs. Tobias had paid him a visit. I couldn't imagine what she would want with Clip of all people. It didn't make a bit of sense to me, but I supposed I was going to have to scarf down some greasy onion rings from Maurice's to find out.

Viva La Coiffure's door was black, with the letters VLC spray-painted on it in blood-red paint. It looked more like a drug dealer's hideout than a hair salon.

I knew I was in the right place when my nose picked up the smell of perm solution and hair spray. If not for that I would have turned around, because the salon was decorated with rusty chains, barbed wire, and warped metal. I feared I'd need a tetanus shot if I brushed up against anything. The staff was dressed in camouflage clothing, as if they were fixing to battle enemy guerrillas instead of dark roots.

I sat down in the reception area, and a girl wearing cat-eye glasses and combat boots got off the cell phone she'd been talking on and approached me.

"Help you?"

"I have an appointment at 3 P.M. They didn't say who with. There was a cancellation."

The girl opened a leather appointment book. "Name?"

"Elizabeth Po—, I mean Hollingsworth."

"Your appointment is with Claude. He'll be with you in a minute."

I glanced through the magazines on the table, hoping for *Good Housekeeping* or *Redbook*. But all they had were thick, oversized fashion magazines. I opened one to a model wearing black lipstick and what looked like an outfit made entirely of rubber bands.

I replaced the magazine on the coffee table. A man with a thinning goatee approached me, his dog tags banging against the front of his khaki-colored T-shirt.

"Hi, precious, are you next?" he asked.

"That depends. Are you Claude?" He looked vaguely familiar.

"I suppose I am." He stifled a cough. "This wretched incense burning in here is irritating my lungs. Would you people go easy on the jasmine, for heaven's sakes?" He waved at the air with his hands and then looked back at me. "What are we wanting here, sugar puss? Color?"

"Yes, please."

He grabbed a strand of my hair and rubbed it between his fingers. "Snookums. I think a cut should take priority. I don't know who's been doing your hair, but you look like you've been cryogenically frozen since the seventies. It's *Charlie's Angels* all over again."

I felt my cheeks getting hot. "I came in for color..." I took a deep breath. "Not for insults."

Claude raised his eyebrows. "Of course you did, pumpkin. Why don't you come to my chair, then?"

I stood up, clasping my purse in front of me. "I'll do that. And if you don't mind, I like being called by my given name. It's Elizabeth."

He squinted at me. "Wait a minute. You're not Elizabeth Polk, are you?"

"I am." I stared at him, and my mouth curled into a grin. "Hey, I know who you are. Cayboo Creek High School. Future Cosmetologists of America. You're Clyde Bodett."

"Professionally I'm known as Claude B." He smiled sheepishly. "I was the only male in the FCA. I thought I recognized you. You haven't changed since high school."

"Same hairstyle, you mean?"

"Sorry if I was a snoot."

"You were, but I accept your apology."

I followed him to his station and sat down.

"You were so talented in the high school cosmetology classes," I said. "You were the star. And now look at you. Working in this salon in downtown Augusta."

He slapped some color in a bowl and began mixing it. "I remember you dropped out of the FCA. What have you been doing with yourself since high school? You were the smartest girl in the class. Are you still living in Cayboo Creek?"

I smiled at his compliment. I never imagined myself as smart. I told him about my job at the Bottom Dollar Emporium and how I'd been promoted to manager. "I've always wondered what my life would be like if I'd just passed pin curling."

He planted a hand on his hip. "Hairdressing has been good to me. I'm making money hand over foot. The women here practically throw it at me. Guess how much I get for a cut?"

"Thirty-five?"

He hooted. "Elizabeth, I wouldn't bother plugging in my blow-dryer for less than fifty-eight dollars a head. And that doesn't include tips."

I whistled. "Dang, that's a lot of money."

He applied a foil to a hank of my hair. "I have a brand-new Lexus, a hot tub, crocodile-skin boots, and a bumper pool table in my rumpus room."

"Sounds nice. I'm proud of you, Clyde. I'm not earning anything like that at the Bottom Dollar Emporium. But I get by."

"I'll say you do." Clyde caught sight of the ring on my hand and he lifted it up for a closer look. "You didn't find this at the bottom of a Cracker Jack box. Sister, where did you get this pretty pebble?"

I withdrew my hand. "My husband, of course. I just got married."

"Judging by the size of this rock, I wouldn't be surprised if your last name was Trump."

"Actually, my last name is Hollingsworth," I said softly, bracing myself for the effect my new surname had on most folks in

Augusta.

Clyde didn't disappoint. He went all bug-eyed and said, "Get out of here."

"It's the truth. I've been a Hollingsworth now for going on two weeks."

"The paper cup people? You married into that family?" he asked.

"It's not just paper cups. It's also napkins, plastic utensils, and plates. Not to mention the condiment division that makes little packets of ketchup and mustard."

"Did you marry a distant cousin or something?" He leaned over me to dab at my hair with his brush. "Because as far as I know there's only one Hollingsworth son and I have it from an extremely reliable source that he's an eligible bachelor."

I gave Clyde a little half smile. "And just who is your reliable source?"

Clyde matched my smile with a smirk of his own. "His very own mother, Daisy Hollingsworth."

I thought I was going to fall out of the chair. "You know Daisy Hollingsworth?"

"She's been my client for years. She stops in for a comb-out every time she's in town."

"She'll be here this afternoon, and tonight I'm going to meet her for the first time." I paused. "Tell me, Clyde, what is she really like?"

He clicked his tongue. "That's hard to say, because she doesn't confide in me like most of my clients. She's very businesslike, frosty even. But definitely a woman who knows what she wants."

I nodded. "That's what I've heard. I'm a little afraid to meet her."

"I can understand that. She reminds me of a younger version of the Queen of England, but, of course, Daisy Hollingsworth doesn't go around wearing those dreadful little hats."

I glanced at my reflection in the mirror. "She's the reason I'm here today. I wanted my hair to look nice when I meet her."

"Well, you can say bye-bye to these roots." He dabbed at my hair and said, "Oh, darn it. I'm getting color on this pretty little necklace of yours. I better take it off."

He unhooked the necklace Mrs. Tobias had given me and as he was handing it to me, the locket slid off the chain and fell to the ground.

"Oh, I'm sorry about that, Elizabeth. I'm a butterfingers today." He leaned down to pick up the locket and examined it. "No harm done. It just picked up some dust and the locket flew open."

He squinted at it. "This is a sweet photograph of you inside."

"What? A photograph of me?" I held out my palm. "Let me see that."

The locket had indeed opened. The fall must have loosened the latch. And just as Clyde had said, inside was an old-fashioned photograph of a woman who looked just like me.

I felt like someone was tap-dancing on my grave. "This is unbelievably creepy."

"What's wrong?"

"This isn't me. I never posed for this picture."

Clyde studied the photograph. "You're right. There's something a little different about the eyes and the bridge of the nose." He looked at me. "But other than that... Where did you get this locket?"

"One of my customers, Gracie Tobias, gave it to me. She also happens to be my husband's grandmother. The latch on it was stuck when she gave it to me, so I'd never looked inside before."

"This is just like an episode of the *Twilight Zone*" His eyes widened. "Oh, my Lord. You don't suppose you've been cloned?"

"I'm sure there's a much more reasonable explanation." I paused and shook my head slowly. "But I don't have any idea what it might be."

Twenty-Eight

If I were in your shoes, I'd walk right back to me.
~ Selection F-9 on the jukebox at the Tuff Luck Tavern

I was about twenty minutes late meeting Clip. I was half-expecting a no-show, but no sooner had I pushed open the battered door of Maurice's than he hopped off the bar stool to meet me.

"Come on," he said. "I got us a booth reserved in the back so we can have our privacy."

I followed him to a yellow vinyl booth with mood lighting courtesy of a neon Pabst Blue Ribbon sign. I could hear the clicking of billiards from the pool table in the back.

Seconds later, a man in a dirty apron plopped down a double order of onion rings in a plastic basket, as well as a roll of paper towels. He set a fishbowl-sized glass of beer in front of Clip. I got a Sprite.

"I went ahead and ordered for you. Hope that's okay." Clip glanced at my drink. "Hey, you forgot the lady's cherries," he said to the man. "That's how she likes her drink."

"I ain't got no cherries," the man said with a shrug, just before he left the table.

"Sorry about the cherries, Liz."

I rubbed my finger over the initials carved into the wooden table, wondering if any of these couples were still together. "It doesn't matter to me, because I don't even like maraschino cherries. They're too sweet."

Clip scratched the hair at his temple. "But I thought it was you—?"

"I like ginger ale, easy on the ice."

Clip knocked himself on the side of his head with the palm of his hand. "It must be my mom who likes the Sprite with cherries, or maybe it's my sister."

"Yeah, right." I pushed the Sprite away from me. Rush Limbaugh ranted on the radio up front, the signal fading in and out. "Okay. Let's get to it. Why did Gracie Tobias come by to visit you?"

Clip smiled his lazy smile again—the one I figured he'd spent hours in the mirror getting just right. Today it reminded me of a smile from a barracuda.

"Liz. You look beautiful with your hair up like that. It shows off that delicate neck of yours."

"Clip, these onion rings are going to be nauseating enough without your cheap flattery as a chaser. Get to the point."

Clip flinched. "What's happened to you, Liz? You can't even take a compliment from me anymore?"

I leaned across the booth. "I am here for one reason only: to find out why Mrs. Tobias came to see you. This is not a social visit."

Clip reached his hand over the table to touch mine. "Can't you and I get re-acquainted first? It's been so long since I've been this close to you, Liz."

I sprung up from the booth. "Okay. That's enough. I'm leaving. Obviously you have nothing to say about Mrs. Tobias and this was all a trick—"

"No, wait, Liz." He stood up. "I do have something to say and it's important that I get it off my chest. Please sit down. I promise I won't touch you again or get out of line."

Clip took a swig of his beer and then set it on the table. "This isn't the easiest story to tell, Liz."

"I'm listening, Clip."

He swallowed. "It all started the night of our engagement

party. You remember that after the party I went out with Dooley and some of the other boys? I was intending to have a drink or two at the Tuff Luck Tavern and then I was heading home. I wished to God I had gone home."

Clip nervously licked his lips and swatted at the bangs that fell over his forehead. "The boys were ragging on me about becoming an old married fellow and they kept putting shooters in front of me. Now, I'm more of a beer drinker, so I wasn't really expecting the wallop that those crazy shooters packed. After a few of those things, I didn't know which end was up. And I swore that if I'd been sober, I never would have ended up in the mess that I did that night."

"What happened?"

"I'm still not exactly sure." His fingers rifled his sideburns. "All I know is the next morning I woke up stark naked in Jonelle Jasper's bedroom."

I realized I'd been holding my breath, so I exhaled slowly. "Oh, Clip," I said in a soft voice.

"I know." He massaged his brow. "I got sick to my stomach when I saw where I was. All I could think of was how you'd react if you found out. I sprinted out of that bed and got out of there as fast as I could, praying you wouldn't find out what happened."

Rush Limbaugh was over and now Charlie Daniels was singing "The Devil Went Down to Georgia." We sat in silence.

"I don't know why you're telling me this now," I finally said. "Months after the fact, I find out that not only did you break off our engagement, but you were cheating on me as well. What's the point of this confession? To cause me more pain?"

"No, Liz." His voice was throaty. "You just needed to know what happened that night so that what I'm about to tell you will make sense."

Tears wet my eyes and I angrily wiped them away.

"Just hurry up and finish what you have to say."

Clip shifted in his seat and took a deep breath. "When I got home that morning, I was laid up on the couch with one doozie of a hangover. Just as I was dozing off, the doorbell rang. When I answered it, I saw this lady all dressed up in gloves and high heels. Her white Cadillac was parked in my drive. I asked her to come in but she said, 'I'd like to conduct our business on your porch, if you don't mind.' I figured her for one of those born-again Christians wanting me to accept Jesus as my savior. But when I stumbled out on the porch she looked me in the eye and said, 'I know where you spent last night, Mr. Jenkins.'"

"What?" I asked in disbelief.

Clip had just stubbed out his cigarette and was lighting another.

"I didn't know this lady from Adam's house cat and here she was all up in my business. I said, 'Look Lady, I don't know who you are or how you know my name, but you best run along now.' That's when she said, 'Mr. Jenkins, if you don't listen to me, your fiancée, Elizabeth Polk, will know exactly what you were up to last night. I hired a private detective who took some very compelling photos of your shenanigans with that dark-haired woman.'"

"I don't understand this." I choked out the words. "This makes no sense at all."

"That's not all," Clip said, folding his hands in his lap. "She offered me thirty-five thousand dollars to break off my engagement with you." His eyes fell to his beer and his voice sounded like it was coming from inside a barrel. "I took it."

My mouth went dry and I took a sip of my drink.

"Let me make sure I have this straight. Gracie Tobias said she would give you thirty-five thousand dollars if you broke off your engagement to me. Is that what happened?"

"That's about the size of it." He shrunk back into the booth as if he thought I might smack him. "It made sense to me at the time. I figured you'd break up with me anyway once you'd heard that I'd spent the night with Jonelle. I decided there wasn't any point in being broke *and* heartbroken, so I took the money."

"Oh mercy. Give me that beer." I grabbed his mug and drained it down. Clip was eyeing me cautiously. "So why have this discussion at all? Why not enjoy your money and keep quiet about this? Why tell me now?"

"Because I made a terrible mistake." Clip's voice was thick with tears. "That money's caused me nothing but grief. First, I couldn't explain where it came from and when I bought the truck, everyone in my family thought I was up to something illegal."

His voice softened and he searched my face with his dark eyes. "I had no idea how much I'd miss you. Every time I passed your house or the Bottom Dollar Emporium I'd just ache inside."

"So you decided to seek comfort with Jonelle," I snapped. "That's very touching."

Clip tugged at his shirt collar. "That woman would not let me be. I didn't want to have anything to do with her, but she kept calling and dropping by. Then she claimed she was pregnant and I was the daddy. That's when I told her I'd think about marrying her, but just to give her baby a proper last name. Later I found out she'd been lying about being pregnant and I told her never to come around me again." His chin dropped. "I knew I needed to own up to my mistakes, so I was going to sell the truck and give Mrs. Tobias her money back, but I could only get twenty-eight thousand dollars for it. I started working the night shift at the Corbitt Can factory after my RC route. I just now made me enough money to pay her off. I've been calling and calling her, but she hasn't been picking up her phone. As soon as I get in touch with her, she's getting every cent of her money back."

I stared at Clip, who looked as spent and limp as an empty seed bag.

"Clip, I'm glad you told me this. And giving back the money is the right thing to do. But if you did it to win me back, it's too late. I'm a married woman now."

Clip rubbed the sides of his face with his palms. "So you still want to be a member of that crazy family?"

"Clip, I'm married to Timothy and he doesn't have anything to do with this."

He snapped his lighter to a cigarette. "How do you know that? Maybe he got his grandma to bribe me so he'd be able to move in on you."

"That's impossible. Timothy was still in California when you got the money from Mrs. Tobias and broke off our engagement. He didn't even come to Augusta until two months later."

Clip rested his chin on his hand. "And you really love this fellow? It's not just a way to get back at me?"

"No, Clip. I do love Timothy. Very much."

Clip cast his eyes downward and his nose reddened. "And you don't love me anymore? Not even the least little bit?"

I watched the jukebox light up as a man stuck in a quarter.

"I'll probably always have feelings for you," I said softly. "You're my high school sweetheart. But I've found the man I want to spend the rest of my life with."

He sniffed. "Liz, that night was the biggest mistake of my life. If I hadn't done it you would be Mrs. Clip Jenkins right now, instead of married to Timothy Hollingsworth. Why do you suppose that Tobias woman went to all that trouble to prevent you from marrying me?"

That was a very good question.

Twenty-Nine

Despite the high cost of living, it's still popular.
~ Notice on the bulletin board in the bingo hall

Why Mrs. Tobias had bribed Clip was the million-dollar question all right, but I didn't have any answers. It was all I could think about after I left Clip stewing at Maurice's and drove home. Why in the world would a woman who was a complete stranger to me only months ago try to prevent me from marrying Clip? And how would she explain the photograph in the locket? As soon as I got home, I was going to call Mrs. Tobias in Hilton Head and get some answers.

I was so lost in my thoughts that I didn't notice until I got out of my car that Timothy's Volvo was parked in front of the house. I glanced at my watch. It was five P.M., and Timothy didn't get home until well after six P.M. I couldn't imagine what he was doing home.

I ran up the steps and flung open the door to find Timothy pacing the living room. His face was ashen.

"There you are, finally. Thank God," he said.

"What's going on? What are you doing home?"

"I've been trying to find you for an hour or more." He scooped his car keys off the coffee table. "We need to go to the hospital right away."

"Who is it? Is it my daddy? Mavis?"

"It's your grandmother. Her friend Boomer called me at work trying to locate you. She's had a stroke. We need to hurry. I'll drive you."

"Meemaw?" I shook my head. "No, Timothy, it can't be Meemaw. She hasn't taken sick a day in her life."

"Sweetie, we need to get to the hospital. There isn't a lot of time." He put a hand on the small of my back and tried to guide me to the door.

"I just talked to her this morning before I went to work. She was beating her rugs for spring cleaning. She's going to give me another cooking lesson this Saturday. We're going to make cornbread."

Timothy grabbed me and hugged me tight. "Elizabeth, it's very important that we get to the hospital... now."

My knees felt as weak as cooked spaghetti. "Oh Timothy. I can barely walk."

"It's okay, honey. Just lean on me. I'll get you to the car."

On the drive to the hospital, I chewed on my cuticles until they bled. Timothy parked in front and led me up to the third floor to intensive care. A nurse pointed us toward a waiting room where Boomer sat on an orange plastic chair. His face was hidden in his hands, over which rose plumes of white hair on either side.

"Boomer?" I said softly.

He looked up at me with eyes tinged red. Then he started bawling.

"Boomer? How's she doing? Where is she?"

Boomer had covered his face with his hands and was stammering through his tears, but I couldn't make heads or tails of what he was saying.

"I'll go find a doctor," Timothy said.

"Too late," Boomer said through his tears. "Glenda's gone. She died five minutes ago."

"No. Boomer," I said, "you're wrong. She would never go without seeing me first. Is she in there?" I pointed to a door beyond Boomer. "She'll want to talk to me."

A doctor who had entered the room with Timothy touched my shoulder. "Are you the granddaughter?" he asked in a gentle voice. His eyes were the same pale gray color as his hair. "We've been waiting for you. Your grandmother went very peacefully a few minutes ago. She never regained consciousness after the stroke."

I bit my knuckle. "It can't be."

Timothy circled his arms around me and held me as I cried into his shirt.

"I just talked to her this morning. How can she be gone?" I said through my tears.

I lifted my head to look up at doctor. "Can I see her?"

The doctor nodded and opened the door that led into the private ICU rooms.

I clung to Timothy and we shambled inside. It was quiet in the room. Although machines loomed on each side of her, Meemaw wasn't hooked up to either of them. She was lying on her back with her hands cupped at her sides as if she'd decided to steal a nap during the day. But I'd never known Meemaw to lie down in the middle of the afternoon. She'd sooner be caught nipping on a shot of whiskey.

I walked to the side of her bed and touched one of her hands, which was still warm.

"Meemaw, are you there? It's me, Elizabeth." I sat down in the bedside chair. "I know the doctor said that you left us a few minutes ago, but I figure you're still hovering around here somewhere the way that lady did in the movie we saw on the Lifetime Channel. I know you wouldn't leave without giving me a chance to say good-bye to you."

I picked up her hand and kissed a freckle on her index finger. She had such strong, loving hands. I'd seen them shell peanuts, can peaches, and stroke my burning forehead when I took ill. A fresh batch of tears seeped from my eyes, and Timothy pressed his cheek against my own.

"Meemaw, why'd you have to go?" I swallowed back more tears as I continued. "I'm not going to keep you because I know Jesus wants you home again, but I just wanted to thank you for taking such good care of me when my mama died. You were like my mama and daddy all rolled into one."

I took a final look at my meemaw. Someone had removed her glasses and her face looked incomplete without the frames, almost as if she were missing a nose or a cheekbone. I spied them lying on a table beside the bed and placed them on the bridge of her nose.

"There, that's more like it. I wouldn't want you to be bumping into things up there in heaven." I kissed her cooling cheek. "I love you, Meemaw," I whispered.

After we left Meemaw's room, a nurse gave me the sweater she'd been wearing. The sleeves were frayed and there were cigarettes and wadded-up tissue paper in the pockets. I held the sweater to my nose, inhaling the scent of tobacco and lilac toilet water, and felt the tears splash my cheeks.

After I pulled myself together, Timothy, Boomer, and I went to the hospital cafeteria to get a cup of coffee.

Boomer's soft, pale hand shook as he set his coffee mug on the table. "I was helping her hang one of the rugs on the clothesline. She had this big brush she was going to beat it with. She gave the rug a good smack and the dust flew out of it. She was enjoying herself, whacking the rug and watching the dirt fly. Then she threw her arm back with the brush, ready to whack it again, and her arm froze in midair. She made a sound like 'omph' and she crumpled to the ground. She never regained consciousness."

Boomer pulled several napkins out of the dispenser and blew his nose.

"I'm so glad you were with her, Boomer," I said.

Boomer and I cried in each other's arms for a few minutes. Then he said he wanted to go home to check on his mother as well as to pick up Meemaw's dog Pierre. He had agreed to care for the pooch until other arrangements could be made.

After Boomer left, Timothy came over to my side of the booth and held me tightly. "Is there anyone who should be called, Elizabeth?" he asked.

"Meemaw has an older sister in lower Alabama who I'll get in touch with," I said. "There's no rush. Marion is in a nursing home and she's at that stage where she's like a faraway radio station, fading in and out all the time. I remember Meemaw used to say she was never going to end up like Marion because she kept her mind sharp working Seek and Find puzzles. She picked up a new puzzle book every time she went to the market."

"I wish I could have known your meemaw better," Timothy said.

"She melted like butter hitting a hot skillet when she first saw you. She always favored curly-haired men. When he was younger, granddaddy had more curls on his head than Harpo Marx."

Timothy squeezed my hand. "Should we call your daddy?"

I scowled. "I'll call him in due time. He and Meemaw were oil and water. They never got on."

I looked up from my coffee to see my godmother, Patsy Ann, standing by our table, wearing a smock printed with pastel teddy bears.

"Oh, Elizabeth, I just got off my shift with the babies in the nursery and heard the news about Glenda," she said. "I am so sorry, lamb." Mascara streaked her plump cheeks.

I hugged her. "I'm glad to see you. Why don't you sit with us? This is my husband, Timothy Hollingsworth. This is Patsy Ann Dinkins, my godmother. She lives behind Meemaw."

Timothy got up to shake her hand, and Patsy Ann nodded so vigorously that her auburn wig shifted.

"Yes, I go over there so often I swear that I've run a groove clean through the centipede grass," Patsy Ann said. Her eyebrows flew up her forehead. "Did you say husband?"

"Yes, ma'am. I'm an old married lady now, going on two weeks. I meant to tell you when I saw you last, but Edward called you away before I could."

She patted her chest. "Edward and I have been in Charlotte seeing a specialist, so I hadn't heard. You poor lamb. Your meemaw is gone for good."

She glanced at Timothy. "Thank goodness our Elizabeth has you to look after her. You better take good care of her, young man, or you'll have to answer to me. I've known this child since she was no bigger than a head of cabbage. I fed her first bottle of formula."

"Patsy Ann was my baby nurse," I explained. "She took care of me in the nursery just after I was born."

"Oh, and what a treasure she was," Patsy Ann crooned. "Prettiest baby I've ever seen in the nursery, and I've seen so many babies that if you'd put them end to end, they'd reach all the way to Timbuktu."

"She's still beautiful," said Timothy. "Won't you sit down? Can I treat you to some coffee or something to eat?"

"Don't mind if I do." Patsy Ann plopped down beside me. "I've been on my feet all day long. We had a couple of colicky ones in the nursery."

"I'll go through the line so the two of you can catch up," said Timothy. "What can I get for you?"

"Coffee, black, and one of those bear claws if they have them. If not, a jelly doughnut will hit the spot," said Patsy Ann.

I put a hand over my coffee cup to show Timothy I wouldn't need anything. After he walked to the cafeteria line, Patsy Ann said, "He's a looker, that one. And such nice manners. I bet Glenda thought he hung the moon."

"Thank you, Patsy Ann."

Patsy Ann jiggled her knee under the table. "It's hard to imagine Glenda gone. So unexpected. She's done gone and left you an orphan and with no other family to speak of."

I stirred my coffee with a plastic straw. "Well, there's my daddy and my half-brother Lanier, but we aren't close."

Patsy Ann sniffed. "I remember Glenda talking about your daddy. Dwayne, is it? Do you wish you were closer to him?"

I shook my head. "Not especially. But with Meemaw gone... Well, I don't expect he'll be much of a comfort. And of course, my mama's been long gone."

Patsy Ann was staring into the distance. She had a funny look in her eyes. Then she turned to me, laid a hand on my shoulder, and said in a low voice, "That's not necessarily true. Your mama may not be long gone after all."

Thirty

Excuse me, but I think your karma just ran over my dogma.
~ Bumper sticker on Reeky's VW bug

Timothy returned with Patsy Ann's coffee and a bear claw the size of a child's baseball mitt. Alarm registered in his eyes when he looked at me. "Elizabeth, are you all right?"

Patsy Ann fanned me with a napkin. "I think the shock of losing Glenda is setting in."

"Elizabeth, honey. Do you need water? Can I take you home to lie down?" Timothy asked.

My lips felt like they'd been Krazy-glued together. Patsy Ann spoke for me.

"No, Elizabeth told me she'd like to stay here and chat with me. There are so many memories of her meemaw to sort through, aren't there, lamb?" She patted my hand. "Why don't you go on home and I'll drop Elizabeth off in an hour or so."

"Is that what you want, Elizabeth?" Timothy asked.

"Uh huh," I managed to say.

Timothy looked uncertain. "I hate to leave you. Are you sure you're going to be all right?"

"I just adore how young men are these days. So sensitive and sweet," gushed Patsy Ann. "Just like Mickey Rooney in all those pictures with Judy Garland." She smiled at Timothy. "Don't worry. She'll be fine with me, sugar pie. Elizabeth and me are like family.

She's my god baby."

Timothy leaned over to kiss my cheek. "I'll wait for you at the house. You have my cell phone number? You'll call me if you need anything?"

I nodded.

"Okay," he said. "I'll see you in an hour or so then. Nice to meet you, Mrs.—"

"Patsy Ann will do." She waggled her plump fingers to say good-bye.

I watched him walk out the door and then counted to twenty slowly in my mind to make sure he wasn't coming back for anything. Then I forced my mouth to form words. "Patsy Ann! What in heaven's name did you mean by that, that my mama wasn't necessarily gone? She's been gone ever since I was a little baby. I put a bouquet of forget-me-nots on her gravesite every year on the anniversary of her death."

Of course, I hadn't seen with my own eyes my mama lying in her casket; I was too young to attend the funeral. But I'd heard the stories of her being whittled away by meningitis until she wasn't much more than a collection of bones with bits of flesh hanging on. Could she somehow have recovered? And did she run away for some reason? Maybe with that mysterious man in her diary?

"Patsy Ann, is my mama alive?" I asked.

Patsy Ann made clucking noises with her tongue. "I've opened a can of worms, haven't I?" she said. "But then again it doesn't seem right to keep it from you. Especially now that your meemaw is gone. Oh, dear me, what am I doing?" She gobbled pieces of her bear claw.

I grabbed the sleeve of her smock. "Patsy Ann, if my mama is alive you have to tell me. I'm her only child."

Patsy Ann wrinkled her forehead. "Lamb, I don't know if your mama is dead or alive." She lowered her voice a notch. "If the facts be known, I don't even know who your mama is."

"Patsy Ann, you do too know who my mama is. Her name's Darlene Polk and she died when I was just a baby."

"I know, lamb, but I'm saying that Darlene ain't your mama. Your mama is someone else entirely."

"What? That isn't possible."

"It's possible, Elizabeth." She paused. "It's possible if somebody went and switched babies at the nursery."

I nearly severed my tongue. "What... are... you... saying?"

Patsy mopped her brow with a napkin. "You have no idea how Glenda fretted over Darlene. Always worried about who she was out with. In a snit if she came home with her hair mussed and lipstick smeared. It's all she ever talked about over coffee. Glenda might not have cared much for Dwayne, but I knew it was a relief for her when Darlene married him. No more late nights pacing the floor of her kitchen, listening for the slam of a car door. No more worrying if Darlene was going to get herself in the family way without being married. Glenda would have fallen to pieces if she saw what I saw that morning in the delivery room."

"What did you see?"

She sighed heavily. "I was holding Darlene's hand for her, cheering her on. I don't normally work delivery but when I heard Darlene had come in with her contractions two minutes apart, I wanted to be there for her. I was so excited. I was going to see Glenda's very first grandchild."

She lowered her eyes to her plate. "Of course, I nearly fainted once the baby slid out from between Darlene's legs and the doctor held her up for all to see."

I took a deep breath. "What was wrong?"

"Nothing was wrong with her health. She had ten fingers and ten toes. She scored an eight on the Apgar and she had a good strong cry."

Patsy Ann's mouth drew up tight like she'd sucked a lemon. "But it was the way that she looked that was all wrong. Her skin was high yellow and her hair was as curly as sheep's wool. There was no doubt in my mind that that child was half-black. I could see what was going to happen. Glenda would have been heartbroken and Dwayne would have divorced Darlene in a flash. It would have been a terrible thing."

"My mama gave birth to a mixed-race baby?"

Patsy Ann nodded

"So you switched babies?"

"I'm afraid so."

"How did you get away with such a thing?"

A note of pride entered her voice. "Shoot. It wasn't that hard. These days mamas and babies have matching hospital bracelets, but in the 70s you just switched bassinets. It was easy as pie."

"But how could you give some other mother a mixed-race baby? You couldn't have gotten away with that?"

Patsy Ann's eyes got bright as dimes. "It just so happened that a young, unmarried society woman gave birth here in the hospital the same evening as Darlene. She wasn't even going to see her baby, because she was putting it up for adoption. That baby was blue-eyed and fair-haired. If you haven't guessed by now—" She squeezed my hand. "That baby was you."

I stared at her wide, plain face. "Patsy Ann, how could you?"

She crossed her arms over her chest. "I don't care what you say. I think I did the best for everyone."

Patsy Ann's news swirled around me like white spots from a flashbulb: Dwayne was not my daddy. Lanier was not my half-brother. Darlene was not my mother, and Meemaw... my dear, sweet meemaw was no more kin to me than a stranger on the street. Moreover, the boy in Darlene's diary, the infamous "B," did get her pregnant, and the reason she kept their relationship a secret was because "B" was black.

"Did you talk to my mama about this? Didn't she see the baby when it was born?"

Patsy Ann shook her head. "She was pretty wrung out, so I don't rightly know. When I brought you to her for the first time, I watched her to see what she might say but she just counted your fingers and toes. If she didn't know that you weren't her baby, she never said boo to me about it."

"What about the other woman, my real mother? Didn't you

know her name? Who was she?"

Patsy Ann scratched the fabric of her slacks. "I thought it was best if I never knew her name."

My mind whirled. "There's gotta be records of women who gave birth that day."

"I wouldn't count on it. The young woman who birthed you came from a connected family and they were hush-hush about her admittance. Trying to save the family some embarrassment, I guess."

"My mama was a rich girl. My birth family was society folk." This was all too much.

"You got blue blood flowing in your veins, sure enough."

"I wonder if my mama or her family is still living in Augusta," I said quietly.

"There's no way of telling, I guess."

I had nothing more to say. I needed a quiet, dark place to think. I asked Patsy Ann to drive me home.

Just before I got out of the car she said, "Elizabeth, do you think I did such an awful thing? Was I wrong to switch those babies?" Her worried face had a blue cast from the light of the dashboard.

"I don't know, Patsy Ann. I just don't." All of a sudden my eyelids felt like they were weighed down with wet towels. "You take care now."

"I wouldn't bother hunting your kinfolk down if I were you, Elizabeth. They gave you away like you were a little gypsy baby. Didn't much care whose hands you fell into."

"Good night, Patsy Ann."

Thirty-One

Never test the waters with both feet.

~ Message in a fortune cookie from Dun Woo's House of Noodles

My knees were like taffy and my hands shook as I fitted the key into the lock of my front door. Timothy stood waiting just inside.

"Oh Timothy," I said, melting into his arms. He rubbed my back and held me close.

"I know, sweetie. I know," he murmured. "Now you need to catch your breath."

I lifted my tear-stained face from his shoulder.

"What is it, Timothy?"

"Elizabeth, my mother is on her way over here. She insisted on coming."

"Now?" I asked. My eyes took in the newspapers piled on the coffee table, Maybelline's rawhide bones strewn across the carpet, and the thin layer of dust that covered every surface of the living room. I glanced in the small mirror on the wall and saw ten miles of bad road staring back at me.

"Why is she coming here now?" I asked helplessly.

"I think she wants to offer her condolences."

I started picking up stuff from the floor and shoving things under the couch. "What did you tell her about me?"

Timothy grabbed my elbow. "Just calm down a minute. Sit on

the couch and I'll make you some iced tea. I don't want you to worry about all this right now. You've been through enough as it is."

"But Timothy, this place looks—"

There was a knock at the door. I grabbed Maybelline and stowed her in the bathroom while Timothy let his mother in the house.

I smoothed my hair back behind my ears and went down the hall to meet her.

"Here she is," Timothy said. "Mother, this is my wife, Elizabeth. Elizabeth, my mother, Daisy Hollingsworth."

The woman standing in my living room was dark blond and rail thin. She was dressed plainly in a lightweight coat and her hair was pulled back tightly in a bun. The bland expression was fit for a vanilla pudding.

"Forgive me, Elizabeth, for coming over at this late hour," she said, "but my son tells me there's been a tragedy in your family." She extended a beautifully manicured hand.

"Yes, my grandmother died today," I said as I shook it. "She raised me since I was just a baby."

She winced. "I'm so sorry. And I also regret our meeting under such troubling circumstances. Have you given thought to the arrangements?"

"Arrangements?" I asked. "No, I haven't. To tell you the truth, I don't even know where to start."

She nodded. "Let me help you, then." Her almost colorless eyes rested on Timothy. "And of course, I insist on paying for everything."

"Thank you, ma'am," I replied. "I'm most grateful." I paused. "But I can't let you pay. I'm sure Meemaw had a nest egg of some sort, and—"

She brushed her hand against my wrist. "Elizabeth, please. I won't hear another word about it."

Timothy kissed his mama on the cheek. "Thank you, Mother. That's very generous."

"It really is," I said. "Too generous. Thank you very much." I managed a weak smile.

She gave me a curt nod in return.

"Oh, my goodness." My hands fluttered around my face. "Excuse my manners. I haven't even asked you to sit down or offered you a drink or—"

She held up her palm. "That's not necessary. I just felt that I had to drop by to let you know that I'm here to help you, Elizabeth."

"And I appreciate that, Mrs. Hollingsworth, ma'am," I said.

"May I see you in the morning around nine? So we can begin the funeral arrangements?"

I nodded.

"It was a pleasure meeting you, Elizabeth," she said.

Timothy escorted his mother to the car and when he came back inside, I said, "Your mama is being very kind."

Timothy shrugged. "She's good in a crisis."

I collapsed on the couch. "What did she say to the two of us being married?"

Timothy sat down beside me. "She didn't say much of anything. All she said was that our news had come as a surprise."

"Well, she doesn't seem upset about it, but then again she's hardly jumping up and down either."

Timothy rested his chin in his hand. "That's my mother for you. She's very hard to read, because she's so unemotional."

"She's certainly being helpful to me." I smothered a yawn.

Patsy Ann's news would have to wait.

Mrs. Hollingsworth arrived at 9 A.M. sharp in her silver Mercedes-Benz. She wore a gray suit and carried an umbrella.

"I hope this won't be too painful for you, Elizabeth," she said as she opened the passenger door. We rode to Bright's Funeral Home in silence. I watched rain sting the car windows. It felt like the whole world was crying for Meemaw.

Mr. Arthur Bright, a short, balding man in a bow tie, greeted Mrs. Hollingsworth fondly.

"Mrs. Hollingsworth, so good to see you, as always," he said.

"Thank you, Arthur. This is Elizabeth. She's just lost her

grandmother."

I couldn't help but notice that Mrs. Hollingsworth didn't identify me as her daughter-in-law.

"I am deeply aggrieved for you, Madam," he said in a grave voice.

Mr. Bright led us into the casket showroom, a large, airy room with plush carpet. "We have The Statesman, a model I know you're familiar with, Mrs. Hollingsworth. There's also a new design in solid bronze that makes a masterful statement. All of Augusta's most prestigious families are ordering it."

We peered into the boxes as Mr. Bright pointed out their various features. "This one has lumbar support and a foot rest," he said of one. "The caskets with fourteen-carat gold overlay are also extremely popular."

I glanced indifferently into half a dozen boxes, but didn't say a word about any of them. Finally Mrs. Hollingsworth looked at me and said, "Is anything catching your eye, Elizabeth?"

"All of these are so... fancy."

"They are the Cadillac of caskets, Madam." Mr. Bright touched his bow tie.

"They're very nice, but the truth is, my meemaw just wasn't the Cadillac type," I said. "Do you have something more modest?"

Mr. Bright raised an eyebrow. "I see. Well, we do have plain pine boxes, of course. There's the Abraham, the Ezekiel, and the Job. But I don't even have those on display. I could show you a catalog."

"Arthur, why don't we go in the other room? Elizabeth just hasn't seen everything yet."

Mr. Bright led us to a smaller room and right away, I spied a nice white box that looked like a suitable resting place for my grandmother. I knew that if Meemaw had her druthers, she would have picked a cardboard box lined in burlap. But the coffins weren't for the dead, they were for the living, and I would feel most comfortable putting Meemaw to rest in that sweet-looking white casket.

I nibbled a hangnail. "How much is this one?"

Mr. Bright cleared his throat and said, "The Primrose is four thousand dollars."

I gasped. "Maybe we better take a look at some of those pine boxes you mentioned.""

Mrs. Hollingsworth interrupted. "We'll take it, Arthur."

Mr. Bright smiled broadly.

"But Mrs. Hollingsworth—" I began.

She put a finger to her lips. "I insist, Elizabeth."

"Excellent choice," Mr. Bright said. "Would you like the interior in pink or champagne?"

I still couldn't get over the cost of that plain, white box, but Mrs. Hollingsworth seemed determined to buy it for Meemaw.

"Well, seeing how Meemaw was a teetotaler, we'd better go with the pink," I replied.

After the funeral home, we drove over to Eternal Memorials and picked out a granite stone with flecks of blue. The engraving would read: "Beloved Glenda: Grandmother, Mother and Servant to her Maker."

Our very last errand, and the most painful for me, was to stop at Meemaw's house to pick out the clothes she would be buried in. As soon as I opened her front door and inhaled the mixture of cigarette smoke and rusty radiators, I burst into tears. Mrs. Hollingsworth rummaged through her purse and pressed a lace handkerchief into my hand.

Meemaw's house looked like the vacant set of a stage play.

There was her half-drunk glass of iced tea on the kitchen table. A recipe for an onion casserole was lying by her pinking shears. Her poodle calendar, featuring two red-ribboned toy poodles posing in the basket of a bicycle, noted a podiatrist appointment today at 3 P.M. Marked in tomorrow's square was a luncheon date with Meemaw's best friend, Cordelia. They went to the Chat 'N' Chew every Wednesday and Meemaw always ordered carrot salad, banana Jell-O, and a bran muffin to keep her bowels in order.

Seeing her calendar was too much for me. Meemaw had jotted

down things on it with such faith, assuming she'd be around to get her corns checked by Dr. Bales and gossip over coffee with Cordelia, and now she was dead. I plunked down on the kitchen chair and launched into a wet, blubbery cry. I was determined to squeeze out every last tear until I was dry as a bone.

Mrs. Hollingsworth disappeared. I didn't know where she'd gone and I didn't care.

After a time, Mrs. Hollingsworth returned carrying some of Meemaw's clothes. She'd gone through Meemaw's things and brought back a white blouse, a black skirt, a full slip, and some black pumps. She also had a favorite brooch of Meemaw's. It was a gold-plated peacock with red rhinestone eyes.

"I hope this is what you had in mind," Mrs. Hollingsworth said. "I've found that you simply can't go wrong when you choose the basics."

She'd picked out exactly what Meemaw herself would have chosen if she could have, right down to the brooch, which I remembered last seeing her wear at my engagement party.

I was grateful to my mother-in-law. I wasn't ready to go into Meemaw's bedroom, and touch her clothes, smell her scent. I felt like giving her a hug for all that she'd done for me, but I was afraid to. Despite all of her kindnesses that day, Mrs. Hollingsworth still seemed as unapproachable as an iceberg.

When she dropped me off at home, I was so pooped I wanted to slide under the covers and fall asleep, but just as I pulled down the bedroom shade, the phone rang.

"Hey there, Lizzie. It's your daddy."

I was surprised to hear his voice. I couldn't remember the last time I'd spoken to him on the telephone. Taffy generally did all the calling.

"I'm calling because I got your message about Glenda."

I waited, and a long silence hung over the line.

"Your meemaw didn't much like me and I wasn't too keen on her," he stammered. "But I'm sorry for your sake, baby girl."

I paused for a moment. "Thank you, Daddy."

All my life I'd hoped for grand gestures from Dwayne, but as Meemaw used to say, you can't get lemonade from a dairy cow. As I hung up the phone, I felt grateful for his small display of sympathy. Even if Dwayne Polk was no more my daddy than the Pope, he was still the daddy I'd always known, and it meant something to me that he'd thought about me during my time of need.

That night I lay awake and heard the soft whistle in Timothy's nostrils that came with sleep. I pictured Meemaw floating around in heaven like an angel, wearing a filmy, white gown, with her sweater over it, to keep away the drafts.

I had a vision of one of the head angels telling her that I wasn't really her flesh-and-blood granddaughter, that the babies had been switched at the hospital. Then I saw Meemaw spread her wings like a giant moth and fly up into his face saying, "Of course I'm her grandmother. Who do you think mashed up Tylenol in her applesauce when she was sick because swallowing pills made her gag? Who smocked her white confirmation dress by hand when she was nine so she'd be the prettiest girl in her Sunday-school class? Who made her morning oatmeal with cinnamon sprinkled on top? It was her grandmother, that's who."

The senior angel flew away all flustered and Meemaw smiled, and I felt like she was right there in the room with me. I knew that even though we might not share the same blood we were definitely family, just the way Attalee and Mavis had been before and the way Timothy would be forever.

Thirty-Two

Still hot! Now it just comes in flashes.

~ Bumper sticker on Attalee Gaines's Skylark

The next morning I went straight to the Bottom Dollar Emporium and fell into Mavis's arms.

"I know, love, I know," Mavis said, as I shuddered against her chest. "I can't believe she's gone."

It was so comforting to bury myself in Mavis's motherly embrace. Thank the Lord she'd taken her house off the market and was planning to stay in Cayboo Creek. I wouldn't have been able to bear the loss of Mavis too.

After I'd spent my tears, I lifted my head from her shoulder and looked around at the store. She and Attalee had been busy marking down items for the Everything-Must-Go sale. Big yellow sale stickers graced every aisle and items were piled up in the clearance bins.

"I feel guilty leaving you short-handed just when you need me most," I remarked.

"Don't give it a second thought," Mavis said, with a dismissive wave. "Birdie's coming by to lend a hand and Hank's been in and out all day today."

I glanced around. "Where's Attalee?"

"I think she's in the stockroom. I don't know what she's been doing back there so long. Maybe you should go and check on her."

I entered the stockroom, but its windowless gloom revealed no sign of Attalee.

"Attalee," I called out softly. When I didn't get a response, I flipped on the light switch. I spotted her leaning against a box of Bridgeford Beef Jerky. She was holding a photograph in her hand. The floor around her was littered with crumpled-up Kleenex.

She honked into one of the tissues. "Stupid birds and bees. Damn pollen is everywhere."

I knelt down beside her and glanced at the photograph. It was a picture of Meemaw and Attalee glaring at one another on each side of a loving cup.

"That was last year when you and Meemaw tied for first place in the Senior Center Bingo Championship," I said.

"Yup," Attalee said with a sniff. "We bickered about who was going to keep the cup. We flipped a coin and she won."

"Would you like that cup for yourself now?" I asked gently. "She's got it on top of the fireplace mantel. She kept her loose buttons in it."

Attalee shook her head. "I cheated to win the championship," she said in a small voice. "I tampered with the cards. When Dixon would call out 'B-9' and I had 'B-7,' I'd use a black pen to change it."

"Attalee!"

She covered her face with her hands. "Your meemaw was just so darn lucky. I ain't never seen anything like it. If she'd gone to Las Vegas, they would have barred her from the slot machines." She parted her fingers and peeked out from behind them. "I didn't mean any harm to her. I just got caught up in the heat of the competition."

"Well, I don't think it's such a terrible thing," I said, grasping her bony hand. "She'd forgive you, I'm sure."

"I hope so," Attalee said. "I wouldn't want her badmouthing me to St. Peter at the Pearly Gates."

"Meemaw would never do that, Attalee." I smiled. "Truth is,

despite your rivalry, she was very fond of you."

"I liked her pretty good too," Attalee said. "Bingo night just ain't going to be the same."

I helped Attalee up and we walked out of the storeroom just as Birdie entered the store.

"My dearest Elizabeth," she said, kissing my cheek. "I can't tell you how sorry I was to hear the news about Glenda."

A copy of the *Cayboo Creek Crier* was tucked underneath her arm.

"Is it in there?" I asked, gesturing at the newspaper.

"On the front page," Birdie said. She spread out the paper on the checkout stand and we all leaned over to take a look at Meemaw's obituary, which was titled "Much Loved Matriarch Meets Her Maker."

"What a lovely tribute," I breathed. "The headline sounds so poetic."

"It's almost as inspired as the one you composed when Burl died," Attalee remarked. "'Burl Gaines Gives Up Ghost.'" She shivered. "It still gives me goose flesh just thinking about it."

Birdie laid a hand on my shoulder. "Elizabeth, tell us how we can help out with the arrangements."

"It's all been taken care of," I said. "Timothy's mother came into town the day before last and she's handled every little last detail. Not to mention that she's paying for everything."

"She sounds like an angel," Mavis said.

"She truly is," I said. "I would have been lost without her."

"But?" Mavis asked.

"But what?"

Mavis shrugged. "I don't know. There was an odd note in your voice just now when you mentioned her."

"She's been such a peach. I couldn't ask for more," I said, twirling a strand of hair around my finger. "But... in some ways I feel like she's just going through the motions, helping me out like she is. I don't think her heart's in it."

"Pshaw," Attalee said. "That's just the way it is between wives and mother-in-laws. They're natural enemies, like cats and mice. Besides, you don't need her heart in this, just her wallet. She's got the dough to throw Glenda the grand funeral she deserves."

"I'll agree with you there," Birdie said. "I'd love to see our dear Glenda go out in style. By the way, Attalee, I brought you that mask I wore to the masquerade party last year." She handed Attalee a paper bag.

"What's this? Halloween coming early?" I asked.

"You're not the only one who has marketing ideas," Attalee said, removing the mask from the bag. "During our big clearance sale, I won't be Attalee Gaines, assistant manager of the Bottom Dollar Emporium." She perched the mask on her nose. "I'll be the Mark-down Mistress," she said in a mysterious voice.

"Mark-down Mistress?" I asked.

"I'll wear this mask and a black cape just like Zorro. But instead of waving a sword, I'll slash prices with my black Magic Marker," Attalee said.

"How clever," I remarked.

"How racy, you mean," Attalee said. She lowered her voice and glanced warily at Mavis who was dusting a shelf. "To attract the male bargain hunters, I'll also be wearing fishnet hose and a bustier."

"I heard that," Mavis said. "And as I've already told you, you will *not* be wearing either of those items. This is a family establishment, not a Hooters restaurant."

Attalee snorted. "I keep trying to tell Mavis that sex sells. But she just won't listen. What do you think, Elizabeth?"

"I think the Mark-down Mistress idea is a stroke of genius," I said. "But when it comes to being sexy, I think less is more. Instead of the bustier and the fishnet hose, why don't you have a rose between your teeth? That's very alluring."

"A rose?" Attalee nodded thoughtfully. "Maybe I'll just do that. I was having a heck of a time finding a pair of fishnet panty hose with tummy-control panels."

"I'm borrowing my grandson's P.A. system," Birdie said. "I'll be announcing the Mark-down Mistress's specials over the microphone like this: 'Come to the home accessory department, where toilet bowl brushes are marked down to two for fifty cents.'"

"Hank will be on hand as a bouncer," Attalee said. "In case the crowd gets out of control."

"It sounds like everything is coming together," I said. "The Everything-Must-Go sale is sure to be a big success and before you know it, the Bottom Dollar Emporium will have a whole new look."

Thirty-Three

When an old person dies, a library burns down.
~ Message in the *Methodist Church Bulletin*

Seeing how she'd been a member there for over fifty years, Meemaw's funeral was held at the Rock of Ages Baptist Church. Reverend Hozey stood at the pulpit in a dark robe, and per my request he did not pound his Bible or use the word "heathens" once in his sermon. Instead he talked lovingly of Meemaw, referring to her as a lamb who'd returned to Jesus's flock.

Mrs. Hollingsworth had programs made up, with Meemaw's name on the cover and her birth and death dates in gold letters.

It had been such a relief to have someone handle all those little details.

The pews were packed with friends and neighbors gathered to pay their respects to Meemaw. Boomer was there with his mother, who wore a nubby purple hat stuck through with a pin that looked like a third eye. She kept snapping her handkerchief at Boomer every time he got emotional during the service.

Most of the Methodist congregation had come, as had a half-dozen ladies from Meemaw's ceramics class. They all sat together like a flock of birds and sang in their quavery voices. Patsy Ann sat in the back with a few of Meemaw's other neighbors.

Timothy, Mrs. Hollingsworth, Mavis, Attalee, and I all sat in the front row, reserved for family members. Before the service began, I motioned for Boomer to come up to join us, but his mama hung onto his arm so hard that I guessed he was staying put.

My composure wobbled during the service. We sang all of Meemaw's favorite hymns, like "When the Roll Is Called Up Yonder" and "Shall We Gather at the River?" while I fought to keep my chest from heaving. Timothy and Mrs. Hollingsworth were on either side of me, supporting me as we sang.

After the service, Timothy and I received guests. He looked so sharp in his dark gray suit that all of Meemaw's friends blushed right through their face powder as he shook hands and flashed them that shy smile of his. I was a little nervous when Patsy Ann came up, because I hadn't yet found time to tell Timothy about my mystery heritage, but she just squeezed both of our hands and dabbed her eyes with a hankie as she passed through the line.

A lady named Emmy from Meemaw's ceramics class approached me and handed me a wrapped package. "Glenda had been working on this for a while. She didn't get a chance to paint it, so we did it for her."

I tore off the tissue paper and discovered a plate with a picture of praying hands in the middle. Praying hands were Meemaw's favorite thing to make in ceramics class; she had half a dozen of them lying around her house. Below the hands were my name, and Timothy's name, and the date of our wedding.

"Thank you, Emmy," I said. "We'll treasure it always."

I ran my fingers over the grooved letters of our names. Here was Meemaw's way of reaching out from the grave and giving Timothy and me her stamp of approval on our marriage.

Boomer came over to pay his respects. He looked colorless and somehow smaller, wearing a salmon-colored suit instead of his usual loud shirt. He bussed my cheek with dry lips and whispered, "Hey there, Toots," in a sad voice, empty of his usual teasing fun. "I better go," he said meekly. "It's time for mother's nap."

After a reception in the fellowship hall and a drive out to the cemetery, Timothy and I went home. I sat on the floor of the den, sifting through all the cards, and I saw Mrs. Tobias had sent an arrangement.

I went into the kitchen to speak with Timothy.

"Timothy? Did you tell your grandmother about Meemaw?"

He looked up from the salad he was tossing. "Yes, I did. I knew she wouldn't forgive me otherwise. I didn't tell her about our wedding. She's due back home from Hilton Head soon and I thought the two of us could tell her together. She's going to be so pleased. She's crazy about you."

She's got a strange way of showing it, I wanted to say, but didn't. I figured there was no point in telling Timothy what his grandmother had done. Not until I had had a talk with her myself.

I stole an olive from the salad and popped it in my mouth. "I'm surprised your mother hasn't told her."

"Mother isn't close to anyone, not even her own mother," Timothy said. "I have to admit, I'm so pleased at how helpful Mother has been to you over the last few days. I do believe she's grown fond of you. In fact, I have business in Charlotte tomorrow and mother has asked if you'd like to have tea with her at her home in Augusta while I'm gone."

"That's sweet of her. I'd be glad to."

"Good." He wiped his hands on a dishtowel. "Maybe things are changing with Mother. Maybe now that I'm married she's decided to try to be closer to her family." His face looked so hopeful.

"When are you going to tell her about the bait shop?" I asked.

"As soon as I get back from Charlotte. That's one of the purposes of my trip. I'm interviewing my potential successor. This fellow knows a lot more about running a company than I do." He grimaced. "I hope she won't be too terribly disappointed in me. I'd hate to let her down just when she's starting to show some interest in me."

I hugged Timothy. "She'd better or she'll have to answer to me," I said.

His face split into a smile. Happiness agreed with Timothy. It was hard to recognize him as the bald bird man that had swept into the Bottom Dollar Emporium just six months before.

Thirty-Four

Stressed is just desserts spelled backwards.
~ Sign outside the Chat 'N' Chew

When I pulled up in front of Mrs. Hollingsworth's house, I thought there'd been a mistake. The house I'd stopped in front of looked big enough to be a museum. I half expected there to be someone at the door charging admission.

Mrs. Hollingsworth's Mercedes was parked in the circular drive, so I pulled the Geo behind it, a little ashamed to be blemishing the view of such a grand structure with my economy car. Its passenger-side door was so deeply dented that even the Ding King couldn't repair it.

I hefted my purse on my shoulder and stared up at the looming mansion. On either side of the house stood four white columns that towered to the height of telephone poles. The looming white structure was as gussied up as a three-tiered wedding cake.

The brass knocker, shaped like a lion's head, summoned Mrs. Hollingsworth's maid. She wore a crisp, black uniform topped by a hat that looked like a doily, just like the maids in the movies.

"Hello. You Elizabeth? Mrs. Hollingsworth is expecting you," she said. The maid was a black woman with the build of a small refrigerator. Her white apron strings strained against her block-shaped belly.

I was fascinated by her, because I'd never met a uniformed

maid before. Once when Meemaw had sprained her ankle, she'd called in a company called Maureen's Maids to clean the house and I'd expected a whole team of maids, wearing black-and-white outfits and shaking feather dusters, to show up at our door. Instead a lone woman arrived, wearing a scruffy-looking sweat suit and dragging an upright vacuum cleaner behind her.

Mrs. Hollingsworth's maid invited me inside and I stepped into a foyer that was about the size of my whole house on Scuffle Road. Enormous portraits of grim-looking people hung in the hall, just like in the Haunted Mansion at Disney World.
I fixed my gaze on a white-haired fellow in a Confederate jacket, wondering if his eyes might follow me as I walked past, but his unblinking glare never wavered.

"Mrs. Hollingsworth is in the living room. I'll lead you to her," the maid said.

I trailed behind her until we came to a room as big as a high school gymnasium. Gold curtains poured from the windows, ending in a puddle of material on the glossy wood floors. Artwork fit for a castle gleamed from every surface. I nearly ran into a life-sized statue of a lady in a loose, flowing gown that left one of her boobs bare for all to see.

A chandelier, bigger around than a washtub, dangled from the ceiling, heavy with a hailstorm of crystals. There was an assortment of spindly carved chairs that looked like they'd split in two if you breathed on them too hard. Once Meemaw and Granddaddy and I'd toured Graceland in Memphis. The King didn't have anything over Daisy Hollingsworth.

The mistress of the house was sitting on a red love seat, flipping through a magazine. Next to her was a white-and-gold dog that looked like it was picked to match the furniture. The animal gave a sharp bark when she saw me.

"Lexie, really." Mrs. Hollingsworth shushed the dog. "Well, hello, Elizabeth. How are you?" She addressed the maid. "Aurora, take Elizabeth's purse for her and store it in the hall closet for the time being."

Aurora lumbered off with my purse slung over her shoulder. I was gawking at an oil painting of a woman in a long white dress with her hair swept up in a chignon.

"Is that you?" I asked.

Mrs. Hollingsworth frowned. "No. That's my sister, Lilly. She died over twenty years ago."

I bent at the waist and made clicking noises for Mrs. Hollingsworth's dog, hoping to coax her to come to me, when Mrs. Hollingsworth interrupted. "Elizabeth, Alexandra is a show dog and her trainer makes a similar sound during their sessions together. I wouldn't want to confuse her."

"Sure," I said straightening up. I looked at Mrs. Hollingsworth. She wore the same expressionless mask on her face.

"A lot of people don't understand that show dogs simply aren't like other dogs," she said in a pinched voice. "They're not meant to be played with."

"I'll remember that." My eyes scanned the room. "This place is gorgeous. I've never seen anything like it."

"Please sit, Elizabeth."

I chose the sturdiest-looking chair. A silver tea service had been set out on the polished coffee table.

Mrs. Hollingsworth poured. "Do you take lemon?" I nodded. She handed me a teacup and passed a plate of powdered sugar cookies on it. I took one and tried to nibble delicately between sips of my tea.

Mrs. Hollingsworth was studying me in a careful way as if she was waiting for me to slip up. My fingers felt big as sausages as I held the teacup, and I fretted about dropping cookie crumbs on the carpet.

"It is a lovely house, isn't it, Elizabeth?" she said in a breathy voice. "Easily the grandest home in Augusta, if not the Southeast."

"Yes ma'am. It looks like you could get lost in it."

"You saw the portraits in the entryway, I assume. Those are Mr. Hollingsworth's ancestors. The Hollingsworth family has an impeccable pedigree. George Walton, the first mayor of Augusta, used to live right next door to Mr. Hollingsworth's great, great, great, great granddaddy." She took a sip of tea and looked at me with eyes that were as cold as seawater. "Timothy hasn't told me much about your family."

"Well, there isn't a lot to tell. There was my meemaw, who raised me, of course."

"What about your father?"

That was a real good question. What about my daddy? But of course, there was no sense in going through all that with Mrs. Hollingsworth.

"My daddy owns a rent-to-own furniture store called the Bargain Bonanza. If you've seen one of his commercials, I promise you, you'd never forget him."

She rattled her teacup on her saucer. "Timothy tells me your father's name is Dwayne Polk."

"Yes ma'am. Do you know my daddy?"

Her lips were colorless, and she shook a little as she spoke. "Why in the world would I know your father, Elizabeth? Do you imagine that we travel in the same circles?"

"Not at all, ma'am," I said in a quiet voice.

Mrs. Hollingsworth lifted her chin and sat board-stiff in her chair. "I don't need to know him, Elizabeth, because I can guess what he's like. He probably drives a pickup truck and no doubt imbibes too much alcohol. I suspect he uses foul language and is quite an uncouth individual. Is that an accurate picture of your father, dear?"

"Somewhat." I swallowed. "He's not a choirboy, but—"

"Aren't you curious as to how I know what your father is like, Elizabeth?" Her voice was so icy, it could have shattered into pieces.

"You can tell me if you want," I croaked.

She lifted her chin and looked at me with an expression that was no longer bland, but full of venom.

"It's quite simply this, Elizabeth. Everything about you says that you are the daughter of a South Carolinian redneck. It's the way you talk, the way you dress, even the way you've been fumbling with that teacup. You may as well wear a sign around your neck."

I put my teacup down on the table and swallowed hard. The tension in the air had gotten so thick it was like breathing cotton.

"I see," I said.

Her lips tightened. "No, I don't think you do see. Otherwise you wouldn't have had the audacity to think that you could actually marry into our family and imagine that I would accept you."

Mrs. Hollingsworth's jaw looked like it was set in cement. I kept thinking to myself over and over, "Jesus in a distressing disguise; Jesus in a distressing disguise." I wanted to run out of the room crying, but I knew I had to stay and face whatever she was serving up.

"Let me tell you, *Ms. Polk,* why I came home from France early. I got an e-mail from my friend Judy Castlewood. Her daughter Marcie had seen Timothy at the Summit Club with, as Marcie said, 'a country bumpkin.' Dear, sweet Marcie nearly fainted when Timothy introduced you as his wife, no less. After I got the e-mail, I immediately made travel arrangements to come home."

The irises of her eyes glittered like quartz under the light of the chandelier as she continued. "Once Timothy told me who you were, I'd planned to pay you a visit to see if I could reason with you. Unfortunately, the next thing I knew, your grandmother had died. I'm not a heartless woman. I felt that we had to get her buried before I could confront you. Now that your grandmother has been given a decent funeral, courtesy of my checkbook I might add, it's time we had our discussion."

She leaned toward me and glared at me with those odd, colorless eyes of hers. "All I really want to know, Elizabeth, is what exactly is it going to cost me to get you out of my son's life?"

I gaped at her. It took me a moment to accept what she was saying. "Mrs. Hollingsworth," I stammered, "I don't want any of your money."

Her expression didn't change. "Elizabeth, I'm losing patience with you. Name a figure so that we can reach some type of agreement."

I sat up straighter in my chair and cleared my throat. "There won't be any agreement. As I said, Mrs. Hollingsworth, I have no interest in your money."

Her expression never wavered. She reached for her checkbook on the lamp table and poised her pen over it. "Don't be foolish. Timothy is bound to tire of you, and then where will you be? Penniless as well as heartbroken. This way you can at least enjoy life a little. Maybe you can even get a decent pair of shoes."

The only sound was the ticking of a grandfather clock in the corner of the room. Mrs. Hollingsworth never once took her eyes off of me. I sat there in stunned silence for a moment and then I got up from my chair.

"Mrs. Hollingsworth, you don't know your son very well because if you did, you'd realize that he loves me very much and the chances of him tiring of me anytime soon are pretty slim."

I glanced down at my feet. "As for shoes, I'd rather wear my little Pick 'N Pay sandals with their genuine leather uppers than the fanciest pair in Paris so long as I could wake up next to Timothy every day." And then in a softer voice I said, "And since we're talking about shoes, I wouldn't want to be in yours, because you've missed the opportunity to get to know one of the finest men alive. It's a crying shame, since Timothy would like nothing more than to be close to you."

Her stony face didn't flinch.

"Thanks again for the beautiful funeral for Meemaw," I continued. "I believe I should go home now. I'll find Aurora and ask her to fetch my handbag."

As I left the room and turned the corner, I saw Mrs. Tobias sprinting down the hallway in her high heels.

"Oh, my stars, Elizabeth, you're already here," she said breathlessly. Her nose was red and peeling from the Hilton Head sun. "I was hoping to catch you before you came. I drove to the Bottom Dollar Emporium and Mavis said you were probably over here, so I rushed right over."

Mrs. Hollingsworth stepped out into the hall. "Mother, what

are you doing here?" she said.

"Well, I wanted to see Elizabeth, of course. Aurora let me in," Mrs. Tobias said.

A puzzled look crossed Mrs. Hollingsworth's face. "The two of you know each other?" she asked.

"Indeed we do, Daisy," Mrs. Tobias said. "I introduced Timothy and Elizabeth to one another a few months ago."

Mrs. Hollingsworth's eyes flashed angrily. "So you're to blame for this fiasco! Mother, what possessed you to do something like this?"

Mrs. Tobias smiled and squeezed my arm. "It was the best thing for the child. Elizabeth has the biggest heart of anyone I know, and Timothy was just so damaged and hurting when he came back to Augusta. I knew she would be the one to draw him out of his shell."

Mrs. Hollingsworth planted a hand on her hip. "Well, she's done a lot more than draw him out. She's also convinced Timothy to elope with her. They've been married for two weeks."

"Married?" Mrs. Tobias's face lit up like a football stadium on game night. "Oh, Elizabeth, what a lovely surprise," she said, as she hugged my neck. "Welcome to the family, my dear."

"So you're not mad at me for marrying Timothy, Mrs. Tobias?" I asked.

"Mad? I'm thrilled. I think the two of you are perfect for one another," Mrs. Tobias said.

"I'm so relieved you're happy about it," I said.

Mrs. Tobias clasped her hands together. "I'm elated. I knew things must have gotten serious between the two of you when Mavis said you were over here taking tea with Daisy. I rushed over because there was something I needed to speak about most urgently. Now that you and Timothy are married and you've met Daisy, it's time for a frank discussion," Mrs. Tobias said.

"Mother. I'm not sure you understand. This is Elizabeth *Polk*. Dwayne Polk's daughter," Mrs. Hollingsworth said.

Mrs. Tobias gave her daughter a stern look. "You're wasting

that tone of voice on me, Daisy. I know Elizabeth's maiden name. In fact, I think I might know more about Elizabeth than she knows herself." Mrs. Tobias touched my wrist. "I have something important to tell you, Elizabeth. I've just been waiting for the right time." She glanced at Mrs. Hollingsworth. "This will interest you as well, Daisy."

"I hardly think so, Mother," Mrs. Hollingsworth retorted.

"I promise you, it will." Mrs. Tobias lifted her finger. "But I suggest the two of you take a seat."

Thirty-Five

Do not disturb! I'm disturbed enough already.

~ Sign outside Mavis Loomis's office in the Bottom Dollar
Emporium

Mrs. Hollingsworth sat sullenly on the love seat while I perched on
the edge of one of the little gold chairs. Mrs. Tobias paced on an
oriental carpet.

"Please, Mother. Give us your revelation and be done with it,"
Mrs. Hollingsworth said.

"I'm just trying to get the timetable straight in my mind,
darling." She rubbed her hands together. "I'm afraid I'm quite
nervous and my mouth's gone dry. Would you ring Aurora for a
glass of water?"

"There's a water pitcher on top of the chevalier," Mrs.
Hollingsworth said with an exasperated sigh.

Mrs. Tobias poured the water into a glass and delicately took a
sip. She cleared her throat after swallowing.

"I believe this all started when I happened to catch one of
those Bargain Bonanza commercials on television," she began.
"Your father, Elizabeth, or Insane Dwayne as he calls himself, was
blowing up a La-Z-Boy. It was quite the spectacle." Mrs. Tobias
paused to take another sip of water. "Naturally that starting me
thinking about Lilly."

"Mother, I don't want to—" Mrs. Hollingsworth said.

"I know, Daisy. It's painful to talk about your sister, but today we must. This story, you see, has a great deal to do with Lilly."

Mrs. Tobias smoothed her periwinkle dress and looked at me as she spoke.

"Lilly was my other daughter, Elizabeth," she said. "Daisy and Lilly were identical twins and they were closer than close. They even had their own special language when they were little girls. When they were very small, they looked and acted so much alike, I could scarcely tell them apart. But as they grew older, it was clear that they were two separate people with distinct personalities."

Mrs. Tobias lightly touched Daisy's shoulder. Daisy stiffened at her mother's caress.

"Daisy was the studious, quiet daughter, while Lilly was more of a social butterfly," Mrs. Tobias continued. "Lilly was a delight to have around, but I'm afraid her judgment wasn't particularly keen. When Lilly was just nineteen, she came to me, quite upset, and told me that she was four months pregnant." Mrs. Tobias tsked at the memory. "Naturally, I was up in arms, particularly when I found out that the father of this baby wasn't the sort of boy we had in mind for our daughter. Lilly wanted to raise the baby, but my husband and I thought it best if Lilly put the infant up for adoption. After a good deal of fuss and some convincing on Daisy's part, Lilly reluctantly agreed."

"Why are you telling Elizabeth this?" Mrs. Hollingsworth said in an angry voice. "The only part of the story that remotely concerns her is the fact that it was her father, Dwayne Polk, who impregnated Lilly. If it wasn't for him, Lilly would still be alive today."

I gasped. "My daddy and your daughter Lilly had a child together?"

Mrs. Tobias nodded.

"Does my daddy even know about this?" I asked.

"Oh no," Mrs. Tobias said. "Lilly decided to keep it from him. When she'd thought about telling him, she discovered that he'd gone and married someone else."

"That was my mama, obviously," I said. "So this baby that Lilly put up for adoption would have been my half-brother or half-sister?"

Mrs. Tobias shook her head and gave me an odd little look. "No, Elizabeth. It's actually much more complicated than that."

Goose bumps rose up on every inch of my body, as I had a sudden flash of insight.

"Mrs. Tobias, I think I know what you're going to say," I said in a near whisper.

"You do?" Mrs. Tobias asked.

My voice came out as a thin squeak. "When did Lilly give birth to her baby?"

Mrs. Tobias touched the top button of her dress. She locked her gaze with mine. "Twenty-six years ago on October 15 my daughter Lilly gave birth to a baby girl at St. Mary's Hospital."

I wordlessly shook my head. "Oh my gosh," I said.

"I wish someone would tell me what's going on," Mrs. Hollingsworth said.

I ignored Mrs. Hollingsworth and asked breathlessly, "How did you find out all of this, Mrs. Tobias?"

"Let me back up a minute," said Mrs. Tobias. "As I told you, I saw your father's television commercial. He blew up some furniture, and then you appeared on the screen. What is that line you say in the commercial, Elizabeth?"

"'Come see my daddy, Dwayne Polk, for savings that will blow your socks off,'" I recited with a blush.

"Exactly!" Mrs. Tobias said. "When I first saw you, I was so stunned I nearly choked on my brandy."

"Why?" I asked.

"Elizabeth, do you have that locket I gave you?" Mrs. Tobias asked.

"Yes, I do," I said. I took the locket from my neck and opened it. "The latch is no longer stuck. It sprung open while you were in Hilton Head."

Mrs. Hollingsworth stepped behind my chair and peered over my shoulder. "I don't see anything peculiar about the photograph.

It's just a picture of you, Elizabeth."

I shook my head no.

"But who—?" Mrs. Hollingsworth began.

"It's a photograph of me," Mrs. Tobias said. "Taken when I was twenty years old."

Mrs. Hollingsworth stared at the photograph with astonished eyes. "My goodness, the resemblance is uncanny. It's almost as if Elizabeth could be—"

"My granddaughter," Mrs. Tobias interrupted. "And she's also your niece, Daisy. Elizabeth is Lilly's daughter."

Mrs. Hollingsworth paled and dropped into a chair.

Mrs. Tobias placed her hand on my shoulder. "When I saw you on those commercials and noted your resemblance to me as a young girl, I suspected that you might be the baby Lilly had given up for adoption so many years ago. I just didn't know how it was possible and I still don't. How in heaven's name had Dwayne even known about the adoption to claim you? I visited the Bargain Bonanza and initiated some small talk with Dwayne. Through our conversation, I found out he had a daughter named Elizabeth and that she worked at a dollar store in Cayboo Creek called the Bottom Dollar Emporium."

"And that's when you started coming in to the Bottom Dollar," I said.

"Yes, and as I got to know you I found that you had no inkling about Lilly's existence and, in fact, thought your mother was a woman named Darlene, who had died when you were an infant. After I found out the date of your birthday, I knew for certain you were Lilly's child, but I still have no clue how you ended up here. The last I'd known was that you were put up for adoption in Atlanta. How you ended up in Cayboo Creek with your natural father is a mystery to me."

"I just recently found out what happened," I said in a soft voice. "It's all been so crazy."

Mrs. Tobias and Mrs. Hollingsworth listened as I told them how Patsy Ann had confessed to switching the babies in the hospital and why she had done it. I told them about the baffling "B" in my mother's diary and how "B" and my mother had kept their relationship secret because they were of different races. Every word I spoke drained a bit more color from Mrs. Hollingsworth's skin.

"I can't believe it," I said. "All this time I was wondering who my daddy was, and here it ended up being Dwayne the entire time." I glanced up at Lilly's portrait on the wall. "It's so sad. She was gone years before I even knew she existed."

Mrs. Tobias patted my hand. "The two of you were alike in many ways. Lilly was something of a spirited young woman, but her heart was pure."

I rubbed the locket between my fingers. "I wish I could have known her."

"Elizabeth, dear. There is one other thing we should discuss." Mrs. Tobias shot me a nervous glance. "Regarding that young man Clip Jenkins. He came to see me today."

"It's all right, Mrs. Tobias," I said, in a gentle voice. "At first, I was upset about the offer you made Clip. But then I realized that if I had married him, I never would've met Timothy."

She bowed her head. "Still. It wasn't my place to meddle in your personal affairs. My behavior was inexcusable."

I rose from my chair and touched her sleeve. "The way I see it, you knew you were my grandmother all this time," I said. "I figure that you were just trying to look after me. Just like Meemaw would."

She lifted her chin and a slight smile trembled at the corners of her mouth.

"I just had this uneasy feeling about Clip. So I hired a detective to follow him. When I found that he was not an honorable young man, I couldn't bear to allow my only granddaughter to marry someone who would be untrue to her."

"It's all right, Mrs. Tobias. I forgive you."

She sighed in relief and fixed her bright, blue eyes on me. "Now that it's been established that you're my granddaughter, calling me 'Mrs. Tobias' just isn't going to do any longer, Elizabeth."

"I don't think I can call you Gracie, ma'am," I said. "It just doesn't seem proper."

"No, no." She laid a finger on her cheek. "I was thinking of a nickname. You called your other grandmother 'Meemaw.' I'd like it very much if you'd call me 'Dear.'" Her eyes shone as she spoke. "It's what I called my grandmother."

"Dear," I repeated. Then I paused for a moment. "There's one other question I have, Mrs. Tobias, I mean... Dear," I said. "Why didn't you tell me you were my grandmother earlier? You knew it all this time and you didn't breathe a word."

She sighed. "I was afraid of turning your life upside down."

"I guess it was a tough call to make," I said. "It all came out in the wash anyhow... Dear."

Calling Mrs. Tobias "Dear" sounded just right to me. Not too cutesie, but nice and dignified. At the Shady Rest Retirement home where Attalee lived there was a sign out front that said, "Caution, Dears Crossing," and I guess Mrs. Tobias was now my Dear, even though I think she'd sort of been that way ever since we'd met. Now, we'd just made it official.

Mrs. Hollingsworth, who had been listening in silence to our exchange, rose unsteadily to her feet. Her face was the pasty color of flour and she held a hand to her chest.

"If you'll excuse me please," she said in a feeble voice. "This has been a very trying afternoon for me."

Before she could reach the foyer, she crumpled headfirst on the parquet floor.

Thirty-Six

Question: What has four legs and an arm?
Answer: A happy pit bull.

~ Dwayne Polk's favorite joke

Later at the hospital, Daisy's cardiologist told Timothy that if I hadn't been around to give his mother CPR, she almost certainly would have expired before she made it to the hospital. As it was, he guessed she would make a complete recovery.

"That's quite a wife you have there, Timothy," he said, with a nod in my direction.

"You don't even know the half of it, Dr. Freedman," Timothy said, squeezing my arm.

Since he'd arrived at the hospital, I'd filled Timothy in about the baby-switching and how we now shared the same grandmother and that his mother was my aunt. His eyes got wide as Mason jar lids and he nearly sloshed coffee all over his trousers when he discovered that he and I were technically cousins, although not by blood, since he'd been adopted.

Mrs. Hollingsworth was released from the hospital several days after her heart attack, and Timothy arranged for a home health nurse to stay with her for the next few days until she got her strength back. Daisy had refused to let him drive her home from the hospital, preferring a limousine service. When Timothy tried to visit her at home, Aurora answered the door and told him that Daisy wasn't seeing anyone except the nurse, servants, and her private secretary. It appeared nothing had changed with Daisy Hollingsworth.

A week after Daisy's release, I was squinting at Meemaw's recipe card for chicken and dumplings when I heard a knock at the front door. I wiped my hands on a dishrag and strode through the living room to answer it.

"Did you forget your keys, Timothy?" I called and opened the front door.

There stood Daisy Hollingsworth. Her face was still pale despite the dusting of rouge on her cheeks. She wore a light-blue silk dress that only emphasized her frail coloring.

"Mrs. Hollingsworth. What are you doing here? Should you be up and about like this?"

"I'm just fine, thank you, Elizabeth. I was wondering if I might come in for a moment." Her large colorless eyes dominated her thin, pinched face. It looked as if she'd lost another five pounds from her already slight frame.

"Sure. Can I get you anything to drink? I just made a pitcher of iced tea."

"No, thank you." She stood uncertainly in the living room.

"Please sit," I said, offering her the best chair in the house, a striped wingback I'd gotten at a garage sale.

Mrs. Hollingsworth smoothed the back of her dress and gingerly sat down.

I perched on the couch and looked up at her expectantly. "Timothy's supposed to be back home directly, so if you can a wait awhile—"

"I didn't come to see Timothy. I came to see you," she said softly. Her eyes rested on the glass shoe collection on the shelf between her chair and the couch.

"Those were my mama's," I paused, catching my mistake, but I didn't bother to correct myself. "She only collected seven of those shoes. I'm always hoping to add a shoe or two, but they're hard to find these days."

Mrs. Hollingsworth stared bleakly at a spot on the wall just above my head.

"I owe you my life, Elizabeth," she said in a barely audible voice. "Thank you."

"I'm just glad I was on hand to help," I said.

"I should have called sooner," she continued. "But I've been doing a lot of thinking since the day of my heart attack. I needed time to take everything in."

I nodded. "That's understandable."

She got up from her chair and picked up a framed photograph of Timothy and me from the end table.

"Timothy looks so content in this picture," she mused. "I never noticed what a beautiful smile he has. He tends to be sullen in my presence." She replaced the photograph. "There are so few things I know about my only child. As you said the last time I saw you, you know him better than I do, Elizabeth."

I shrugged. "Maybe."

"I hadn't bothered to get close to him. Not once in his entire life," she said with a sad little sigh.

She turned to face me. "I never wanted children," she said. "But my husband, Bettis, insisted we have a male heir who could one day take over the family business. We compromised by adopting a baby. That's how we ended up with Timothy."

"You don't like children, then?"

She rubbed her forearms as if she were cold. "I'm afraid I don't like people in general. Children less so because they tend to be needy. I shouldn't have married, but my social position demanded it."

"I see."

She shook her head. "No, Elizabeth, I don't think you do see. You're the opposite of me in almost every way. You have a genuine affection for people and it shows. You're very like your mother, Lilly, in that respect."

"Am I?" I said, experiencing a flush of pleasure at the unexpected mention of my mother's name.

"Yes," Mrs. Hollingsworth said with a nod. "Lilly was the sociable, warm twin, whereas I was the shy, guarded one. That was all right when I had Lilly. She was my link to other people. When she died I felt cut off from everyone."

"You must have felt terribly lonely, losing your identical twin like that."

"More than you can imagine," she whispered.

I waited for her to continue. Two feverish spots of color burned in each of her cheekbones as she stood on the braided rug in my living room.

"Dwayne was a fling for Lilly," she said. "He was so handsome, your father. And Lilly appreciated a good-looking man."

Her eyes lingered on my face, but I could tell she wasn't seeing me. She was tangled in memories.

"After she learned she was pregnant, the two of us stayed up all night, discussing her options," Mrs. Hollingsworth said. "I urged her to have an abortion, but Lilly wouldn't hear of it. After much discussion, she finally agreed to put her baby up for adoption. However, after she gave you up, she was inconsolable for weeks. She scarcely left the house and she vowed to find you as soon as you reached your eighteenth birthday."

Ms. Hollingsworth's voice diminished to a weak whisper. "Not a month after she gave birth to you, she was on her way to her morning classes at the University when she ran her Karmann Ghia into a telephone pole. Her little car crumpled like it was made of tissue paper. She was distracted and upset about the adoption. I'm certain that's why she had her accident."

I winced. "I'm so sorry, Mrs. Hollingsworth."

Moisture shined in her eyes. I expected her to wipe her tears, but her hands stayed clasped tightly in front of her.

"Eighteen years after Lilly died, I searched for you. I was desperate to find you, as you were all that was left of my sister. I went to the adoption agency in Atlanta and they couldn't tell me anything. My only hope was that you'd seek us out. And now here you are."

I nodded.

A lone tear trickled down her pale cheek. "I've really made a mess of things. I don't suppose Timothy will ever forgive me for trying to bribe you to leave him. I fear our relationship will always be damaged by my foolishness."

"It might be," I mused. "That is if Timothy knew about your monetary offer to me, but seeing how he doesn't—"

"You didn't tell him?" she gasped.

I shook my head. "I didn't see any reason to."

A look of genuine gratitude registered on her face. "Thank you, Elizabeth. Thank you so much."

She looked so helpless, so unaccustomed to reaching out to anyone. I took a deep breath before I spoke.

"I know Timothy well enough to say that he'd like nothing more than to be close to his mother."

She bit her bottom lip and her hands shook slightly as she spoke.

"And what about you, Elizabeth? How do you feel?" she asked softly. "I know I said some terrible things to you."

I looked at her face, which looked so soft and hopeful as she spoke. It was as if ten years had been washed away by her tears.

"Why don't we just put all of that behind us, Mrs. Hollingsworth?"

The corners of her mouth turned upward and she exhaled noisily, as if she'd been holding her breath during our entire conversation. "Please, Elizabeth. Call me Daisy."

Thirty-Seven

Fear knocked and faith answered.

~ Sign outside the new and improved Bottom Dollar Emporium

Daisy was initially disappointed that Timothy didn't want to carry on with his position at Hollingsworth Paper Cups. However, she took his decision to buy the bait shop gracefully and decided that she would stay in Georgia indefinitely, so she could look after the corporation and be closer to Timothy and me.

Daisy and I had leisurely lunches at the Wagon Wheel at which she tried to tell me all that she remembered about my mother. Talking about Lilly after so many years of silence proved to be a real catharsis for her. And I was thrilled to learn so much about my birth mother.

During our lunches I also mentioned my interest in marketing. I told Daisy about the new business plan I'd developed for the Bottom Dollar Emporium and how certain I was of its success. I also told her I'd registered for the SAT and that if all went well, I would be applying to the business program at USC in Aiken.

She listened to my plans with rapt attention. Once I'd finished, she smiled broadly. What would I think, she asked, about coming to work in the marketing department of Hollingsworth Paper Cups? She really wanted a family member to be in a key position in the company and she thought I was the perfect candidate. I was so bowled over by her offer that I told her I'd have to think about it.

I tried to imagine me, a dollar-store girl, wearing tailored business suits and talking to the board of directors about quarterly profits and marketing strategies. The excitement of it kept me up at nights. After much hand-wringing on my part and lots of encouragement from Timothy, I told Daisy that I would be thrilled to accept a position at Hollingsworth Paper Cups. We agreed that I would start my new position right after I enrolled in the business program at USC.

Speaking of which, Mavis, Attalee, and I'd been working ourselves into a tizzy, trying to get everything just right for the grand opening. We were checking in merchandise and smartening up the interior in preparation for our big day. Timothy had seen to it that the soda fountain was assembled and shined up to a high gleam in the back of the store. He also signed the final papers to purchase the bait shop.

Meanwhile, Timothy and I found a cottage near the creek with a big, wide porch, a sunny kitchen, and a fenced-in yard for Maybelline. There was also a freshly painted room just off the master bedroom decorated with a border of teddy bears. We made an offer, and after a little dickering on my part, the cottage was ours. We planned to move in by the end of the month.

On the morning of the grand opening of the new and improved Bottom Dollar Emporium, Timothy tied the bow in the back of my frilly candy-striped apron. We all got new uniforms to go along with the old-timey theme of the Bottom Dollar.

"Are you nervous?" Timothy asked.

"A little," I said, twisting in front of the hall mirror to catch a glimpse of the apron from the back. "Last night I dreamed that nobody came to the grand opening."

Timothy laughed. "Well, you know that won't happen. You sent press releases to every newspaper within a two-hundred-mile radius. Plus it's the one thing this town has been talking about for days. Even the guys at the bait shop are excited. Lots of people are eager to hear that Elvis impersonator you booked for the opening."

"Yes, well, I just hope he'll go over with the crowds," I said.

The Elvis impersonator I'd hired was Dun Woo from the House of Noodles. I'd been skeptical because Dun Woo was under five feet tall and Chinese to boot, but when he sang "Love Me Tender" to Attalee and me, we got shivers up and down our spines. Dun Woo also promised to wear elevator shoes for the gig.

Besides the Elvis impersonator, I'd lined up a clown, Pam's Portable Petting Zoo, and the Cayboo Creek Cloggers. Buddy, who was a Shriner, had arranged for some of his fellow Shriners to wear their flowerpot-shaped hats and make figure eights in the parking lot with their little cars.

Matilda had agreed to read tea leaves for folks, and members of the Methodist Church were going to sell baked goods out front. I wanted the grand opening of the Bottom Dollar Emporium to be the biggest event to hit Cayboo Creek in decades.

Timothy pecked my cheek just before I left. "Everything's getting underway around noon, right?"

I nodded.

"Okay, Sweetie. I'll knock off at the bait shop and see you then."

When I got to the store, Mavis and Attalee were just opening up. The porch was decked with an assortment of geraniums in gleaming copper pots and an old-time vending machine filled with ice-cold root beers. A line of rocking chairs swayed in the breeze.

Mavis's hand shook as she worked the key in the lock. To match her uniform, she wore red lipstick, nylon stockings, and a pair of white pumps. Attalee had her teeth in and her hair in an elaborate bun swirled like the ice cream in a DQ cone.

"I declare, I'm more nervous today than I was on my wedding night," Mavis said as she pulled open the door.

We bustled inside and although we'd all seen it the night before, the differences in the store still stopped us short.

Hank had restored a hand-cranked antique brass cash register he'd bought for Mavis at an auction, and it gleamed on the checkout line like an Aztec shrine. Beyond the cash register were rows of wooden barrels brimming with jawbreakers, Red Hots, and

Chocolate Babies. Mason jars displayed gourmet lollipops and candy sticks in every flavor.

I could smell the roasted coffee beans in their burlap sacks, the bundles of cinnamon sticks, and the hand-dipped candles that came in every scent from English lavender to spiced pear.

In the grocery section, jars of home preserves like jams, jellies, relishes, and pickled fruits winked from the shelves. Along with the preserves, there were small sacks of stone-milled grits and boxes of buckwheat pancake mix and Moon Pies.

I personally favored the mysterious tinctures in the health-and-beauty section. There were dark bottles of Yager's Liniment, tins of Cloverine Salve, and containers of pine tar soap.

The toy section was a child's paradise. It spilled over with Chinese checkers, stick horses, cast-iron banks, and sock monkeys.

Finally, the houseware section was stocked with gadgets of all sorts, like cherry pitters, Jew's harps, and Gerber knives.

Attalee picked up a drawstring bag filled with lye soap. "All of this stuff sure does bring back some memories," she said in a wistful voice.

Although the merchandise was old-fashioned, the marketing behind the store was anything but. In addition to all the press releases I'd sent out, a Web site and distribution plan had been designed for the Bottom Dollar Emporium so eventually merchandise could be shipped to people all over the Southeast.

In the back of the store, cordoned off with a low picket fence, was the soda fountain. It was marble-topped with red swivel stools. Attalee had proclaimed herself the official soda jerk. She wore a starched white jacket, matching hat, and a jaunty red bow tie.

"In my day, the soda jerk was one of the most respected members of the community," Attalee said, clapping her hat to her head. "It was a highly sought-after occupation." She'd spent the last few days brewing up a menu of egg creams, phosphates, malteds, and floats.

Mavis stood in the center of the store, just taking it all in. She withdrew a handkerchief from her bag and dabbed at her eyes.

"I've never seen anything so beautiful in all my life. Thank you so much, Elizabeth."

Mavis and I embraced just as Birdie trotted into the store.

"Extra! Extra! Read all about it!" she said, holding up the front page of the *Cayboo Creek Crier*. "I used the biggest type I had. Just as big as back in 1969 when the first man landed on the moon."

The headline, which splashed across half the page, said, "Bottom Dollar Emporium is a Blast from the Past! Grand Re-Opening Scheduled Today." Sidebars included, "Elizabeth Hollingsworth, Store Manager, Is Marketing Maven" and "Attalee Gaines Named as Head Soda Jerk of the Bottom Dollar Emporium."

"I almost forgot," Birdie said. She rummaged into the miniature Igloo cooler she'd brought. "I have some orchid corsages for the three of you to wear on this auspicious occasion."

Birdie pinned the corsage to my apron strap. "Elizabeth, it's going to feel downright peculiar not having you with us. Mavis, have you found a replacement for Elizabeth yet?"

"There is no replacement for Elizabeth," Mavis said in a soft voice. "But I do suppose I'll have to hang a help-wanted sign in the window one of these days."

Hank entered the store wearing an ill-fitting corduroy jacket over his overalls and carrying a horseshoe made of carnations with a banner that said "Congratulations."

"I thought I'd come over and rub elbows with the women of the hour," he said. "And maybe help myself to a stick of peppermint candy."

Mavis patted her hair. "Oh, Hank, that's a lovely arrangement. I'm putting this right up front so everyone who comes in can see it."

Mrs. Tobias (or "Dear," as I was trying to remember to call her) came in cradling three dozen long-stem red roses, which she gave to Mavis, Attalee, and me. When she toured the interior of the store, she kept squeezing my hand and marveling over what a wonderful granddaughter she had.

By 9 A.M. a sizeable crowd had arrived to watch Mavis cut

through a strip of red ribbon that was stretched across the doorway. One half hour after we opened, the checkout line wound all the way back to hardware and every stool at the soda fountain was occupied. Chiffon assisted Attalee in preparing malts and egg creams, and Timothy had arrived to help me bag purchases at the checkout. Everyone who came in raved about all the new merchandise and most filled their baskets.

"This town has needed a community gathering place for a long time," Birdie said to me. "Elizabeth, you've not only saved Mavis's business but you've given Cayboo Creek a place to meet and socialize with their neighbors."

By noon, the parking lot was mobbed. Folks had brought blankets and coolers and spread themselves out on the grassy areas around the store to watch the cloggers and listen to Dun Woo, who wore wraparound sunglasses and a miniature rhinestone-studded jumpsuit, sing "Jailhouse Rock."

That day everyone I knew dropped by the new and improved Bottom Dollar Emporium for a visit. Even Taffy and Daddy paid their respects—without Lanier. Turned out he was back in jail for hot-wiring a Miata.

Taffy, who looked like a matador in a bolero jacket with gold braiding, appeared to miss the point of the Bottom Dollar Emporium entirely.

"Betty D. About these washboards. Why in heavens would anyone buy such an old-fashioned contraption when they can toss everything into their Kenmore?" she said with a smirk. "And you really should consider updating your candy inventory. You're selling sweets that were around when I was coming up."

Daddy, on the other hand, beamed with a pride I would never have expected from him. He kept patting my back, saying he was proud to call me his daughter.

"Who's my baby girl?" he drawled, slinging an arm around my shoulder. I started to deflect his question, but it occurred to me that I was my daddy's baby girl after all. I'd certainly inherited some of his acumen for business.

"I'm your baby girl, Daddy," I said, planting a kiss on his cheek.

I hadn't yet told Daddy about the baby-switching or that Lilly had been my true mama. I decided that someday he and I would sneak off together, without Taffy, and I would tell him everything.

Boomer came by and bussed my cheek. "Your meemaw would've have been so proud of you, Elizabeth," he said. "I just wish she was here to see this."

"Boomer, I do believe she *is* seeing this." I placed my hand on my heart. "As a matter of fact, I feel her here with us right now."

Matilda had taken a break from reading tea leaves and asked to see me outside for a minute. "There's something I wanted to show you," she said in a mysterious voice.

We went around to the back of the store, where we could have some privacy.

"Is anything wrong?" I asked. "You haven't seen anything terrible in my future, have you?"

"Absolutely not," she said with a shake of her beautifully shaped head. "Your future is very bright. This has to do with your past."

She handed me a photograph, and I startled when I saw Darlene's face smiling up at me.

"Look what's written on the back," Matilda said.

"'To Bradley with all my love, Darlene Givens,'" I read. "Who is Bradley?"

"Bradley is my husband Frank's brother. He died several months ago from a massive coronary. We were going through his things and we found this. I saw the photograph and I knew Darlene Givens was your mother's name, or rather the woman who you believed was your mother all these years."

Matilda knew all about the baby-switching. I'd told her the entire story shortly after I'd found out about it.

"So Bradley is the 'B' of Darlene's diary. The mystery is finally solved," I said, softly.

"He kept her photograph all these years along with a stack of love letters. They were the only things in his safety deposit box."

I ran my finger along the edges of the photograph. "What was Bradley like?"

"He was Frank's older brother. He was groomed to take over the family's insurance business, which he ended up running for years. He never married. Most people considered him a workaholic."

I leaned against the brick of the building. "He broke Darlene's heart."

"I know," Matilda said with a nod. "Knowing his family as I do, I'm sure they forced him to choose between the business and Darlene, and I guess he chose the business. Money is a powerful incentive. Still, the way he kept the memory of her all these years makes me wonder if he questioned his decision. I think he really loved her."

I handed back the photograph. "You know what this means, don't you? Frank has a niece somewhere out there."

"I know," Matilda said. "Maybe we'll try and find her one day. Why don't you keep the photograph? I'll also get the letters to you."

"Thanks," I said, tucking the photo into my purse. "I'd like to read them. Even though Darlene isn't my mama, I still tend to think of her that way."

At eight P.M., our official closing time, everyone was a little worse for wear. Mavis had nibbled off her lipstick and there was a long run in her stockings. Attalee had a splash of cherry phosphate on the front of her white jacket and one of her eyebrows had worn off. I sat on a chair with a heart-shaped back by the soda fountain with my shoe off. I massaged my left foot while Timothy kneaded my shoulders.

"You need to wander over this way, child," Attalee said to Timothy. "I've got me a crick in my neck that needs working out."

Timothy obliged, and Attalee sighed contentedly as he worked his fingers around her neck. "This is one handsome hubby you have, Elizabeth. He reminds me of a young Tony Curtis." After a few minutes of Timothy's ministering, Attalee snored in her chair.

It was decided that Timothy would see her home. Mavis and I assisted him as we guided a sleepy Attalee out to the car. Timothy kissed my cheek and said, "I'll be right back, sweetheart."

Mavis and I plodded back into the store. Mavis cut off the outside light.

"I'm like Attalee. I'm too pooped to pop," Mavis said with a yawn. "But I also can't recall when I've had a more magical day. Thank you so much, Elizabeth. I'm sure going to miss you."

"I'm going to miss y'all too," I said. "But we'll still see each other. We just won't be working together every day."

"That reminds me," Mavis said. "Attalee and me got you a little going-away gift."

She disappeared into the stockroom and came back carrying a black leather briefcase that looked just like the one Timothy used to carry. She handed it to me, and when I opened it up I saw a brass square monogrammed with my name: Elizabeth Hollingsworth, Esquire."

"What's the 'esquire' for?" I asked.

"Oh, that was Attalee's idea," said Mavis. "She thought it would make you sound really important."

"This is just what I needed, Mavis," I said. "Thank you so much."

Mavis smiled and ran a finger along the ornate columns in the Bottom Dollar Emporium. "This started out as a grand place. It was never meant to be just an ordinary dollar store. I feel like this building has come into its own again." She paused and looked at me. "Not unlike some people I know."

"Oh now, Mavis. I've enjoyed every minute that I've worked for the Bottom Dollar Store."

"I know that, Elizabeth, but it's clear that you were meant for bigger things than ringing up candy at a cash register." She slowly shook her head. "I've always suspected that. When you walked in here ten years ago, I thought to myself 'someday that girl will go places.'" Her soft gray eyes filled with tears. "I just didn't know it was going to hurt so much when you did."

I threw my arms around Mavis and we hugged until I saw the headlights from Timothy's car shine through the plate glass window.

"I'll go out there and tell him that I'm going to help you close up," I said.

She shook her head. "No. I'll take care of that, Elizabeth. You go on now. Go home with your husband."

I took one last lingering look at the Bottom Dollar Emporium and then left through the front door. Through the window I saw Mavis ease into a rocking chair. She shucked off her pumps and put her feet up on an empty box. I couldn't remember the last time I'd seen such a look of contentment on her face.

Meemaw's Oatmeal Cookies

Makes enough cookies to fill up a good-sized cookie jar

1 cup shortening (I like Snowdrift, but Crisco or even lard will do.)
1 cup granulated sugar
1 cup brown sugar (If it's gotten hard on you, instead of banging it against the kitchen counter stick it the microwave for a spell with a dab of butter and it'll soften on you.)
2 eggs
1 teaspoon vanilla extract
1 ½ cups White Lily all-purpose flour
1 teaspoon baking soda
1 teaspoon salt
3 cups quick cook oatmeal
1 cup chopped nuts (I'm partial to pecans, but you can use walnuts.)
2 cups sweetened shredded coconut, raisins, or currants (I tried dried cranberries once, but they got stuck in my teeth.)

Preheat oven to 350° F.

Cream shortening and sugars; add eggs and vanilla. Add flour, baking soda, and salt. Add oatmeal, nuts, and coconut (or whatever you decided on). Drop teaspoons of batter on a cookie sheet. Bake for 10 minutes.

Karin Gillespie

Karin Gillespie is national bestselling author of five novels and a humor columnist for *Augusta* Magazine. Her nonfiction writing had been in the *New York Times*, *The Writer* Magazine and *Romantic Times*. She maintains a website and blog at Karingillespie.net. Sign up for her newsletter on her website, follow her on Twitter or connect with her on Facebook.

Books by Karin Gillespie

GIRL MEETS CLASS
LOVE LITERARY STYLE

The Bottom Dollar Series

BET YOUR BOTTOM DOLLAR (#1)
A DOLLAR SHORT (#2)
DOLLAR DAZE (#3)

Henery Press Books

And finally, before you go...
Here are a few other Southern charmers
you might enjoy:

GIRL MEETS CLASS

Karin Gillespie

(from the Henery Press Chick Lit Collection)

The unspooling of Toni Lee Wells' Tiffany and Wild Turkey lifestyle begins with a trip to the Luckett County Jail drunk tank. An earlier wrist injury sidelined her pro tennis career, and now she's trading her tennis whites for wild nights roaming the streets of Rose Hill, Georgia.

Her wealthy family finally gets fed up with her shenanigans. They cut off her monthly allowance but also make her a sweetheart deal: Get a job, keep it for a year, and you'll receive an early inheritance. Act the fool or get fired, and you'll lose it for good.

Toni Lee signs up for a fast-track Teacher Corps program. She hopes for an easy teaching gig, but ends up assigned to Harriet Hall, a high school that churns out more thugs than scholars.

What's a spoiled Southern belle to do when confronted with a bunch of street smart students who are determined to make her life as difficult as possible? Luckily, Carl, a handsome colleague, is willing to help her negotiate the rough teaching waters and keep her bed warm at night. But when Toni Lee gets involved with some dark dealings in the school system, she fears she might lose her new beau as well as her inheritance.

Available at booksellers nationwide and online

Visit www.henerypress.com for details

LOVE LITERARY STYLE
Karin Gillespie

(from the Henery Press Chick Lit Collection)

They say opposites attract, and what could be more opposite than a stuffy literary writer falling for a self-published romance writer?

Novelist Aaron Mite meets Laurie Lee at a writers' colony and mistakenly believes her to be a renowned writer of important fiction. When he discovers she's a self-published romance author, he's already fallen in love with her.

Aaron thinks genre fiction is an affront to the fiction-writing craft. He often quotes the essayist, Arthur Krystal who says literary fiction "melts the frozen sea inside of us." Ironically Aaron doesn't seem to realize that he's emotionally frozen. The vivacious Laurie, lover of flamingo-patterned attire and all things hot pink, is the one person who might be capable of melting him.

In the tradition of *The Rosie Project*, *Love Literary Style* is a sparkling romantic comedy which pokes fun at the divide between low and high brow fiction.

Available at booksellers nationwide and online

Visit www.henerypress.com for details

THE BREAKUP DOCTOR

Phoebe Fox

The Breakup Doctor Series (#1)

(From the Henery Press Chick Lit Collection)

Call Brook Ogden a matchmaker-in-reverse. Let others bring people together; Brook, licensed mental health counselor, picks up the pieces after things come apart. When her own therapy practice collapses, she maintains perfect control: landing on her feet with a weekly advice-to-the-lovelorn column and a successful consulting service as the Breakup Doctor: on call to help you shape up after you breakup.

Then her relationship suddenly crumbles and Brook finds herself engaging in almost every bad-breakup behavior she preaches against. And worse, she starts a rebound relationship with the most inappropriate of men: a dangerously sexy bartender with anger-management issues—who also happens to be a former patient.

As her increasingly out-of-control behavior lands her at rock-bottom, Brook realizes you can't always handle a messy breakup neatly—and that sometimes you can't pull yourself together until you let yourself fall apart.

Available at booksellers nationwide and online

Visit www.henerypress.com for details

CPSIA information can be obtained
at www.ICGtesting.com
Printed in the USA
BVHW092106210922
647611BV00004B/250